SEE HOW SHE RUNS

A Cape Trouble Novel

By Janice Kay Johnson

ISBN-10: 0989041875
ISBN-13: 978-0-9890418-7-4

See How She Runs

Cover Design by Seductive Designs
Photo copyright: Couple © 123RF.com/Tatjana Strelkova
Photo copyright: Woman Running © Depositphotos.com/Viktor Cap
Photo copyright: Crosshair © Depositphotos.com/Radek Mühl

PROLOGUE

Naomi Varner clutched her cell phone in a shaking hand as she strained for any sound. She'd squeezed herself into a corner, completely alone in a vast and usually noisy, bustling restaurant kitchen.

Had they seen her?

She gazed longingly at the back door, but didn't dare do anything so out of the ordinary as take off when there were still people in her restaurant. She already knew at least one off-duty cop was patrolling inside, and what if there was another one outside, walking the perimeter?

Her stomach cramped painfully and she bent forward. Oh, God, was she *crazy*? Why hadn't she run the second she heard instead of trying to get some proof? Her effort at being a good citizen might make her a dead citizen.

She could not believe any of this. How was it possible she had just heard a guy she had been dating agree to kill someone for money? A shitpot full of money. And be collected and businesslike about it.

An hysterical laugh rose in her throat. She clapped her free hand over her mouth barely in time to silence it. He'd told her he was a businessman. That the private meetings she'd been letting him hold here in her restaurant after closing were *business* meetings. Negotiations. And, oh God, they were, just not any kind of business she could ever have imagined.

Greg Cobb was a contract killer.

She tried to wrap her mind around the idea.

No, worse than that; he must have some kind of criminal organization, or he'd be more of a loner than he was. She'd teased him about needing bodyguards, assuming his problem was being rich enough to have to worry about getting kidnapped. Now she thought those off-duty police officers who worked for him must have a lot more of a clue as to what he did for a living than she'd had. Cops, working for some kind of crime boss. What that said about them—

Her teeth chattered.

There'd been a freaking *FBI agent* sitting at the table during the meeting. The one during which Greg had matter-of-factly told a rising politician he'd take care of his opponent and make it look like an accident. Even better – he'd find a way to add a hint of scandal to the death. Make sure there was a whore in the car with him. Something like that.

On an electric zap of hope, she thought, if the third man at the table really was FBI, what if this was a sting? Greg could have agreed to go along with it.

Wouldn't he have told her? Maybe not, if the FBI had asked him not to.

She closed her eyes. No, that made no sense. A sting didn't include the FBI agent sitting at the table and offering proof of his identity. The leather folio might have been a fake…but from her glimpse, it looked real enough.

Anyway, why would Donovan Greer, California State Senator now running for the U.S. House of Representatives, open his big mouth in front of the agent unless he *knew* the guy was dirty? In fact, now that she thought about it, Senator Greer's tone had suggested all he was doing was putting a face with a name he already knew.

All of her was quaking now. Her stomach roiled. The square-edge of counters was all that held her up.

If anyone had caught a glimpse of her, they'd have come after her right away, wouldn't they? *Yes*! So if she was just cool enough, she'd be okay. She had to pull herself together.

Any minute now, Greg would push open the swinging door and say, "We're done, babe. Thanks for letting me use your place again. Hey, let me walk you out to your car." Where he'd want to kiss her, and right now she was afraid she'd puke if he tried.

He'd been in profile to the door, open just a couple of inches, when she'd run the video function on her phone to catch him and Greer in living color *and* sound. What if he'd seen?

She'd never done any acting, but tonight had to be a first time. Yep. If she could stop hyperventilating, that would be a good start.

Even better would be getting her phone out of sight. She dropped it in her bag.

Barely in time. The door opened and he strolled in, sandy-haired, handsome, sharp in a beautiful dark suit even though the tie hung loose and he'd undone the top couple buttons on his white shirt.

"Sorry to keep you waiting so long." He raised his eyebrows, studying her. "You okay? You look hot and bothered."

Naomi wrinkled her nose at him. "Thanks. *Hot* might be a compliment. *Bothered*, not so much."

He laughed, but she had the feeling he was still assessing her. Not believing her act.

She huffed out a breath. "I just checked for some ingredients I need tomorrow, and we're low. I'm pissed. Somebody dropped the ball."

"Will you have to change your menu?"

"Tell diners they can't have something on the menu? No, I'll have to pay premium prices to get what I need in here before I start cooking. In fact, I'm going to do a more thorough check right now, before I go home. Shoot off some emails." He knew she had a small office off the kitchen.

"I don't like to think of you here alone." The pause felt significant. "It's not safe."

Something seemed to skitter up her spine.

The words were okay. Sort of…concerned. But his eyes were flat. It came to her suddenly that they always were. He smiled, he said the right things, but he had really cold eyes.

And she was projecting because of what she now knew.

Naomi forced a smile "I'll be fine." Shaking knees or no, she started toward her office, praying he'd just think she was preoccupied because of her potential disaster.

Yesterday, she would have thought running out of serrano peppers or cornichons a disaster. Time for a new definition.

His arm swept out to catch her half way across the kitchen. She flinched, despite all her resolve, then raised a horrified gaze to his. They stared at each other. His expression never changed.

After a moment, he shook his head. "Naomi." Was that regret she heard?

"I'm…just in a lousy mood," she managed, apologetically.

His arm dropped from her waist. Those cold eyes swept over her one last time. "I'll leave you to it, then. Don't walk me out. I'll lock behind myself."

Her "thank you" wasn't much better than a whisper.

He nodded, and was gone. No "I'll call you." Looking down, she saw the tremor in her hands. Had he felt it? What had that last look meant?

Nothing. It meant nothing. He'd left, hadn't he?

She had to stay for a few minutes, in case he'd been suspicious. He'd expect the lights in the kitchen to stay on, her car to remain in her spot for…she didn't know. Twenty minutes? Half an hour?

She desperately wanted to run the video, see if she'd actually captured what she thought she had. Whether faces were recognizable, words clear and not indecipherable mumbles.

Not here.

Her mind wasn't ready to grapple with the problem of who she could go to with the recording if it was any good.

A faint shush of sound came from the other side of the swinging door. She went rigid, ice sliding over her skin. Had Greg not left? Or…had his help not left?

Maybe she was hearing things.

But a man slapped open the door with such force she sprang back several feet, pulse racing. Eyes on her, he crossed the kitchen.

This wasn't the off-duty cop she'd seen before, the one who'd been in the men's room when she eavesdropped. This guy wore a rumpled sports coat that didn't go all that well with his slacks. He was maybe early fifties, hair graying and receding, eyes weary. And when her gaze dropped to his waist, she couldn't miss the police shield on his belt. Seeing where she was looking, he swept the coat back with one hand, exposing a big black handgun.

"Ms. Varner."

Naomi backed up until she bumped against the huge, stainless steel refrigerator, then edged sideways. She kept her body angled, hoping he couldn't see her right arm and hand. He never took his eyes off her.

"You're a police officer, right?" Her voice was too high. "I have to tell you, you're freaking me out. How did you get in?" Panic balled in her throat. "What do you want?"

He didn't say anything.

"If you have questions," she said in a rush, "can't they wait until tomorrow?"

"No." A resigned note in his voice made her heart squeeze in terror even before, with shocking speed, he drew his gun and pointed it at her. "I'm afraid not. No good in putting off something that needs to be done."

A pained look in his eyes said he didn't want to kill her, but he was going to. That's what he meant.

The unthinkable filled her head: *I'm going to die.*

CHAPTER ONE

Detective Adam Rostov was bored out of his skull. Being stuck on hold was his idea of hell, and he spent a lot of time there. This was not the life of thrills and chills his rookie self had imagined.

He growled an obscenity. The detectives at neighboring desks didn't so much as turn their heads. Malone was hammering at his keyboard, mumbling under his breath, Santiago glowering at his computer monitor with a telephone tucked between ear and shoulder. On hold, sure as shit. Four desks away, Ryan Farrell had his chair tilted back, his feet planted on his desk, and was staring into space. *He*, at least, was free to think without that bland music numbing his brain cells.

Another day in the office.

When Adam's cell phone rang, he grabbed it. Right this minute, he'd have welcomed a call from a creditor dunning him. The number that did show sent a trickle of adrenaline into his blood stream.

"Weismann," he said.

"Rostov."

The fact that FBI Special Agent Sam Weismann was keeping his voice low had the adrenaline production increasing. The two of them maintained a cautious, generally friendly relationship. Sam's brother was married to Adam's sister. On a couple of previous occasions, they had had an exchange of information not strictly authorized.

"You know about the wiretap on Gregory Cobb."

Even as the elevator music was abruptly cut off in his other ear and a voice started speaking, Adam hung up his desk phone. He switched the Samsung to his right ear. "Yes." Thanks to Weismann.

"They've found the chef."

The hand on the desk fisted. He'd been waiting a long time for this. "They saying what they're going to do about it?"

"The indication is that she's got something on them. They're nervous. I think it's safe to say there will be an…approach."

Adam grunted. If Cobb's organization wasn't already moving, he had every intention of beating them to Naomi Varner.

"How'd they find her?" he asked, the roughness of his voice betraying more than he'd have liked.

Perhaps in response to it, Sam Weissman paused. "She opened another restaurant."

He shook his head. No need to comment. First rule when you wanted to disappear: do not follow your previous career. Also previous hobbies, relationships, habits. But first and foremost: do something else for a living.

"Little place in a town called Cape Trouble. Oregon coast."

He grunted. She shouldn't have stayed on the west coast, either. "You get a name?"

"No name. No address or phone number. But how many restaurants can there be?"

"If it's tourist country, quite a few." Didn't matter. "Thanks, Sam. I owe you one."

"You going to be okayed to go after her?"

No. His lieutenant professed to be puzzled by his obsession with a woman who had never been considered a suspect despite the fact that a homicide detective – *his* homicide detective, Adam's partner – had been stabbed to death in her restaurant kitchen, with her knife that had *her* fingerprints on it. That she was the one to find the body. The lieutenant's puzzlement at Adam's continuing questions had become irritation, which then moved right along to a chilly refusal to hear one more goddamn word about Naomi Varner, and could he please - add in a couple of obscenities - remember the investigation wasn't theirs?

Then there'd been the near-career ending incident when Adam had overheard that asshole Roy Valdez loudly telling another cop that Frank Donahue had to have been dirty. "Restaurant was closed, and it's not even in our jurisdiction. Better yet, Greg Cobb was having some kind of private party. You gotta ask yourself what ol' Frank was doing there."

Adam knew too well the damaging effect of that kind of talk, however little it was based on reality. By God, Frank's wife and kids weren't going to live under that suspicion, not if he had anything to do with it.

Enraged, he'd confronted Valdez and stopped just short of removing a few of his teeth. The lieutenant hadn't been real pleased with him. He also hadn't shut Valdez's speculation down, undercutting any loyalty Adam had felt for him.

Now, studying a map he'd pulled up on his computer, Adam said only, "I'll see if I can get a flight into Portland tonight. I can be in this Cape Trouble by morning. If you learn anything more, I'd appreciate a call."

"Watch yourself."

The way his lips drew back from his teeth might have been misconstrued as a smile if anybody had been looking. He said goodbye and pushed away from his desk.

Lucky he had weeks of vacation saved up. Most people went to the Caribbean or Hawaii in late November, but him, he thought he might enjoy a good storm. Made a change from southern California's eternal sunshine.

*****

"We're full up, and have three people waiting for tables," Anita Barnes said cheerfully, clipping two new order slips on the line in the window separating pantry/service area from the kitchen.

Naomi glanced at the two additions and opened the industrial refrigerator. "Locals won't like having to wait."

"All three are tourists." Anita frowned. "Visitors, anyway." She grabbed the coffeepot and disappeared.

French toast was especially popular this morning. Dipping thick slabs of whole wheat sourdough bread in the delicately spiced egg batter, Naomi reflected briefly on her waitress's unexpected expression. Apparently, one or all of the people waiting for tables were unfamiliar to Anita, but not standard issue tourist. If there was such a thing.

The momentary zing of anxiety was understandable, after the article she'd seen last night on her laptop. She had a few Google Alerts set to be sure she saw anything that came up about them. The piece was short, from the *Los Angeles Times*. The investigation into the murder of a California state senator that had taken place two years ago had been reopened. No hint why. Had a new witness come forward?

Wondering had kept her awake half the night. Just the reminder now was enough to make her skin prickle, as if there was too much electricity in the air.

Stupid. She'd be glad if they really solved that murder. There was nothing about it to lead anyone to her. This morning was no different than any other morning.

People did conduct everyday, average business in Cape Trouble, just like anywhere else. Almost every businessperson dealt with suppliers. The new resort being built north of town, on the other side of the point crowned by the lighthouse, had a lot of strangers coming and going. Long timers in town were alternately excited by the prospect of increased business, and irritated because they didn't expect to have to wait in line in the off season for a cup of coffee or to buy a book – or to get a table when they went out for breakfast. Only a few months ago, townsfolk had mostly united in an effort to preserve fifty acres on the south side of Mist River from the evil developers. They'd succeeded – but progress couldn't be halted.

And progress, like it or not, had the Sea Watch Café considerably busier than it had been in November last year.

Naomi turned out food as fast as she could, until Anita, a comfortably plump, middle-aged woman, appeared with dirty dishes, no new orders, and an expression of satisfaction.

"It's clearing out," she reported. "Four people sent compliments to the chef. Three for the French toast, one for your Spanish omelet."

"Thanks." She already had mixing bowls and pots soaking in the deep sink and was thinking about today's lunch specials. Curried lentil for soup and—

"One of the men asked about you. Wanted to know your name."

She went absolutely still, not turning until she was sure she could control her expression. "Why did he care?"

Anita shrugged. "He really liked the French toast."

"Is he still here?"

Anita ran a credit card through the slider. "He was one of the late-comers. Back corner table."

Heart drumming, Naomi debated with herself. Look? Don't look?

What good would it do *to* look? They were unlikely to send anyone after her she'd recognize. Still…knowing someone out there was curious about her personally made the hair on her nape raise. It was a creepy sensation, like knowing you're being watched even though you can't spot the watcher.

And – the back corner table. Naomi had noticed before that the local cops eating here almost all chose that table when it was open. Apparently they preferred to keep their backs to the wall. Maybe other paranoids – say, criminals – had the same preference.

Finally, she couldn't stand it. She took a couple of hesitant steps out of the kitchen, through the service area, just far enough to be able to peek into the dining room.

Anita was currently clearing one table while chatting with a couple at a neighboring one – Linda and Palmer Ellenbogen, frequent diners. A retired money manager and city council member, Palmer was signing the credit card slip Anita must have just handed him.

Two small tables were occupied by single men, both strangers to Naomi. The one in the back corner appeared at first sight to be harmless. He was texting on his phone or checking email while groping for his coffee cup with his free hand. Strongly built, he was late thirties at a guess, wearing jeans, work boots, a navy wool shirt open over a T-shirt. Disheveled, dark red hair and stubble suggested he was not a sales rep planning to make some calls, or not today, anyway. A lumberjack or construction worker, maybe, or the rare single male tourist. Heck, maybe his wife just wasn't a breakfast eater. He didn't send up a flare for Naomi, which didn't keep her from stepping back quickly when he raised his head.

Only then did she see that the second guy here alone was looking straight at her.

For no known reason, he scared her. Heartbeat accelerating, she scuttled back into the kitchen, her wild gaze going to the back door.

Run.

Instead, she retreated far enough to press her back to the counter edge right beside the rear exit. There she waited, trying to control her breathing. If he appeared—

Instead, Anita did, ringing up another charge while calling, "Have a nice day." The bell above the door tinkled as someone apparently departed.

The flood of fear retreated like a wave, exposing clean-washed sand. Playing with the unwary, Naomi reminded herself. The next wave might be a monster that would fling itself higher on the beach and pull any fools out to sea.

Nonetheless, her tension loosened by increments. The man was somebody who'd stopped for breakfast. That's all. Restaurants, by their very nature, served strangers. She'd been in this particular stranger's line of sight by chance. His thoughts had likely been elsewhere. People rarely even took in their waiter's face, not to remember. *She'd* been background clutter.

It really sucked to have become such a scaredy-cat, to have to deal with these too-frequent moments of terror, her body reacting with a primitive fight or flight reflex that left her feeling like a soggy, wrung-out dish rag afterwards. Most often, the cause wasn't even logical.

She might have made an appointment to discuss her problem with a doctor and request a heavy-duty dose of anti-depressants or anti-anxiety medications, except for one, teeny little reality check – she had real enemies who would like very much to kill her, if only they could find her. And then there was the fact she'd just as soon avoid coming to the attention of law enforcement, too.

But her second anniversary in Cape Trouble was approaching, and no one had found her yet. She had to be doing something right.

Keep to herself. Stay out of sight. No contact with anyone from her past. No artless confidences to new acquaintances. Don't be foolish enough to completely trust *anyone*. And never, ever, ever let down her guard.

She was smart enough to know a killer wouldn't necessarily look dangerous. It could even be a woman who came hunting her.

Finally calm, she started the enormous pot of soup cooking, then rolled out pastry dough for peach tarts that would bake while she juggled preparations for the dozen entrees on her lunch menu, not including the simpler salads and sandwiches that Anita would help with.

So…what about the one guy had set her off?

Once upon a time, she'd have thought he was sexy. Maybe that was reason enough. The last man she'd gone on more than one date with had turned out to be an assassin-for-hire. Gee, maybe any hormonal reaction to a man fired up her panic. Good thing she wasn't looking for romance or even just sex, then, wasn't it?

This guy had been leaner than the other one, more like a greyhound beside a mastiff. Hair darker than hers, eyes…she wasn't sure. Gray or hazel, maybe. Lighter than you'd expect with his coloring. Striking bone structure, the cheekbones broad, prominent and blunt. Almost brutal. There'd been something exotic about that face. And – his expression might have had nothing to do with her, it might have reflected whatever he'd brooded about while eating breakfast, but it wasn't pleasant. He hadn't been debating whether his next activity should be checking out the tide pools or climbing the path to the lighthouse to take photos.

She shivered, listening to Anita's cheerful voice and the faint tinkle of the bell on the door as more diners left. Too early for any to be arriving; the café didn't close between breakfast and lunch, but the few people who wandered in before eleven-thirty or so usually wanted only coffee and a muffin.

The lunch rush had her too busy to worry. It wasn't until Anita was gone, the sign turned to closed and the door locked that Naomi thought again about the two men. She was adding up the day's receipts and preparing for a quick stop at the bank. Either man or both might have paid cash - in fact, it appeared most people eating breakfast here this morning *had* paid cash - but an excess of caution had her flipping through the credit card slips, starting at the bottom of the pile.

The names were mostly familiar. She made note of the two that weren't.

Julian A. Granath. Julian's signature consisted of a few loops and a couple of straight lines. Unreadable, if his name hadn't been on the card.

Randall Bresler. No middle initial, handwriting with perfectly formed letters.

Neither name seemed to fit the guy with the sharply sculpted cheekbones, although – well, that was dumb, wasn't it? He could just as well be a Joe Smith. The man with the dark red hair could go with either name, she supposed. Or neither. There'd been plenty of genuine tourists in the café this morning.

The Cape Trouble Chamber of Commerce had run ads in several recent issues of *Oregon Coast Magazine* as well as the *Portland*

Oregonian and the *Seattle Times* trumpeting the appeal of winter getaways. Pounding surf, twining mist, unspoiled beaches, heaps of driftwood, sand dollars and Japanese floats. Either because of the ad or the improving economy, tourism was up. She'd prefer not to think people had chosen to vacation here because of the other press Cape Trouble had recently gotten, when a serial killer had been arrested this summer. No matter why, inns were full on Friday and Saturday nights despite the season.

She zipped cash along with a deposit slip into the bag for the bank, and placed the credit card slips into a plain envelope to take home with her. Bag over her shoulder, she let herself out the back door into the alley, where she had wedged her compact car in beside the dumpster. The earlier rain had subsided into a barely-there drizzle that felt cool and clean.

Her usual careful look up and down the alley was aborted when she saw Monica Sanchez, who owned the art gallery two doors from the Sea Watch, heaving a full bag into the dumpster. Relieved to have safe company, Naomi started toward her car.

The lid clanged shut and Monica turned and saw her. "Hey. Looked like you were busy today."

"Swamped. What about you?"

"Busier than usual for this late in the fall." A voluptuous brunette, Monica smiled with satisfaction. "I sold an Elias Burton original this morning."

Naomi grinned. "Bet that made your day."

Elias Burton was a local boy made good whose watercolor and oil originals went for prices in the neighborhood of $5,000. Naomi didn't know what Monica's commission was, but it seemed likely to be in the 30-40% range. Naomi had wondered a little if he and Monica had something going that had nothing to do with art, mainly because they were both, in their own ways, spectacular looking.

"Was it the one in the window?" she asked. She hadn't been able to help noticing the watercolor depicting a single person walking through the fog on a rocky stretch of beach. The first time she saw it, Naomi had stood on the sidewalk staring, gripped by loneliness so intense, she'd felt hollowed out. That was the power of his art – usually landscapes that somehow still evoked emotion. It was rare for him to paint people at all. Studying that particular painting, she'd kind of been glad.

"No. That one is…unsettling. I warned Elias it might be a hard sell. Draws people in, though. No, this couple bought an oil of a tide pool. A little less distressing to look at."

"I wonder about him sometimes," Naomi said impulsively, then regretted what she'd said. Friendly but not very personal was more her style.

"You and me both." Monica's tone was wry. "Listen, I left the store unmanned. I'd better get back in before someone robs me blind."

"Good idea." With a last smile, Naomi unlocked her car and slung her messenger bag into the passenger seat. "See 'ya." She hit the button to lock the minute she was in.

Four blocks from the café, Naomi parked and went into the bank. The teller, an older woman she'd come to know, counted quickly, gave her a receipt and wished her a good day.

A couple of turns, and Naomi reached the Pacific Coast Highway, where she turned north. Her small rental cottage was in Jasper Beach, the next town up the coast – although calling it a *town* was an exaggeration. Jasper Beach was more a cluster of elderly homes, a few of which had once been stately, the rest shingled cottages, one ramshackle old resort, a two-pump gas station and small grocery store, a gift shop and a couple of artists' studios. The small crescent beach had been named for the tiny, polished pebbles, many deep red jasper, that washed up to mix with the sand. Naomi preferred the quiet and intimacy of a village where everyone knew their neighbors to the larger Cape Trouble, where a good percent of the houses were rented by the night to tourists. To her regret, the huge new resort on the bluff now dominated her view from the cottage, and when it was complete, the mostly empty beach she loved would be flooded with strangers.

Men were swarming the skeleton structure right now and a crane seemed to be lifting roof trusses into place.

Her cottage didn't even have a detached garage. She felt lucky to have a sagging carport that allowed her to come and go through a side door without getting wet.

Often when she arrived home, the next door neighbor's curtain twitched, but not today. Come to think of it, Arthur Tuchek's boat of a car had been missing. It might feel as if he was always home, watching her comings and goings, but he did have to grocery shop now and again.

Naomi unlocked and stepped into the tiny utility room, hearing the silence. From habit, she locked behind her. Two steps took her into the kitchen, where she went completely still.

Her junk drawer jutted open about an inch. It tended to stick. But she hadn't needed anything out of it in…oh, a week, at least. And…the cupboard door right beside the refrigerator was partially open, too. Enough that she could see the way the shelf paper was peeling up – or had been lifted so someone could look under it.

Run.

Instead, she inched backwards, trying not to make even the smallest of sounds until her shaking fingers found the latch for the deadbolt.

*****

She'd barely gone inside, and next thing she rushed out to her car and leaped in.

Adam sat up straighter.

Her Ford Focus shot out of the driveway so fast, he wondered if Naomi Varner aka Kendrick had even glanced into the rearview mirror to ensure she didn't slam broadside into some poor sucker who happened to be passing.

Not that there was much in the way of traffic, in this odd little cluster of homes on the other side of the point from Cape Trouble.

He set aside the binoculars, prepared to follow her, but had barely put his rented SUV into gear when she did a mid-block U-turn and stopped on the other side of the street from her house.

There she sat.

Through the binoculars, he saw that she was speaking on her cell phone, her gaze riveted on her house.

Huh. She hadn't been brought out by an urgent call demanding her presence elsewhere, then. Something inside had alarmed her. He turned the binoculars on the house, looking for any hint of movement behind the small-paned windows. Closed curtains in almost every window blocked his view. Had she left them drawn, or had a visitor closed them to keep anyone from watching as he…what? Rummaged through her possessions? Or lay in wait for her?

If he'd laid in wait, why hadn't he grabbed her, whoever he was? And, if that wasn't the case, what had scared her?

Interested and mildly annoyed, Adam settled in to wait. He'd known he wouldn't be the only one to show up in Cape Trouble to hunt down the chef, but he'd hoped to have a day before he faced any competition.

No such luck, he thought philosophically.

He'd give a lot to know what she had on Gregory Cobb or someone else in his organization that made them so nervous.

*****

Naomi watched a large gray sedan round the corner and stop in front of her cottage. No flashing lights or siren. It was unmarked but also, with the distinctive antennas and the cage separating front and back seats, unmistakably police issue. Why hadn't her 911 call brought a blue and white sheriff's department squad car?

Her engine still ran. She stayed where she was, watching as a solidly built, sandy-haired man wearing a suit and tie got out. His hand slipped inside the suit coat, and withdrew holding a huge black handgun.

He looked vaguely familiar, although she couldn't summon his name. She didn't think he was a regular, but he ate sometimes at the café, she was sure. Some of her tension dissipated, although in its wake she wasn't sure her knees would hold her if she got out and walked across the street to join him.

He was moving quickly, staying close to the cottage walls as he eased into the carport toward the side door she'd told the dispatcher was unlocked.

Maybe it would be better if she stayed put until he came back out.

At that moment, he disappeared from her sight. Anxiety grabbed hold again. She stared so fixedly, her eyes began to burn. She remembered to blink, but it didn't help much.

And then the front door opened, and he appeared, his seemingly casual glance taking in the entire street, all the cottages, and, of course, her small blue car.

Naomi put it into gear and returned to her own driveway. The tall cop strolled to meet her.

"Ms. Kendrick?"

"Yes."

"I'm Detective Jason Payne." His eyes were an unusually light shade of brown. Naomi guessed him to be in his mid-thirties. He was handsome, although in a smooth way that didn't move her personally.

Good thing, she thought semi-hysterically, considering her new theory about the connection between her sexual and panic responses.

"What did I do to deserve a detective?" she asked.

"I happened to be passing. Wasn't a mile away when I heard the request for a unit."

"There's…nobody inside?"

"No. I…can't quite tell what alarmed you." His tone was neutral enough not to suggest he thought she was a nut. "Why don't we walk through together."

She bit her lip and nodded. "I went in the side door."

He took a long narrow-eyed look over her shoulder. She turned enough to see that he was studying an SUV she hadn't noticed earlier. No, she was sure she would have, if it had been parked just around the corner from her cottage when she turned down the street. It must have arrived since. Someone sat in the driver's seat, although through the tinted windshield, she couldn't make him out well.

With a chill, she had to wonder if he had searched her house and was now watching to see what she did about it.

Right. To break in and then sit there in plain sight made so much sense. He was probably waiting for someone.

The detective must have come to the same conclusion, because he finally gestured her ahead.

Inside, she stopped a few feet into the kitchen. "I didn't get even this far. It was the open drawer that caught my eye. That's my junk drawer. You know, screwdrivers, rubber bands, extra sticky notes, anything I don't know where else to put."

He nodded.

"I haven't opened it in a week or more. It's warped a little and needs a little sideways jiggle to close it." She nodded toward the cupboard. "And…I was sure I didn't leave that open, either. And, um, look at the shelf paper."

Oh, God. That sounded so weak. Old cottage, damp climate, and some shelf paper laid who knew when that was peeling up.

The cop had returned his weapon to a holster hidden beneath his suit coat. Now he produced a pair of latex gloves from a pocket, snapped them on and fully opened the cupboard door.

The dishes were at least more or less where she'd stacked them.

One by one, he opened the other cupboards. Same deal. A couple of other places, the shelf paper gaped, but…would she have noticed?

Her certainty wavered.

"Look," she said a little shakily, "I think the refrigerator might have been pulled out, too."

As if it had been pushed back in a little too far, an indentation and slight tear in the aging vinyl floor showed that she didn't remember.

He contemplated the worn floor, then her, the very tilt of his eyebrows skeptical.

Beginning to feel like a fool, she led the way through the small cottage – living room, single bedroom, bathroom with an ancient, deep, claw-footed tub and inadequate storage. She kept seeing objects that might have been moved, drawers slightly askew, but she didn't dare even say, *I do think someone has been in here.* And…the truth was, she began to fear that she *was* nuts. Or, at least, that her earlier panic attacks at the restaurant had primed her to see something where there was really nothing.

"All right," the detective said finally. "Why don't we sit down in the kitchen?"

"Would you like a cup of coffee?" she asked.

"Not at the moment, thank you." His mouth lifted on one side. "Reluctant as I am to turn down anything from your kitchen. You're a fine cook, Ms. Kendrick."

"Thank you. I recognized you from the cafe."

He pulled a small spiral notebook out of an interior pocket, flipped it open and held a pen poised above it.

"You didn't say." His eyes rested thoughtfully on her face. "Is anything missing?"

She shook her head. "I don't wear much jewelry except for earrings, and…well, I can look more carefully, but they seemed to be there."

Detective Payne nodded. He'd seen her open the wooden jewelry box on the dresser. "I saw a printer, but no computer."

"I take my laptop with me every day." She nudged it with her foot. "It's right here. The TV – well, it's nothing special."

He nodded at that, too. His expression remained pleasant. He hadn't said, *You're wasting my time*, but he was thinking it, or worse.

After a minute, when she didn't rush into speech, he said, "Ms. Kendrick, you did the right thing to back out of the house the minute you suspected an intruder had been in it. Any signs were very subtle, however. I can't help wondering if you don't have reason beyond the ordinary to be nervous. If so, we're here to help, you know."

Peculiar, alternating hot and cold sensations made her wonder if she was beet red one minute, blanched bone white the next.

Oh, dear God, she shouldn't have called the police at all. Because now…well, she either had to answer that question, or lie.

And then what? Find a safe place to call Greg and say, *We had a deal, and you just violated your side of it?*

When – it was entirely possible the whole thing was in her imagination?

Probably was in her imagination. *Please God it is.*

Because the idea of starting all over again was appalling. It was like teetering on the edge of an abyss. She'd spent almost two years trying not to stare down into that nothingness. She didn't know how to disappear again. Didn't have enough money saved to fund a new beginning.

I put too much back into the business, she realized, belatedly. For all those panic attacks, she'd let herself feel too safe.

Maybe this morning's jitters were meant as a reality check. Her sub-brain saying, *Complacency is dangerous.*

She managed a shaky smile. "I'm sorry. My home was broken into a few years ago, long before I came to Cape Trouble. When I walked in and saw a few things that seemed off, well, I guess I had a sort of flashback."

"I see." Detective Payne studied her for a long moment before he restored the notebook and pen to that inside pocket and rose. "Don't be embarrassed. And please don't hesitate to call the next time. Most often, when our alarms go off, there's good reason. Tamping them down isn't smart."

She nodded and stood. "Thank you for saying that. And for coming so fast. Really."

He gave her a card with his cell phone number scrawled on the back. One more speculative look, and he departed, leaving her not so sure he had bought her little story there at the end. That bit he'd said, about listening when that voice inside said *run*, made her wrap her arms around herself for comfort. Had she just done something really stupid, awakening the interest of a cop? And not just any cop, oh, no. A detective?

Run.

No. She'd been on edge all day. No one had been in her small house. A busy detective wasn't going to investigate her past out of idle curiosity. It was silly even to think he might.

After a minute, she very carefully closed the junk drawer, the way it should have been.

CHAPTER TWO

Adam followed Ms. Varner – no, get used to calling her Kendrick, so he didn't slip up – to work the next morning, making sure she made it safely inside through the back door of her restaurant via the alley.

Didn't she realize the perils of parking in a deserted alley, for God's sake? Even if she didn't have enemies, she was a woman. A woman on her own should avoid lonely places like alleys. Especially a young, pretty woman.

Hovering at one end of this alley in his rented SUV, he scowled at his own mental addendum. What difference did it make what Naomi Kendrick looked like? He was here because of his belief that, at the very least, she'd lied to the cops after finding Frank's body in her restaurant kitchen. The fact that she closed the restaurant and disappeared so soon thereafter had cemented his suspicion into certainty. And then there was the fact that she'd been dating Gregory Cobb. Nice women didn't usually snuggle close with killers.

No, she might not have murdered Frank herself – hard to see how she could have, given their relative sizes and strength – but by God she knew something.

It wasn't as if she was a raving beauty, anyway. More… It took him a minute to settle on a word, which was *intriguing*. Small, slight enough to qualify as skinny, which seemed unnatural in someone who could cook like she did. Didn't she eat her own food? Her skin was unusually pale, particularly given her dark hair and brown eyes. The sharp chin and slant of her eyes made him think of pixies and other, mythical beings. Her ears should have been pointed at the top to complete the picture.

Forget the fact that, in other circumstances, he might have been attracted to her. Wasn't happening.

At least she had a recognizable face. There was no question this Naomi Kendrick was the Naomi Varner he'd seen only in a photograph. The one significant change she'd made in her appearance was the hair, which had been long before, and was now boy-short, except on her all the feathery cut did was emphasize that subtly fey quality.

Short of a gunman bursting in the front, she should be safe enough for now, tucked away in the back of her café. Adam decided he'd get breakfast elsewhere this morning, then go back to the Sea Watch Café for lunch. If she showed her face at all, he wondered if she'd recognize him from yesterday morning.

The remainder of yesterday afternoon and evening, he'd kept an eye on her and tried to plan his own approach, altered by the fact she'd already had a scare. He couldn't be positive her small house had actually been searched, although her reaction made it seem likely. He doubted she'd stowed whatever Cobb's organization sought in anyplace easily found, anyway. The restaurant kitchen, now, might be worth a look, if he were willing to risk an arrest for breaking and entering.

Under other circumstances, he'd have used these free hours to make contact with local authorities.

He'd done his research enough to know that the Cape Trouble police chief, a guy named Daniel Colburn, had come from the San Francisco P.D., where he'd served in homicide. Adam had made a few calls and was left with the impression Colburn had been solid on the job. No one seemed to know how or why he'd ended up in a backwater like this. Still, he was likely more competent than your usual small town cop.

Even if his own intentions had been in the clear, Adam would have been wary of the detective who had showed up yesterday in response to Ms. Kendrick's call. He might have come by chance – say, was the nearest officer in the good-sized rural county where average response time might run as much as half an hour – but it was also possible she'd called him personally. The fact they hadn't touched made it unlikely the relationship was romantic, but they could be friends.

Didn't matter. For the time being, Adam had no intention of alerting any local law enforcement. The last thing he wanted was them to verify he was who he said he was with his lieutenant.

After breakfast, he needed to find a place to stay. What catnaps he'd managed in the front seat of the Tahoe had left him tired and stiff this morning. He wanted a shower. To shave. A place he could stretch out. He needed to start looking as if he belonged. He'd been lucky yesterday that no one had called the cops on the strange vehicle parked on their block.

There seemed to be no available rentals in Jasper Beach. He had spotted two *For Sale* signs, though, and written down the phone numbers for the agents handling them. Both houses were vacant. He could be persuasive.

After using a gas station restroom to shave, he ended up having breakfast at a place called The Waves, attached to a beach-front hotel. Pancakes heavy in his belly as he left, he wondered that anyone chose to eat there when they could be having Naomi Kendrick's French toast.

Then, instead of phoning, he dropped in at the real estate office for the smaller of the two houses, and the nearest to Naomi's. He found the listing agent in. She was young and eager, and, while her disappointment was obvious when he admitted he wasn't in the market to buy, she agreed to call the absentee owner. This was the son, she explained. The former resident had recently passed away. She murmured that part, almost apologetically: *passed away*.

He figured that meant dying of old age, versus the kind of deaths he saw day in and out. Those tended to be too ugly to qualify as a gentle *passing*.

She provided him with coffee in a styrofoam cup and left him in the tiny conference room. He could hear the murmur of her voice coming from across the hall. She reappeared, bright-eyed.

"If you're willing to make a refundable, three hundred dollar damage deposit in addition to the daily charge, Mr. Ingersoll has agreed to rent you the house for the two weeks you've requested. In fact, he's offered to add some very basic furnishings – a bed and a kitchen table and chairs, at least. The appliances stayed with the house," she added. "Mr. Ingersoll had hoped for a quicker sale, so the idea of renting the place out occasionally appealed to him."

His smile made her blush. No ring on her finger. Maybe his lack of interest could be attributed to tiredness. He hoped that was it.

Turned out, the agency managed a number of rental properties, so she was able to quickly produce a suitable contract. She said she'd call a local furniture store and have them deliver the promised furnishings.

"Oh! And linens," she added, making notes.

He'd have been okay with throwing a bedroll on the floor and maybe buying a lawn chair, but wouldn't mind being a little more comfortable than that.

After writing a substantial check in return for a key, he headed inland rather than doing his shopping in Cape Trouble. The scenery during the drive was pretty, he had to admit. He'd noticed the ribbons of mist that clung to the aptly named Mist River near its mouth. They thinned and then vanished not far up-river, where the water, impressively clear, rushed between and over boulders. Occasional deep pools made him think trout. The trees weren't big, but the forest was denser, wetter, with a thicker understory, than any he'd hiked in California's Sierra Nevada mountains.

The town of North Fork turned out to be somewhat larger than Cape Trouble, and also the county seat. As the Realtor had promised, he found a thrift store where he bought some basic cooking utensils and dishes. He'd do the next renter a good turn and leave them behind when he left. A grocery store was his second stop.

Half an hour later, he let himself into his very own rental, situated not quite a block from Naomi Kendrick's. From the front window, he could just see her place at an angle.

The furniture hadn't been delivered yet, but he plugged in the refrigerator, hoped it cooled quickly, and put away his groceries. There was no microwave, but he hadn't expected one. He flipped on a burner to be sure the stove hadn't been unplugged, too. It turned red. Good enough. With a little exploration, he found a washer and dryer as well. Handy, if he was to stay any length of time.

He wandered back to the front window and gazed broodingly down the street to Ms. Kendrick's bungalow. Here he was, in place, but lacking a plan. He'd been in such a goddamn hurry to get here, he hadn't bothered worrying about his strategy.

What might have worked before she had a good scare wouldn't now. She'd be extra cautious. Still…something else was bound to happen. She wouldn't have kept anything important shoved under her bed. No, if her place had really been searched, that was just the opening move.

So…watch and wait, he decided. See if he couldn't find an in with her.

He grunted his dissatisfaction at what was no plan at all, checked his watch, and saw that it was almost lunchtime. Despite the heavy breakfast, his stomach growled. Meals eaten during a surveillance usually came in a greasy white bag. The café would make for a nice change.

*****

He was there again. Same table, even. When she looked out, those curiously light eyes met hers. He tipped his head the slightest bit in some kind of acknowledgement, but he didn't smile.

The other man had had breakfast at the Sea Watch again that morning. She'd been relieved this one hadn't, but here he was for lunch, instead.

Yet another lone man had taken the table in the corner. She'd come out to get a look at him, but she couldn't tell if he saw her. He was older, forties or even early fifties, brown hair touched with gray at the temples, so ordinary in appearance she wasn't sure she'd recognize him if she bumped into him on the street half an hour from now. He wore chinos and a sweater. The lack of drizzle today had brought colder temperatures, and everyone had added a layer. Naomi had, too, although she'd peeled hers off once she got to work. It was always hot in the kitchen.

Once again, she retreated, her heart beating faster than it should.

He's back because he likes my food.

Plenty of visitors ate once or even twice a day here, while they were in town. Without arrogance, she knew her food was the best to be found on this stretch of the coast.

Calmer, she checked the newest orders Anita and Brianna, her newly hired second waitress slash dishwasher, had brought to her. Today's soup was a spicy tomato and the specials a vegetarian chili and her own take on lasagna. Almost everyone was topping off lunch with one of the two pies – today, apple and chocolate walnut.

She was almost grateful she didn't have a larger dining room. She couldn't have kept up alone, which would have meant more employees. More bookkeeping and paperwork. And a bigger kitchen, too, of course. No, she'd been there, done that, receiving the acclaim that had once been her dream. In one night, it had all crashed and burned, and she had expected to ache for what she'd lost.

Instead, to her bemusement, she was satisfied with this small café. Locals weren't exactly foodies, so she couldn't get too creative, but she could still make good food, and she didn't subsist on something like five hours of sleep a night anymore. She didn't have to supervise half a dozen other chefs, there was no pressure to startle and delight restaurant critics, and yes, she often had to wash her own pots and pans, but didn't actually mind.

She might even have been happy, if only she could know she was safe, that she wouldn't have to take off at any time. If she could make real friends.

Both Anita and Brianna stayed to help with dishes. Anita left via the front door, accompanied today by Bri, whose boyfriend was coming by to get her. Since for once it wasn't so much as drizzling out there, Anita had walked today.

Naomi regularly listened to stories from Anita's life, about the kind, balding husband who was an insurance agent, the teenage son who played tight end on the high school football team, and the daughter who had applied for early admission to Willamette University and expected to get in. Making encouraging noises, she sometimes felt like a foreigner trying to understand this so-American family. *She* had never lived anything like that.

If she had, she might not be able to bear the loneliness now.

Annoyed because she'd let herself feel momentarily wistful, Naomi let herself out the back. She almost swore when her gaze went straight to her usual parking spot only to find it empty. She'd almost forgotten. That morning, she'd turned into the alley to find an unfamiliar pickup had taken her usual spot, forcing her to park a little farther from her door than usual. Now she walked quickly, staying observant. It was with relief that she reached her car and inserted the key in the lock.

The blur of movement came from nowhere. Slammed face first into the still closed car door, she was helpless when her bag was yanked from her shoulder.

"No!" she cried, and pushed off, swinging around.

All she saw was a back. The man was charging away down the alley, her messenger bag – her computer! – clutched like a football in front of him. A black knit hat covered his head, leaving her without a clue who he was or what he looked like. Scared and furious, Naomi raced after him, yelling for help.

Another man appeared at the head of the alley. Seeming to understand instantly what he was seeing, he put down his shoulder and met the other guy in a block that had to hurt.

They grappled, and went down. Naomi saw fists flying, and heard them connecting. There were grunts of pain and effort, too. And – was that her screaming?

She'd almost reached them when the original attacker rolled away. It wasn't a hat he wore, it was a face-mask. No, a death mask. She could see only dark pits where his eyes should be and teeth as he snarled. He reached behind himself –*Gun!* a voice in her head screeched – but her rescuer lashed out with a booted foot, connecting with the masked man's arm. Her bag dropped with a thud to the ground.

Voices sounded behind her.

Clutching his arm as if it hurt, her attacker stumbled to his feet, that death's mask turned to her. She felt the eyes burning into her, and then he turned and ran again. The second man swore, leapt up, too, and took off after the first, leaving her bag where it lay.

Whimpering, Naomi snatched it up.

"Naomi? Are you all right?" It was Monica, but she wasn't alone when Naomi turned. With her was Elias Burton, the artist, tall and rangy, with his gilt hair and silver eyes.

He reached her first, but was looking past her. She swung around again to see the second man limping back toward her. And – oh, dear God – it was *him.*

Shaken, she had the odd thought that he was as beautiful as Elias, but was the dark to Elias's light. Except for those eyes, not dark at all.

And he had lifted a hand to the side of his face, where redness surrounded an abrasion right where skin stretched taut over his cheekbone.

"You're hurt." She sounded shell-shocked.

"Nothing serious. What about you?" His voice was a little gritty, as was the scrape, she saw when he got close enough. It needed cleaning and antibiotic ointment.

"I'm okay." She thought.

"I've called 911," Monica said breathlessly.

Second time in two days. Different departments, but…would whoever responded know?

She had to tell them. It would look…odd, otherwise.

"I'm sorry I couldn't catch him," her rescuer said. "He disappeared in that damn parking lot."

The good size lot was right in front of the beach access, where there was also a narrow strip of grass with picnic tables, a public restroom, and outside showers so people could wash off sand before returning to cars.

He frowned. "I saw the car he jumped into, but I couldn't read the license plate. Looked to me like it had been deliberately coated with mud."

They all heard the siren, cut off as a squad car turned in to the alley but stopped a short distance up it, blocking that end. At least in Cape Trouble, you got a quick response.

Naomi didn't know whether to be relieved or not when the police chief himself got out. She had managed to avoid even meeting the man during the first ten months of his tenure, but had let herself get drawn into planning the auction that was part of the Save the Misty Beach campaign. When Doreen Stedmann, the woman who had launched the campaign, was murdered in the storage unit where auction donations were kept, Police Chief Daniel Colburn had scrutinized all the volunteers. Naomi hadn't liked the thoughtful way he had looked at her. He suspected something about her, but enough time had gone by now, she assumed he had either let it go, or she'd been imagining things. She'd gotten to know him a little better, since she'd become almost-friends with his fiance.

His blue eyes took in their small group. "Naomi, Monica." His eyebrows raised a little, as if in surprise. "Elias." Then that gaze settled squarely on Naomi's rescuer.

"Chief Colburn," he said, holding out a hand.

"Adam Rostov."

They shook.

She had a name to go with that extraordinary face now. It fit better than the ones she'd come up with from credit card slips. Rostov sounded as if it could be…she didn't know, Romanian, Russian, Ukrainian. *Dracula*, she thought, in a completely unsuitable flight of fancy, given where they were and why.

And the fact that her back was starting to hurt. Her stomach, too, for some reason. That jerk really had barreled into her hard. She shifted, trying to get more comfortable. Gaze resting on her, Rostov seemed to be the only one who noticed.

Daniel wanted to know what happened. The story came out in bits and pieces. Naomi realized events had a weirdly fragmentary quality already in her mind. She described getting smashed into her car, feeling her bag being wrenched away. The guy taking off, intercepted by Adam Rostov.

"Him, I recognized. He's eaten in my restaurant a couple of times," she said. She looked shyly at him. "Although I didn't know your name, of course."

"I still don't know yours, except I gather you're Naomi."

"Oh. Kendrick. I'm Naomi Kendrick." She introduced the other two, at which point they offered what little they could as witnesses, then allowed themselves to be dismissed by the police chief.

His interest was in Adam Rostov, who said he'd had lunch at Naomi's café. "Great chili," he told her, his gaze resting on her face briefly before he turned his attention back to the police chief. "Then I wandered down to the beach for a few minutes. I'd just gotten back to my rental—" he nodded the direction from which he'd first appeared, "—when I saw what looked like a mugging. I thought I could at least get the lady's bag back."

When Daniel asked if her assailant had been armed, she frowned, remembering her impression.

"For a minute I thought— But I don't know. He just sort of whammed into me. I didn't actually see any kind of weapon."

"He had a handgun," Adam Rostov said flatly. "He was reaching for it when I kicked him. Fortunately, at that point Ms. Sanchez and Mr. Burton had appeared and he panicked and decided to take off."

"How did you know—?" Naomi asked.

"It was holstered in the small of his back, visible when he ran."

She should have seen, too, but…everything had happened so fast.

"Thank you," she said suddenly. "I haven't said that yet, have I? Everything really important is in this bag. My laptop, my wallet, my phone. It would have been awful if he'd gotten away with it."

His mouth curved. "You're welcome."

She looked at Daniel. "This probably doesn't have anything to do with what happened, but, um, yesterday I thought I'd had an intruder at home."

The gazes of both men sharpened.

"Did you call it in?" the chief asked.

"Yes. I don't live within the city limits, you know. A Detective Payne came. He said he'd been the closest. He walked through the house with me, but—" This was embarrassing. "The more I looked, the less sure I was that anyone had been in there after all."

"What made you think someone had?"

She explained.

"It's…odd, to have the two events so close together."

She didn't like the penetrating way Daniel Colburn was looking at her. It was all cop. He *knew* there was something she wasn't saying.

As a diversion, she turned to the other man. "You should go to the clinic so they can clean up that scrape. And…you're not hurt anywhere else, are you?"

"I'll stop at the pharmacy and pick up some antibiotic cream." The grit in his voice seemed to be natural, not the residue of the fight or the chase. "I just rented a house for a couple of weeks. I'll go back there and clean up." He glanced down ruefully. He was not only wet, she saw a tear in his dark brown trousers – and, through it, another red, seeping scrape. The reason for the limp, she realized belatedly.

"Oh, no!"

The grin that flashed was disarmingly boyish and sexy. "I played soccer through college. Intramural rugby, too. Believe me, this is nothing."

"You'll be here in town, then?" Chief Colburn asked. His tone was not-quite casual.

"Actually, the place I found is on the other side of the point with the lighthouse." Her rescuer frowned. "Jasper Beach? Is that right?"

That momentarily chilled her. What were the odds…? But how could he possibly have known someone was going to grab her bag?

"I wasn't aware any of the houses there were available for short-term rental," the chief remarked.

"The house is for sale. I guess the owner decided he'd like to make a little money while he's waiting for a buyer."

Daniel Colburn nodded, his relaxation noticeable only because she was watching closely. "Makes sense."

He took a description of the car, which sounded like the average rental, then wrote down Adam Rostov's cell phone number. Adam didn't know the address of the cottage he'd rented. "I have the paperwork in my SUV, if you want it. The owner's name was Ingersoll, if that means anything to you."

"Oh, that's just down the block from me," Naomi was surprised into saying. "Bert Ingersoll was a nice old man. I remember when—" She stopped, realizing somebody planning to sleep in that house probably didn't want to know about the owner's death.

But he raised his eyebrows, those compelling eyes on her. "When…?"

"Well… He'd been dead several days when his next door neighbor began to wonder why newspapers and mail were piling up. That's all. But I know the house has been thoroughly cleaned."

He grinned again. "Don't worry. I'm not that sensitive. Although I can see why that Realtor didn't tell me."

"I shouldn't have," she said remorsefully.

"Don't worry about it." He glanced at Chief Colburn. "You done with me?"

"Yes, thank you. And for getting Naomi's bag back."

Rostov nodded politely at both of them and walked away. The limp was no longer in evidence. He moved the way she'd thought he would, fluid and contained. It was easy to believe he'd been an athlete. Daniel had that unnervingly thoughtful expression on his face as he watched him go, but he shuttered it after a moment, raising his eyebrow at her. "You okay to drive?"

She assured him she was. Yes, she'd let him know if anything else out of the usual happened. He held open her car door as she lowered herself carefully into the seat, then slammed it closed. Because his car blocked the way she usually exited the alley, she went the other way. She had reached the cross street and put on her turn signal when she glanced in the rear view mirror and saw that he hadn't moved. From this distance, she couldn't read his expression, but she knew he was thinking hard about her.

The temptation was there: to go out to the highway and start driving. Don't stop. She had everything really important with her. She could get a long ways before tomorrow morning, when Anita arrived to find a dark, locked café.

Of course, she'd have to get rid of this car and buy another. Figure out, eventually, how to create a new identity.

Fingers gripping the steering wheel tight as she waited for a light to change, she tried to believe this had been a simple mugging. The guy hadn't tried to hurt her, after all. He just wanted her bag. He could probably tell she carried a laptop, and assumed she'd have money and credit cards besides.

Yesterday…had been all in her imagination.

And even if it wasn't, she had been reluctantly considering one option to fleeing. Back in southern California, she hadn't known anyone in law enforcement she could be sure was honest. Daniel Colburn would be trustworthy, she did believe that. Whether he could protect her, or would want to once he knew the whole story, though… How could she be sure?

She couldn't, of course. But…if the choice came to running again, her possibilities even more limited this time, or going to Daniel… She still didn't know.

As she passed the road leading to the resort that was under construction, a couple of protesters waved placards at her. She couldn't imagine what they thought they were going to accomplish now.

Her turn signal went on when she reached Jasper Beach, although she suddenly wished she'd asked for an escort home. What if the guy who'd grabbed her bag really had searched her house? He'd already gotten in once. He could be waiting for her.

She stopped a block from home and called the Cape Trouble Police Department, reaching Ellie Fitzpatrick, who served as dispatcher, receptionist and who knew what else. Naomi identified herself and asked if the chief was in.

He came on the phone. "You reached home yet? Has somebody been there?"

"I don't know," she admitted. "I'm having a panic attack. I guess I should have called the sheriff's department, but that would take a lot of explanation, and…"

"I should have offered," he said immediately. "Sit tight. I'll be right there."

"Thank you," she said meekly.

He was as good as his word. In less than five minutes, he passed her, stopping in front of her cottage. She followed and pulled into the driveway.

Here she went, going in the side door again with a police escort. This one pushed the door quietly open and went in first.

They were alone. He had her check doors and windows while he opened closets and even bent to peer under the bed. Frowning, he looked around.

"I'm going to have my officers drive by regularly. And yeah, it's out of our jurisdiction, but it's not far, and adding the loop here won't kill any of 'em. Tonight, leave both outside lights on. If either is off, we'll take that as a signal."

Naomi nodded, almost speechless at his kindness.

Maybe I can trust him.

He was still a cop. What if he didn't believe her?

As he was going out the front door, an unfamiliar black SUV approached. No, wait – could it be the one that had been parked around the corner yesterday? It swerved to stop behind the Cape Trouble squad car. Adam Rostov got out and came up the cracked walkway.

"Tell me somebody wasn't waiting for you here."

The slight roughness of his voice felt like the touch of calloused hands. Hearing it, seeing him again, gave her goosebumps.

"Were you sitting over there yesterday?" she asked abruptly, nodding toward the corner.

Daniel stayed silent, but she felt his awakened interest.

Adam turned and looked. "Oh, yeah. I was parked there for a while yesterday afternoon. I saw a cop show up here. I should have realized this was your place. A lot of these houses don't have numbers, and street signs seem to be in short supply, too. I was waiting to get into the house, but it turned out I was in the wrong place."

"Oh." That made sense. She relaxed infinitesimally before giving him a stern look. "You should already have put ice on your cheek. You still haven't cleaned it up, either. You might end up with a black eye."

He smiled at her. “I went to the pharmacy, as ordered, ma’am. I now have first aid supplies.”

He’d saved her today. Well, not her, but most of her important possessions. She ought to offer *something* besides a thank you.

“Why don’t you come in?” she suggested. “I have ice, and you probably don’t, do you? And…was the hot water tank turned on?”

He looked taken aback. “I didn’t think to ask. Or check. If you’re sure…”

“I’m sure.”

Daniel eyed him narrowly, but only nodded at Naomi. “Remember what I said.”

“I will.” She smiled at him, too. “Thank you. You’ve gone above and beyond. I may have to make a huckleberry cobbler just for you.”

He grinned. “Bribery. Turns out I’m susceptible.”

“I could be susceptible, too,” her rescuer put in hopefully.

She laughed. “I do make very good huckleberry cobbler. And you definitely deserve your very own.”

It wasn’t until she turned to go into the house that she saw the way Adam watched Daniel walk away. It was speculative. Cold. In fact, it looked an awful lot like the way *Daniel* had watched *him.*

She didn’t know anything about this man.

No. I do. We aren’t friends or even acquaintances, and yet he jumped in without hesitation when he saw I needed help.

That was recommendation enough, wasn’t it?

“Let me get some ice for you,” she said.

He followed her in, reassuring her again by the careful distance he kept from her. He must have guessed she’d be easy to alarm.

This was the decent thing to do, that’s all.

CHAPTER THREE

He felt like a vampire stunned to receive an unanticipated invitation. *Please, come in.* No extraordinary effort on his part required. All he'd had to do was loiter with an eye on where Ms. Kendrick would emerge from her café, and *bingo*.

She sat him down at her small kitchen table and took out a bag of frozen peas rather than the ice he'd expected.

"I think this will work better," she said, seeing his expression. She wrapped it in a dish towel and handed it to him. Then her gaze fell to his knee. "Maybe a second one would be a good idea."

Adam shook his head as he pressed the cold pack to his cheek. After wincing at the sting of the ice, he said, "The knee really is just scraped. Let's talk about you, instead."

She didn't move a muscle, but he had the fleeting image of a doe that had just spotted a predator. Paralyzing fear. *If I don't even breathe, he won't see me.*

Adam was disconcerted to discover he didn't enjoy being responsible for that expression in her eyes.

"You're walking carefully," he said. "You can't tell me something doesn't hurt. Did he knock you down? Hit you?"

Her relief was like seeing someone who'd been concussed regaining consciousness. Warmth, humanity, a sense of self, came back online. His guilt ratcheted up a notch until he reminded himself who Ms. Naomi Kendrick was - a hired killer's girlfriend, and a liar.

"He...shoved me against my car. I think I wrenched something in my back." Her forehead creased. "I don't know why my stomach hurts."

Setting the frozen peas aside for the moment, he reached for the hem of her T-shirt and said carefully, "May I?"

She quaked. "You want to *look* at my stomach?"

"Yes."

"Why...? Oh, never mind. You can... Oh, my," she finished, staring down at the beginnings of what was going to be a bruise closer to black than the usual purple. It was an obscenity on her smooth white belly.

"What the hell?" he growled. It looked like she'd been stabbed, lacking only the cut.

"Oh," she said again, but this time on a rising note. "My keys. I'd put them in the car door, and he shoved me flat against it. That's...right where they would have hit me."

"Jesus." He had trouble tearing his eyes from her torso. Women in southern California tended to bake themselves in tiny bikinis whenever possible. Had Naomi Varner when she lived down there? If so, she'd lost any vestige of a tan. There was something about the purity of her snow white skin that spoke of innocence. Her ribs looked as delicately made as the rest of her body. It was all he could do not to lay his hand flat on her belly, feel the texture of that skin, the give to the softness beneath.

He cleared his throat and made himself let go of the thin stretchy fabric of her T-shirt. It fell to cover her bare flesh. Too bad he was still eye level with her small, high breasts. "Okay," he managed to get out. "What about your back? Can you bend over?"

He had her do some careful twists, too, and concluded she'd probably strained a muscle. She took some painkillers, insisted he do the same, and went off to get a bag of cotton balls.

After dampening several at the kitchen sink, she added tiny drops of soap. "I can...wash your cheek, if you'd like." She sounded shy. "Since you can't see to do it."

Adam didn't point out that he could go use the mirror in her bathroom, although that might have been smart. Instead he said, "If you think it needs it."

Again he laid down the frozen pack. Naomi stepped close to him and touched one fingertip beneath his chin to tilt his face up to her. Damn. Her eyes dominated that pixie face. With her focused utterly on him and not her own fears or inner pain, her eyes weren't just brown, they were the color of melted caramel, warm and swirling.

Her touch was gentle, too, until the soap stung and he winced.

"I'm sorry, I'm sorry!"

"I'm being a wimp," he said gruffly. "Ignore me."

This smile produced a dimple at one side of her mouth. He wanted to lay his finger over it, feel the pucker.

Damn it. He blinked and tried to fix his gaze anywhere but her face. Unfortunately, her breasts were strategically placed straight in front of him.

They weren't especially impressive, he reminded himself desperately, trying to picture what-was-her-name's generous bounty. The image came and went without being any help. He couldn't so much as summon the former lover's name, either.

He closed his eyes. *Please finish. Get this over with.*

There were another couple of soft touches, after which she stroked her finger over the scrape. It felt cool. "Ointment," she murmured. "I hope the ice pack doesn't wipe it off. Oh, well. We can put more on."

He opened his eyes, groped for the towel-wrapped peas, and held it up to his face, wishing he could hide behind it.

"Why don't I clean up your knee, too?" she suggested.

Oh, hell. She was going to kneel in front of him? How was he supposed to hide his reaction to these...intimacies? He couldn't think what else to call them.

Say, *Gee, no, thanks.*

But it was too late. She'd already taken a handful of those cotton balls to the sink and was dampening them with warm water and soap. The next thing he knew, she crouched in front of him. Not quite as bad as kneeling - not so symbolic - but bad enough.

He wasn't sure he could have gotten a word out.

Her hair looked baby fine, wisps clinging to her forehead and cheeks, baring neatly formed ears. Tiny gold birds took flight on her earlobes. He'd noticed the glint of gold before without focusing on the earrings. Were they symbolic for her, of the flight she'd made? And if that was so...what did it mean?

Recovering his usual state of cynicism was taking more effort than usual. To accomplish it, he had to turn his head and look toward the gingham curtains closed over the small kitchen window. Closed curtains, because she was hiding. Remember why?

Yeah, okay. His arousal didn't immediately subside at the dose of reason, though. Apparently his body didn't care whether she was an amoral bitch or not.

Could she really be, and still feel the obligation to take care of him out of gratitude? Could hands as gentle as hers have thrust a knife up beneath a man's ribcage into his heart?

Adam sat forward, slightly hunched, hoping his chinos tented enough to keep him from shocking her.

"There," she said at last, brightly, and rose to her feet. Her gaze didn't quite want to meet his.

"Thank you," he said roughly. "I think my face is numb now."

"Good." She accepted the now dripping pack from him and carried it to the sink. "Would you like a cup of coffee or...or something?"

"No, but thanks." He frowned. "You think this guy was after something in particular?"

Her pupils flared before she looked ostentatiously around. "Like what? Do I look wealthy? I don't have a single valuable possession. I mean, the laptop is probably the priciest thing I own, but second-hand?"

"If he searched your house and then went after your bag, that's pretty persistent."

Her teeth closed on her lower lip. "I really think I imagined that someone had been in the house. Why would anyone bother? It just doesn't make sense."

His thoughts were more clinical now. *Sure it makes sense, Ms. Varner. And you damn well know it.*

"So, listen," he said. "Let me give you my phone number. I'm barely a block away."

"When you're not at the beach or whatever you plan to do for fun."

Was there a hint of a question there?

"I just...needed to get my head together," he said. Nicely vague. The last thing he wanted was for her to ask what he did for a living, although she probably would eventually. Truth or lie? "I'll probably do some hiking, walk the beach. The usual. No nightlife, though, so I should be around evenings or during the night if anything scares you."

Those warm eyes searched his. "If you mean it."

"I mean it. You have a pad of paper?"

She produced one along with a pen. He scribbled down his name and phone number. Looking at his name, there in blue ink, he suddenly wondered if anyone had ever mentioned the name of Frank Donahue's partner to her.

Couldn't have. She wasn't that good an actress.

A certainty that gave him pause, because if she wasn't...

Letting the troubling thought go, he dropped the antibiotic ointment back in his small white sack and rose to his feet. He felt an ache or two along with a creak in his knee, all from the violent encounter in the alley. Could have been worse. Man, he'd have liked to rip that mask off the guy's head. Then he'd know who he was dealing with. Getting a license plate number wouldn't have been as good; the car was sure to have been rented under a fictitious name.

He might have been smart to have used one himself, except he didn't have a choice of fake I.D. lying around the way anyone in Cobb's organization would. Too late to worry about anyway.

He went to the front door, pausing when he opened it. "I'll see you tomorrow." Her surprise made him grin. "I had breakfast at that beachfront hotel this morning."

Naomi Kendrick's nose wrinkled the tiniest bit.

"Your French toast is better," he said simply.

Her dimple flickered. "Live and learn."

He was laughing when she closed the door behind him.

His drive was short. The furniture, as basic as it came, had been delivered in his absence. He stood in the kitchen looking around. *Her* cottage was homey. His wasn't.

Feeling irritable, he dragged one of the cheap metal and vinyl-upholstered chairs to one side of the front window in the living room. While he was at it, he grabbed a beer - one should be safe - and his binoculars. Then he sat back to examine his troubled awareness of contradictions between the woman she appeared to be and the one he had expected her to be.

To think, and to wait.

*****

Naomi was grumpy and exhausted when she let herself into the Sea Watch come morning.

She would have given a lot yesterday afternoon to go for a run, but had been afraid she'd aggravate the soreness in her back. Plus, running wouldn't have the usual zen-like effect if she had to listen for footsteps behind her and search every outcropping or tree for a predator lurking behind it.

And then, of course, she couldn't sleep. Despite her fears, she had slept better in Cape Trouble than she ever had before. The steady sound of the surf, so near, was like a mother's heartbeat to a baby, she'd come to believe, reaching deep into her psyche, where the most primal instincts lurked. Nights were otherwise miraculously quiet, traffic almost nonexistent, sirens rare. None of her neighbors threw wild parties. She suspected she was the youngest resident of Jasper Beach by at least twenty years if not closer to thirty. The small enclave might almost qualify as a retirement community. With her nonexistent social life, she fit right in.

Last night, though, she'd heard every faint sound. She would stiffen at what she knew was only the passing of a car on Highway 101. A tiny creak - the house settling. What might have been a voice - she did have neighbors. A car occasionally driving slowly by – patrol car.

Her eyes seemed to have sunk into deep holes when she'd looked at herself in the mirror this morning. She shuddered, remembering the holes in the ski mask that had seemed so empty until that last, inimical stare.

In defiance of the agreement every downtown merchant had signed, she parked on Schooner Street this morning and unlocked the front door of the cafe instead of the back. The time might come when she'd feel safe - semi-safe - to park in the alley again, but not this week.

Tomorrow was Monday anyway, the one day of the week the cafe remained closed. Normally she looked forward to it. Now...well, she'd have to do her shopping, but otherwise she knew she'd huddle at home, listening for more creaks.

Alone in the cafe, she indulged herself in a strangled moan.

She didn't always have a breakfast special, but today she carefully wrote on the blackboard, *Huckleberry crepes*. After breakfast, she'd make those two promised cobblers. She'd frozen plenty of huckleberries she had picked herself.

"Oh, yum," Anita announced, after she'd arrived and seen the blackboard.

They were so busy this morning, Naomi didn't have a chance to think about anything but cooking. Anita popped into the kitchen once and said, "A Mr. Rostov sends his compliments on the crepes, and says to tell you as good as they are, they don't let you off the hook. Does that make sense?" she added doubtfully, before tacking on, "What a gorgeous man!"

Naomi smiled. "It makes sense. And he is. He also came to my rescue yesterday when a guy in the alley slammed into me and snatched my bag."

Anita gasped. Naomi had to give her a few more details, but they were too busy for her to exclaim too much.

A couple of hours later, the orders trickled to an end, and Anita told her another man had asked to speak to her. "It's the guy who wanted to know your name, I don't know, a couple of days ago? He was at the corner table?"

Naomi nodded, hiding her perturbation. She could hear voices from the dining room, so she wouldn't be alone with whoever this man was.

She dried her hands and went out. Half the tables were still occupied with people finishing their coffee. She knew most. Adam, of course, was long gone.

This time, the large man with auburn hair sat by the window. He was over-sized for the small table. He saw her immediately, not looking away as Naomi pinned on a smile and wended her way across the room to him.

"I understand you asked for me?"

"Yes, do you have a minute to sit down?"

She hesitated, then pulled out the chair opposite him. "Literally a minute. I need to get started on lunch."

"I understand." He extended a big hand to her. "Randall Bresler." He appeared expectant.

She recognized the name, but not, she suspected, for whatever reason he thought she should. She let him engulf her hand and shake. He didn't try to hold onto her longer than felt comfortable.

After a moment, he smiled faintly. "I'm building the new resort on the bluff."

"Oh." Duh. She should have recognized his name from articles in the *Cape Trouble Tribune*, not only from his credit card slip. It did ping in her memory now. He wasn't a construction worker; he owned the whole shebang. "I hope you'll join our merchants' association even if the resort is outside the city limits."

"The chamber of commerce has already sent a representative." He sounded wry. "Somewhat prematurely. We won't be opening until spring. Late spring, probably. I hope." The last was muttered.

Her gaze strayed toward the kitchen.

He noticed. "You're a superb cook, Ms. Kendrick. I do understand the pleasures of owning your own business, but I know the hassles, too. If you came to work for me, the hassles would be gone. You'd be free to cook - and I'd give you a completely free hand with the kitchen, I promise. You tell me what you're taking home after expenses here." There was the smallest hint of condescension in his tone. "I'll top it. Substantially." He shook his head when she started to open her mouth. "No, don't say anything yet. Obviously, you have months to consider my offer. But please do give it serious consideration."

He only wanted to hire her. She almost laughed.

"I can promise that much," she said. "But be warned. If I had to make a decision today, I'd say no."

He nodded and held out his hand. Once again, they shook, after which she returned to the kitchen.

Naomi prepared and baked three cobblers, cutting one up to offer as a dessert during lunch. The other two, she cooled and covered. When she was eventually ready to close, she had to make two trips to get both to her car.

This being Sunday, she left the last two days receipts locked in the cafe's small safe, which made her even more nervous than usual, given the events of the week. Taking a large amount of cash home didn't seem like a good idea, either, though. She was careful never to have more than two days take sitting around. If she ever was robbed, that way the loss wouldn't be crippling.

She stopped first at the police station. Daniel greeted the sight of the pan in her hands with a huge grin.

"I've died and gone to heaven."

"Don't tell Sophie it took my huckleberry cobbler to take you there."

He gave a shout of laughter. "Don't worry, she takes me to heaven pretty frequently."

The reminiscent gleam in his blue eyes made Naomi's cheeks heat. The pang she felt wasn't jealousy, not exactly. It wasn't as if she'd ever wanted Daniel Colburn. In fact, if she'd been alone, she'd have snorted at the idea of her having any kind of relationship with a guy in law enforcement. Even this tentative step toward friendship with Daniel made her nervous. Her experience with cops was more than a little tainted.

Daniel thanked her again for the cobbler and walked her out to her car. The last thing he said was, "You be careful, Naomi."

Seeing that he now serious, she nodded. "Cowardly me, I parked on the street today instead of the alley. Don't tell on me," she added, trying to lighten the moment.

His chuckle told her she'd succeeded. "Keep doing that for now."

Some hesitation at the end told her he had intended to tack something else onto that sentence. *Until...?* Until what? Until nothing else happens for weeks and weeks? *Is that when I'll start to feel safe again? Or...almost safe?*

She didn't know. Maybe she'd never feel safe again. She imagined herself in her eighties, rocking slowly away, head cocked as she listened for the creak of floorboards outside her room in the nursing home.

When she reached the traffic light at the highway, a black SUV loomed in her rearview mirror, stopping right behind her. She tensed. For some absurd reason, the blink of its turn signal reassured her. Did bad guys signal their intentions? Probably, she realized ruefully. They'd pass unnoticed better if they were careful not to commit any trivial infractions.

The windshield of the SUV was tinted enough it took her a moment to be sure Adam was the driver. Coincidence that he should happen to come up behind her, or something more sinister?

Oh, God, she was so tired of living in fear.

He followed her sedately back to her neighborhood. She drove to his cottage instead of hers and pulled to a stop at the curb. He turned into the driveway. Naomi was taking the baking dish from the passenger seat when he walked toward her, carrying a bag she recognized. Sweet Ideas: Books 'n Fudge. Hannah Moss's bookstore, across the street and a block down from the Sea Watch Cafe. Naomi's relief was so enormous, her knees wobbled. Although the wobble might have had something to do with the lazy, purely masculine stride that held such leashed strength, she had no doubt of his ability to hit a dead run between one step and the next.

She nodded at the bag. "You've been shopping."

His grin was devastating. "Spent a mint. Hey, pun. Mostly on books, since I'm not much of a chocolate eater. But she has these caramel truffles with a scattering of sea salt on top..."

Naomi laughed. "And here I come, daring to bring more sweets."

"Is that my cobbler? You actually meant it?"

She opened her mouth to say *I don't lie*, which of course was a lie, so instead she went with, "I keep promises."

"Do you."

She couldn't quite read that.

"Come on in," he said. "I think I can make room for a first helping right now. I just happen to have some French vanilla ice cream."

"Do you." She made it as bland.

His low, rough laugh gave her satisfaction, until it occurred to her in alarm that she had almost sounded as if she was flirting with him. Was she? Horrifying thought.

"May I offer you some dessert?" he asked.

She'd skipped lunch altogether, except for a few tastes, a necessary part of cooking. Her stomach cramped. And…it wasn't as if she looked forward to going home to her empty house.

"Actually...that sounds good."

"Good." He led the way up a concrete walkway buckled by the thick root of an aging, now leafless, maple tree. As he let them into the house, he asked how her back was. "I suppose you've been on your feet for hours."

"I perched on a stool a little more often than usual today. The answer is, sore. I'd love to go for a run, but I have a feeling I'd better hold off for a few more days."

"You're a runner, huh?" He appraised her with a sidelong glance that left tingles of warmth in its wake.

"Yes, I even did one half-marathon." Thank heavens, she'd managed to sound like usual. "I don't aim for anything that ambitious anymore."

"I run, too. Let me know if you want company next time you go out."

"Your legs are longer than mine. I'd slow you down."

He shook his head. "Even if that's true, taking it a little easy isn't the worse thing I could do. Speed has never been my goal."

She almost opened her mouth to ask what was, but stopped herself. That would be flirting, too. And...what if he told the truth and she didn't like it? What if he lied?

Takes one to know one.

She jerked her attention from the very sexy man to the house. She'd never been inside although she'd often stopped by the peeling picket fence to chat with old Mr. Ingersoll when she was returning from a run or just out walking. Whatever the interior had looked like then, now it was a blank slate, any personality wiped away. The furnishings were beyond bare bones. A cheap kitchen table and two chairs were tucked into a corner in the kitchen, and she saw another, matching straight-backed chair in the otherwise empty living room, by the window.

Following her glance, Adam said, "Taking advantage of the light to read."

"It's too bad you don't have a view of the ocean."

"There's one from the bedroom. Between houses, but I can see the surf."

From bed? Oh, she so didn't want to picture him in bed, shoulders bare and sleek, hair rumpled, eyes heavy-lidded.

"Where do you usually run?" she blurted. Gee, why not just say, *So, where are you from?* "I mean, do you have to pound city sidewalks, or do you at least have a park you can take advantage of?"

"Sometimes one, sometimes the other." He took the ice cream out of the freezer and a spoon from a drawer. "I'm from southern California. Lotta city streets, but some decent parks, too. When I can, I run on the beach."

Oh God, oh God. But...he'd said it so casually, not even looking at her. And people from California must come to the Oregon coast for vacations, too.

"Why here?"

A dark arch of his brow made his face even more devilish. "Here?"

"Cape Trouble."

"Oh. I liked the idea of someplace that actually has an autumn. For some reason, November is when I'm hit every year by this intense dislike of unrelentingly sunny, unchanging days."

"I know what you mean," she said softly. "I...used to live down there, too." Fear stampeded through her. Was she nuts?

"Yeah?" He peeled the aluminum foil off the cobbler. "Where'd you live?"

"It was a long time ago. Um... I've lived in L.A. and West Hollywood."

"You ever run on the beach?"

"Of course I did. Great way to get over any delusion that I was in good shape."

He laughed. "Anywhere you can here?"

"Yes, but you need to drive around to the other side of Mist River. It's technically trespassing, but everyone does it. The beach over there is sandy and goes on and on. I jog along Jasper Beach sometimes, but the cove is so small and you can't really get around the points except at low tide, and even then you're clambering over rocks instead of running. Mostly I take a trail that heads up and over thataway." She gestured. "Great views, mostly doesn't get too muddy."

"You'll have to show it to me." He handed her one of the plates, a giant scoop of ice cream atop an even bigger square of cobbler. "No microwave," he said apologetically. "So I can't warm it up."

"It's good either way. Although I'll never be able to finish a serving this size."

"That's okay. I'll finish mine and yours." Again, his gaze swept her. "I've been wondering how you stay so little when you cook so magnificently."

Magnificent, she liked. *Little* made her feel like a nondescript dab of nothingness. Which is good, she reminded herself. She wanted to be nondescript, for the eye to pass right over her.

"It's hard work," she told him. "I forget to eat. Plus, it always seems to be hot in the kitchen, which keeps me from being hungry." Chronic, low-level fear tended to depress her appetite, too.

He took his first bite and closed his eyes until he'd swallowed. Then he made a sound in his throat, a little gritty like his voice. "Damn. And I thought that truffle was good."

Would he make that sound when he—?

Don't go there! Naomi thought in alarm.

Knowing he was watching, she popped a bite into her mouth, savoring it, breaking down the flavors, searching for nuances, and generally satisfied she'd gotten it right. "Mmm," she finally murmured.

"Nirvana," he agreed.

"Daniel Colburn called it heaven." Her mouth curled up at the memory.

"You've already been to see him?" The question was unexpectedly sharp, surprising her into lifting her head.

"I dropped his off at the station."

"You're friends?"

There was still an edge there, one she didn't understand. "More with his fiancée. I worked with her on the auction we held this summer to help raise the money to buy the old Misty Beach Resort."

The set of his shoulders eased. "I heard about that. Is it a done deal?"

"Not yet. We're close to having enough money, though. The real holdup is the legal complications. You know the plans for the land?"

"Only that it's to be saved from the evil developers."

She laughed. "Right. Well, the old man who owned the resort died last spring and left it to his nephew since he didn't have any kids of his own. Instead of selling it right away to developers, the nephew very generously gave us all the time we needed to raise the money to buy it instead. Our contribution is being matched by a conservancy group that will also manage the land as a preserve," she added.

Adam nodded.

"Unfortunately, it turned out Benjamin Billington wasn't brimming with generosity because he wanted to honor his uncle's wishes. The truth was that he had killed a bunch of women around here, years before when he was working at the resort summers, and he'd buried them on Uncle Harlow's land. He was afraid that, with bulldozers tearing up the ground over there, the bodies would be unearthed."

"Hey, I remember reading about that. It happened here, huh?" His eyes darkened. "It wasn't you he went after at the end...?"

"No, that was Sophie, Daniel's fiancée."

"Jesus." It sounded prayerful. "That must have made him crazy."

"I...didn't see him that night, but people talked about it later. 'Crazy' is probably an understatement."

Looking disturbed, he said, "Yeah." Then, "So the legal complication is whether a serial killer actually can sell the land?"

"Something like that." Wanting to get away from the grim subject, she told him, "You know, people *really* talk in Cape Trouble. It's sort of creepy when you're used to the big city where you don't even know the names of your neighbors on each side of your apartment."

He grinned. "I can see that. Hey, what's with the protesters out by the highway?"

"There's a small group of people who apparently still delude themselves they can stop construction of the resort. Everybody ignores them. I mean, any ecological damage has already been done, right?"

"Except for increased traffic, sewage, water usage."

She made a face at him. "Okay, you're right."

He asked what most locals thought about the new resort, and she told him more than he probably wanted to know. Everybody in town had an opinion, frequently expressed in her café. What she didn't hear, Anita reported to her.

Adam said reflectively, "I see your point about gossip. Tough to get by with anything around here, isn't it?"

The way he said it, the way he looked at her, sent a chill through her. She actually shivered.

"Yes." She forced a smile. "I hope you're as hungry as you said you were, because I think I'm full." She pushed the plate toward him and then rose to her feet. "I'd better get home."

Lines deepened between his eyebrows. "You okay?"

"Sure. Just...things to do. Tomorrow is my only day off, you know."

"I did notice I'm on my own for meals tomorrow."

Somehow she kept the smile in place. "Sorry." Only belatedly did she wonder if he was angling for an invitation. She'd think about that later, when she could forget the cool speculation she might or might not have really seen in eyes that changed from crystalline gray to stormy in a heartbeat.

He stood, too, and walked her all the way out to the street. "Thank you for the cobbler."

"You're very welcome." She made sure her open car door formed a barricade between them before she faced him. "It's not exactly an even trade, you know. Not after what you did."

A strange expression crossed his face, one that held frustration and uncertainty. "Naomi..." But whatever he'd thought of saying, he cut off. Instead, he only stood there looking at her, those same lines carving his forehead.

"Bye," she said hastily, got in and closed the door. She gave a vague smile in his general direction before driving away.

CHAPTER FOUR

Adam didn't enjoy feeling like scum.

Call him low, but he made every effort to alter his shame into resentment squarely aimed at Naomi for playing the innocent so well, she damn near had him fooled.

This was the lady who'd dated Gregory Cobb, a killer-for-hire. Who'd reputedly stayed late several times so he could host "business" gatherings in a private room in her restaurant.

This was also the woman who'd pulled a vanishing act the minute the shit came down. Pretty damn skillfully, too, except for the glaring mistake of opening another restaurant. She'd disappeared so fast and so effectively, he had to believe she'd already been prepared to decamp if things went wrong. Innocents didn't have alternate I.D.s in their dresser drawer, ready to pull out at need.

Yeah, but...damn it. Even their brief acquaintance had doubt stirring. What if she'd bolted because she was scared, not because she was guilty? What if she really had entered her restaurant one morning to stumble over a cop knifed to death in the kitchen? For a person who'd never even seen a body, the sight would have been hideous. He could imagine the revulsion she would have felt at the idea of someone using one of her knives to kill with. Was it really so unlikely she'd refuse to cook another meal in that kitchen? That she'd close the restaurant and walk away?

No. But that didn't explain the name change. The fear he saw in her eyes.

What if she'd seen something and been threatened because the killer suspected?

Why not tell the cops?

Because the one threatening her was Cobb, and she guessed local law enforcement couldn't protect her from him?

Damn it, he thought again, fear didn't excuse her for not cooperating with the investigation, for letting Frank's killer go free.

If Gregory Cobb hadn't murdered Frank, he'd had someone else do it. Cobb had been there that night. He'd admitted as much. Frank had to have been on his tail. He'd learned something, suspected something. Could he even have hoped to corner Naomi, late, only to find someone else waiting for him in the kitchen?

What if she *hadn't* left yet, though, making her a witness? Or at least knew who had still been lurking in her restaurant when she left? Even if she was normally a law-abiding citizen, could she have felt mushy enough about Cobb to buy some crap explanation from him? Say, that Frank was the dirty one? Or, worse, not buy the explanation but still be willing to let whatever she'd seen slide?

Maybe, but she wasn't willing to continue a relationship with the guy, Adam reminded himself. In fact, she'd obviously laid her hopes on the concept that out of sight was out of mind.

Clearly, from the wiretap, she was shit out of luck if she'd been that foolish.

He'd spent most of the night and the following morning after she'd presented him with the huckleberry cobbler brooding. It was like trying to ride the surf in. Thinking he'd caught the wave just before he was dumped from his board and sucked back out.

Was he thinking with his dick even to imagine she could be an innocent? Hey, he wanted her, and it wasn't okay to have her if she'd played any part at all in Frank's murder? He didn't like to call what he felt *hope*; truth was, the only loose thread he could pull in his determination to prove Frank had been killed on the job, doing his duty, was Naomi Varner aka Kendrick. He *wanted* her to be that thread. He owed Frank his loyalty.

But fitting the shy, reserved, frightened woman he was getting to know into the frame designed for a liar and accessory to murder had turned way too quickly into a struggle.

He already knew, after a stint while he had been assigned to the gang unit, that he didn't like undercover work. He wasn't enjoying it this time, either. He didn't mind being a hard-ass. Deceit, though, rubbed Adam the wrong way. And tonight he was suffering a boatload of guilt, because he'd talked Naomi into going out to dinner with him.

"Unless you hate eating in other people's restaurants, let's get out of town," he'd suggested when he knocked on her door midday. "I think you need a break."

"I...don't go out very often," she had said hesitantly. "But that sounds nice."

He was pretty sure she had surprised herself by agreeing. After browsing online, he suggested a bistro in Pacific City that seemed to have good reviews. Naomi agreed she'd heard about it and would like to try it.

He couldn't do dressy, not out of the one duffel bag, but he changed to black trousers, low black boots and a sports shirt before returning to pick her up in the early evening. Leaving his weapon in the glove compartment tonight ought to be safe.

When he pulled into Naomi's driveway, she popped right out, not waiting for him to come to the door. His mouth went dry at the sight of her. He wasn't sure if what she had on qualified as a dress or a tunic top, but it was rust-red with what looked like a black vine climbing her side. Long-sleeved, high-necked, stretchy and snug fitting, it just covered the subtle curve of her hips and ass. Below were black leggings and what looked like black ballet slippers. Black lace wrought in metal danced from her earlobes. Even though it wasn't actually raining right this minute, she carried a coat draped over her arm along with her hefty messenger bag.

The first thing she did was apologize for bringing it. "I just thought I'd be happier keeping it with me. You know. After…"

Smart girl, was what he thought.

"I don't blame you. You look sensational," he said, with complete honesty.

Her eyes were warm, free of the shadow of pain and fear. Maybe it was the idea that nobody could find them, that for a few hours she would be safe. If so, it hadn't occurred to her that they could be followed.

Or that *he* was a danger to her.

"Thank you," she said, smiling. When he opened the passenger side door, she hopped in.

The drive down Highway 101 wound dizzyingly. Sometimes they were surrounded by forest, then would unexpectedly emerge on a cliff's edge high above the turbulent, gray Pacific Ocean. Views would have been even better on a clear day, but the low gray clouds and occasional drizzle added atmosphere.

Conversation stayed light. They talked about books, movies - although she hadn't seen many these past two years, as Cape Trouble had no theater and she said she only rented DVDs occasionally - and music. Their tastes intersected enough that they at least spoke the same language. She didn't ask what he did for a living, thank God.

She would, sooner or later.

He kept stealing glances at her, disconcerted by how different this woman was from the wary one of their previous encounters. Adam remembered thinking he might have been attracted to her, under other circumstances. He'd already accepted that, like it or not, his body reacted to her; no *might have been* about it. But now...damn. Lit with humor, animated, her face was extraordinarily pretty. More mischievous elf than shy, fey creature barely glimpsed before it fled. And, while she was definitely slight in build, her curves were more pronounced than he'd guessed. His hands wanted to explore every dip and hollow on her body.

Not happening, he told himself grimly. At least, not yet. Not until he could be sure of her, one way or another.

Turned out eating with her was an adventure in itself. They shared crab cakes with an aioli that he'd have pronounced fine until she decreed it too strong on the paprika.

He frowned on the next bite. "You're right."

The merry smile made her eyes sparkle. "Of course I'm right."

"Modest, too."

"Excellence requires a level of confidence, don't you think?" she said matter-of-factly.

He smiled. "I concede your point."

Over a really fabulous steak for him and halibut for her, he asked if she'd lived in other parts of the country.

"Florida, when I was really little. My dad died when I was six. I hardly remember him." She must have seen the question in his eyes, because she said, "Nothing dramatic. I mean, he didn't plummet to his death in a sky-diving accident and he wasn't killed serving overseas. He just...dropped dead. According to Mom, he was grilling on the back patio and *wham*. He was gone. Turned out he had a flaw in his heart that nobody had ever had reason to notice. I suppose it's a good way to go, except he was only thirty-seven." A hint of that shyness returned to her eyes. "That's probably more than you wanted to know."

"No. I'm curious." Insatiably.

More to disconcert him.

"Oh. Well, then, um, Mom remarried a couple of years later." Her expression was no longer as open or good-humored. Was it because his curiosity was too strong, reminding her to be wary of *him*? Or did this reserve have to do with her stepfather? "After that we moved a lot," she said, in a tighter voice. "He'd get bored with a job, or just restless, and we were off again. I hardly ever stayed in the same school for more than a year, if that. So really I've lived all over, but mostly in the Southeast. I quit bothering to make friends."

"My father was military," Adam heard himself telling her. It was a whopping lie. A useful one, though, to create a nice sense of affinity. The words came easily, too, because this history was borrowed from a friend. "We usually stayed put for three years at a time, and the friendship thing was a little easier for me because all the kids had the same experience. Still, you don't graduate from high school with your best friend from kindergarten."

"No." She sounded sad. "All my favorite books when I was growing up were about these deep bonds of friendship. I was so jealous."

He wanted to take her hand. Instead he reached for his wine glass.

"I've told myself I grew up more independent than I would have if I'd ever put down roots."

"There's that," he agreed.

"Where are your parents now?" Naomi asked.

"Dad's retired." Another lie; Dad never got there. After having to resign from LAPD even though there was never any solid proof he'd taken bribes, Adam's father had been lucky to get hired as sheriff in a small crime-ridden town down by the Mexican border, where he treated his bitterness with booze, grew a gut that sagged over his belt, and woke up angrier every morning. Eventually there'd been a divorce. And then – hell. Adam's jaw tightened. He wasn't going to think about the end.

Back to fantasyland. "One of their last stops was San Diego, and they liked it so they stayed. They have a nice little house, and Dad's become a gardener." He managed a smile as he told her about Ramirez's dad, a stocky, tough former Navy chief, deadheading his roses and conducting war, now, only against aphids.

Adam had been an adult by the time he became friends with Juan Ramirez and was as good as adopted by his parents. Adam didn't like knowing he'd just used some really good people in a way they wouldn't approve.

Naomi laughed, though, as if he'd restored her effervescence. He was gladder of that than he should be, which triggered a warning ping.

"How about your mom and stepdad?" he asked, wanting to turn the subject from him and his life before he had to think up new lies he'd have to integrate with the ones he'd already told – and remember.

She hesitated just long enough, he wondered whether she was concocting a lie of her own.

"My stepfather was abusive." Face and voice both told him this was raw truth. "Mom died five years ago, just before I—" She stopped so fast Adam heard the rubber burning. She swallowed. "He didn't kill her, but he might as well have. She was broadsided by a drunk driver. Pure chance that driver wasn't him."

Hell. "I'm sorry," he said, and discovered in shock that this time he'd laid his hand over hers on the table without even realizing he was doing it.

She stared at their hands, too. Neither of them moved for a moment. He didn't so much as breathe. And then she turned hers and gave his a grateful squeeze. His heart threw in a hard thump as he looked at those intertwined fingers, hers pale, fine-boned, his so much darker, thicker. Her nails were short and unpainted - practical. He wanted those small, competent hands touching him. Anywhere, everywhere.

Don't be an idiot.

Yeah, yeah. His goal had been to get close to her. That was happening. Holding hands was like...a bunt, he decided. Not even close to a base hit, never mind a double, triple or home run. Nothing he had to feel guilty about later.

He just wished holding hands with her didn't feel so good, as if the simple touch had become a conduit.

He cleared his throat. "I assume you don't speak to the son-of-a-bitch."

Her eyes met his squarely. "Not a chance."

"Good for you."

"He didn't hurt me. Mostly he ignored me. Sometimes I almost wished he'd hit me. I think when I made him mad, he took it out on her." She gave her head a little shake. "Let's change the subject. Tell me something about you."

First thing that entered his head was to confide his youthful dream of becoming a fighter pilot. Not smart, because that would lead to him having to say what he actually did do for a living. The subject would inevitably come around, but later was better than sooner.

"I was a hell of a soccer player."

Her smile lit that piquant face. "Modest, too."

He grinned at that. "Got me through college on a scholarship. I still play in an adult league." He was a forward, Ramirez a dynamite goalie. "How about you? Are you strictly a runner, or do you play any sports?"

She wrinkled her nose. "I'm an okay swimmer, but I never competed. I did gymnastics when I was little, but I'm kind of a coward. Flying through the air, feeling the bar slip through your fingers and landing on the mat with a big *whump*?" She mock-shuddered. "I was scared to death on the balance beam. Mom gave up." She smiled. "We played a little soccer in P.E. I think I would have liked it. I was always the last picked for basketball teams. Can't imagine why."

He chuckled as he lifted a hand for the waitress. Naomi declined dessert, and he did the same. "Can't be as good as yours," he said, and was rewarded by her smile.

The waitress heard what he said, though, and Naomi mentioned her cafe. Next thing he knew, the chef had emerged from the kitchen and they were engaged in shop talk. He stayed at the table sipping coffee while she disappeared to inspect the kitchen, not emerging for a good fifteen minutes.

Cheeks flushed, she apologized, but he shook his head.

"Did you enjoy yourself?"

"Yes, actually. There's not really anybody else in Cape Trouble..." She didn't finish, obviously feeling she'd gone out on a limb on the arrogance scale, but so far as he'd seen, she was right. There were cooks, and then there were chefs. Tonight's dinner had been cooked by another chef.

He thought about suggesting a walk on the beach since night had yet to fall, but unlike her he hadn't forgotten that they could easily have been followed. He didn't like being unarmed and feeling exposed, either. Besides, he discovered when they stepped outside that a faint drizzle had started, enough he had to use the wiper blades to clear the windshield.

In his SUV, pulling back out onto the highway, he nudged the conversation to siblings. None for her, a sister for him. Pets - no and no. His mother had a cat now, if that qualified. He'd hardly set eyes on it, since it shot behind the couch whenever he stepped foot in her condo.

"You haven't said what you do—" she began, but he talked right over the top of her as if he hadn't noticed she'd asked a question, too.

"Have you owned your own restaurant before, or always worked for other people?"

He sensed a startled glance, but after a moment she said, "I actually did own one before this. It was...bigger. We offered lunch and dinner, so I worked really long hours."

Adam filed away the "we". Had Cobb been an investor in her restaurant? He wished he knew whether investigators had looked into the possibility of a financial entanglement.

"I was thinking about this recently," she continued. "I should have brought in someone to take more of the business stuff from my shoulders. I had a bookkeeper, but I supervised the staff myself. I'm a perfectionist, and I liked keeping control. And when you're on top and want to stay there, you have to constantly strive for new, startling, better—"

Adam wondered if she was talking to him anymore, or only herself. Purple-gray dusk was settling, blurring detail.

"I think you forget about *better*," she said softly. "I actually enjoy preparing simpler food now. Trying to make the familiar as good as it can be, while still satisfying people who think, oh, macaroni and cheese, I like that."

"I understand. And I can attest that your food is amazing."

"Thank you," she said, letting him hear her smile.

Night was coming swiftly now, and either there was no moon or clouds covered it. They'd encountered hardly any other traffic on the highway. He recognized the curve ahead and knew they'd be crossing Mist River into Cape Trouble in just a minute.

Naomi said suddenly, "Thank you for suggesting this. I mean, getting away. It felt...really good."

It had, even for him. He'd set aside his job more than he probably should have and let himself enjoy taking a woman out for dinner.

"I had a good time, too."

"Partly, I don't do much in the evening because I have to get up so early in the morning. If I had my own house, I might enlarge the kitchen so I could do some of the baking in the evening instead, but as it is..." She shrugged.

"Why'd you sell your other restaurant and move?" he asked. "Was it because you wanted to go smaller?"

Cape Trouble wasn't exactly lively at this time of night, but streetlights and hotel and restaurant signs were lit, letting him see Naomi's face better than he had a minute ago.

"No-o," she said slowly. "Something happened. I just...I wanted to leave the area."

"Southern California?"

Careful not to look at her, he was still aware of being scrutinized.

"Yes," she said finally.

"I might have eaten in your place."

Earlier silences had felt...comfortable. This one stretched long enough he had to glance her way.

"As many restaurants as there are in the greater L.A. area, it's unlikely." She sounded almost snappish, as if she was hoping like hell he hadn't.

He wondered what she'd say if he asked the name of her restaurant. Cape Trouble fell behind them. He had his signal on for the turn into Jasper Beach when instead he asked, "Why don't you like the idea that our paths might have crossed before?"

"This is my new life. Ne'er the twain shall meet," she said lightly.

The nice man who'd taken her out to dinner would have accepted her less-than-subtle evasion and not pursued the subject. The cop observed, "The *something* that happened must have been a humdinger."

She turned her head to look out the window. "I don't want to talk about it."

"I'm easy to talk to," he said mildly.

But, damn, they were pulling up in front of her cottage, and she unfastened her seat belt and had her door open before he set the emergency brake. Apparently he'd killed the mood.

"Hold on," he said. "Let me do a walk-through with you."

Uh oh, he thought. Walk-through? He sounded like a cop or a real estate agent. But if she'd noticed, he couldn't tell, because she was already out of the SUV. From the set of her shoulders and the stretched length of her neck, all the tension eased this evening was back. Adam guessed she'd have loved to say, *Thanks, but no thanks,* except that the strain on her face told him she was also scared to go into her home alone. After a moment she gave a short nod before slamming the passenger side door.

He wanted to grab his Glock from the glove compartment, but she turned towards him rather than the house as she waited, providing no opportunity. Not much choice but to go in unarmed.

They walked the short distance to the side door in silence. *His* nerves and muscles tightened in readiness. He scanned the interior of her little Ford on the way. No surprises there. None inside, either, that he could see. Her gaze darted this way and that as they entered each room, but didn't settle anywhere and he didn't detect any alarm, so he guessed she hadn't had a repeat visitor, and nobody hid under her bed or crouched behind her dryer or the clothes hanging in her closet.

No invitation to stay for a cup of coffee was issued, although she relented at the front door to the extent of saying, "Thank you for offering to come in. It's dumb to keep being scared every time I get home—"

"No. You have good reason to be cautious. Cautious is smart."

A little frown furrowed her brow as she studied him. "That's what the detective said the other day."

"It's common sense."

"Yes, but if someone really did break in, he'd have discovered there isn't anything here worth taking. Why would he come back?"

Keeping his mouth shut, he couldn't resist a significant glance at the messenger bag she'd dropped on the sofa. Naomi turned enough to see what he was looking at, and her cheeks flushed.

"I almost always have it with me."

"You know that. I didn't until now."

She frowned. "Now you're scaring me! Knock it off."

Adam flattened a hand on the doorjamb beside her and looked down at her. "I want you to stay safe."

Which was *not* his principal goal here, or shouldn't be, anyway.

"Oh." Her face softened.

Caramel, he thought again, looking into her eyes. Warm and melted. He leaned forward.

They looked at each other. For all her wariness, she felt the same pull, he could tell. Even yearning. *I shouldn't…but I want to.* That's what she was thinking.

He shouldn't, either, but, damn, he did want. A polite guy kissed his date goodnight, he told himself. He didn't slap her on the back and say, *Good talking to you.* He should play this to the end.

Naomi didn't step back. In fact, she tipped her face up and her eyes fluttered shut when his mouth brushed hers. The contact was barely a whisper, but he felt zinged as if by static electricity, only in a good way. He went back for more, no longer bothering to think up justifications.

This time he covered her lips with his and took advantage of what might have been a gasp to slip his tongue into her mouth. The tiny sound she made shot straight to his groin. So did the feel of her small, strong hands when they settled on his shoulders.

A part of him knew he was kissing her way too seriously for the circumstances, but he couldn't seem to help himself. Instead of exploring her mouth, he was devouring it, but, God, her tongue met his and she leaned into him even as he gathered her tight, lifting, fitting her to his larger frame.

A groan rumbled in his chest, and he tore his mouth away long enough to kiss the tip of her cheekbone, her temple, her closed eyelid, back to her cheek, then take a nip at her earlobe that had her quivering. Everything about her worked for him, even the way she breathed, fast and light like a bird captured in his hand.

His hand was sneaking around to cover her breast when light flashed against his closed eyelids. Adam opened his eyes fast, just as headlights played over them. A powerfully protective instinct had him pushing her back over her doorstep so his body blocked her completely. His right hand went for his weapon, before his brain caught up with the memory that he was unarmed. Which was lucky, or he'd have ended the game he was playing with her prematurely.

Fortunately, the car continued past at fifteen miles an hour, tops, as hasty as anyone in this neighborhood ever drove. Adam didn't like knowing the eyeful the driver had probably gotten, though.

She'd gone rigid in his grip. "Who was that?" she whispered.

"Nobody. I mean, probably a neighbor. You do have neighbors," he joked, when he didn't feel anything approaching humor. Adam was painfully aroused, angry at himself for kissing a suspect the way he just had, and even angrier because he'd let himself become blind to their surroundings even though he knew someone had it in for her.

"Oh. Oh!" With that second small cry, she leaped back, her self-consciousness fully restored. "I don't want gossip."

He was irked to hear how appalled she sounded.

"What's so scandalous about having your date kiss you goodnight on your doorstep?"

"No, I know you're right," she said after a moment. "But, um, I'd better really say goodnight this time." Her eyes didn't meet his. She was still embarrassed, or something else.

"Okay." What else could he say? "I enjoyed myself tonight," he repeated.

"I did, too." She sneaked a look at him. "Thank you for dinner."

"Sleep tight." He stepped forward, kissed her lightly on the cheek, then walked back to his Tahoe when that was the last thing he wanted to do. Just before he reached it, he heard her front door close. The porch light remained on, as did the one over the side door. He'd noticed last night that she was keeping both on when she hadn't the first night he'd sat outside her place. Lighting the darkness, that was another human instinct to keep fear at bay.

He drove to his less-than-cozy home away from home and let himself in, only he didn't turn on any lights. Instead, he sat in the dark and watched Naomi Kendrick's small house, interested not ten minutes later to see a Cape Trouble P.D. unit creep past, pretty obviously checking out her place.

Had to be the police chief's doing, and above and beyond, considering they were outside the city limits here.

Which told Adam he wasn't the only one who knew damn good and well that the guy who snatched her bag would be back.

For future reference, he was glad to find out he hadn't misjudged the city cop who had inexplicably become police chief in tiny Cape Trouble, which – given the summer's happenings – wasn't as untroubled as you'd expect.

*****

Naomi lay awake for hours. She heard more traffic than usual and, unlike last night, timed the intervals. Almost exactly forty-five minutes apart. Comforted to know it was the extra patrol Daniel had promised her, she relaxed, until she thought about the long stretches *between* patrols, and then she started to worry about whether, if the man behind the knit mask was watching, he could clock the appearances of the patrol cars and know exactly how long he'd have in between. Which left her more awake than ever.

She thought about the evening and how…happy she'd felt, except for the unsettling moments when she remembered the way Adam Rostov's eyes had burned into hers the first time she saw him across her small dining room, and how conveniently he had then popped up when she needed him.

Sometimes she was sure he was being straight with her. When they talked about their childhoods, their parents. The uncertain moments might be in her head, because she was paranoid and even more jittery than usual.

The something that happened must have been a humdinger.

He could have been interested only because he picked up on her emotions about it.

He'd been all-in when he kissed her. No faking there. And – would he have kissed her at all, if he'd been hired to come after her?

Naomi made a face at the dark ceiling. Why not? Face it, for most guys, sex was just sex, and moral qualms didn't enter into it. If someone working for Greg, or Donovan Greer, or… Would an FBI agent hire a confederate? She couldn't imagine. All she knew was, everyone sitting at the table that night lacked moral compass. She'd known that for sure when, two weeks after she had closed the restaurant and taken off, Greer's opponent in the race for congressional office, a man named James Heath, had been found shot to death, parked in an alley in a really sketchy part of town, lipstick on his face, his pants unzipped and pulled down to his thighs. He'd supposedly given a talk to big supporters in Newport Beach where he raised bucko contributions, then told his aides he wanted to drive home on his own. The assumption was, of course, that he'd taken a detour for a quickie and maybe pissed off a pimp. Who knew? Only that he was dead, his wallet missing and his reputation trashed, too, just as Greg had promised.

She hadn't even finished reading about the death on Yahoo when Naomi had had to run for the bathroom. She'd barely made it. Afterwards, rinsing her mouth, she thought about James Heath's wife, who had to suffer humiliation and savage hurt along with grief.

Lying here, Naomi relived for the couple hundredth time that last conversation with Greg, secretly ashamed she'd made up her mind to let him kiss her, to pretend she liked it, even though she knew he was a monster. Would it have made any difference if she *hadn't* shrunk from him? Was that when he knew for sure she'd heard too much? Or – would he have kissed her even if he'd already made up his mind to have her killed?

Her mind jumped sideways. The electrifying kiss with Adam might not have meant anything to him except the possibility of getting some. A vacation fling. Men were wired like that, even the ones who were basically good people.

She groaned and rolled over in bed, slapping the pillow over her face.

She shouldn't have trusted him – but how did you go through life not trusting *anyone*? And…he had come to her rescue once. His number was in her phone, already called up before she crawled into bed so that all she had to do was touch 'send', grateful to know how quick he could get here.

A thought came coldly to her. Even if he was one of the good guys, she couldn't forget he was here only for a short time. He wouldn't be around that much longer, and then she'd erase his number from her phone and be totally on her own again.

Unless she decided to trust Daniel Colburn, another man she didn't know that well, with her Pandora's box of horrors, not to mention her safety.

At three in the morning she gave up on sleep, pulled a sweater over her pajamas, and turned on the kitchen light before opening cupboard doors and pulling out pots and mixing bowls. Some people went for comfort food; she went in for comfort cooking.

CHAPTER FIVE

Adam might have had breakfast or lunch at her café, but Naomi never stuck her head out of her kitchen to find out. This Tuesday wasn't as busy as they'd be closer to the weekend, but that didn't mean she was standing around, either.

She was able to leave at the same time as Bri, and out the front door, too. After a quick stop at the bank to make the deposit, she went home.

To combat her desperate need for a nap, she decided to go for a run. There really wasn't any reason to think the mugging was anything but her being a lone woman in a deserted alley, she thought. She wouldn't be carrying her laptop or wallet on a run. Plus, she'd go crazy if she didn't do *something*. She hadn't gotten any exercise in days, which had to be contributing to her sleeplessness and anxiety. Her back wasn't as sore today, and exercise should be therapeutic, right?

Naomi twitched aside a curtain and peeked down the street. The black Tahoe sat outside the Ingersoll house, but she didn't see Adam. She wanted to call and ask if he'd go with her…and she didn't. Staying to herself was healthier for her. The contradictions she sensed in him had her twitchy. No matter what, she couldn't start counting on him, not when he wouldn't be around long.

She changed into stretchy running gear, including calf-length pants instead of shorts because the day was really chilly. Long-sleeve shirt, but breathable fabric. Before she went out the door, she removed the square door at the back of her closet and stowed her bag. She'd discovered the cache early on, after moving in. It was a space roomy enough for suitcases and the like. A really thorough search would find it, but the boards were old and didn't look that different from the ones surrounding them. She tucked her key and phone in pockets, debated sneaking out the back door and decided not to. She did her stretches in the carport, then trotted out to the street, waving to Arthur who was looking out his window.

Her route took her past Adam's rental. Somehow she wasn't surprised when he burst out and called after her, "Hey! Wait up and I'll go with you."

Relieved and, damn it, dismayed by how powerful that kick of relief was, she turned and jogged in place. "Why don't you just catch up with me? Keep going, and you'll see a trailhead."

He cursed when she kept on, but she guessed it wouldn't take him long to change, and with his longer legs he wouldn't be far behind her.

Her muscles had loosened by the time the trail began the climb to the promontory that formed the other arm encircling the crescent of Jasper Beach. A dense but low-lying fog was advancing in off the ocean, as it often did in the afternoon, but hadn't yet reached the cove.

The trail switchbacked up the steep, rocky slope, between small, twisted Sitka spruce and shore pines that clung wherever they could embed roots in pockets of thin soil. If she looked back, she'd have a great view of the lighthouse on the point, and of the bones of the new resort rearing over Jasper Beach. Instead, she concentrated on her footing, on the burn of muscles, on the flash of movement lower down that told her Adam was gaining on her.

The sleepless night and ever-present anxiety along with taking – what? – a week or ten days off exacted a toll. She was breathing harder than she ought to be this early into her run. No rule said she couldn't cut this shorter than usual. She shouldn't let pride push her too far.

Adam still hadn't caught her when she crested the top, where a semi was passing on the highway something like three quarters of a mile away. To her left, a cliff dropped to the ocean, where waves crashed against rocks instead of beach. The evergreens and madrone up here had a better foothold, but were still too battered by winter storms to achieve much size. The smell of the ocean filled her nostrils and she kicked up speed.

Droplets of moisture clung to branches that she had to dodge. She was smiling when something slapped her arm hard enough to spin her around – and the next second a *crack* overrode the sound of the surf.

*****

God damn idiot woman, Adam fumed, watching her lithe body in form-fitting, pumpkin orange disappear over the ridge above him. One minute, she was as nervous as a doe in season, the next she lost all sense and trotted out into the open with a target painted on her back.

Crap. He should be back at her place, figuring out where she'd stashed that bag. She'd be gone long enough for him to prowl her computer, unless her passwords were better chosen than most people's. He'd have liked to get a look at the phone, too, but she might have that with her.

But here he was instead, chasing her down before someone pushed her off the edge of the cliff—

Crack.

Rifle, not handgun. He turned on the after-burners. Sprinting, sweat burning his eyes, he tried to calculate where the shot had been taken from.

Crack.

God *damn*. If she'd gone down—

She was down, all right. The bright color showed up against a basalt outcropping topped with stringy yellow grasses and long whippets of something that might be a wild berry. A fireball gathered force in his chest, but then her head turned when she heard him.

Relief transformed her face. He felt some wild relief of his own, until he saw the grip she had on her arm and the blood running between her fingers. She'd been hit. Wrenching his gaze from her, he yanked out his Glock and slowed, scanning for movement, color that didn't fit among the monochrome of misty greens and grays and tans.

The shot could have been set up from a hundred yards away, two hundred, farther, depending on how skilled the sniper was. His own black running pants and tee didn't stand out the way Naomi's getup did, but they weren't much better. He'd have rather been in khakis. The landscape was too open up here, too, the available cover made skimpy by the advent of winter, with branches bare.

He passed her with a terse, "Stay down," not letting himself think about the shock in her eyes as she stared at his weapon. He kept going, moving from one tree contorted by winds to another, his skin crawling from his awareness that none of the trunks were broad enough to shield his body. Bending over, he ran for a pile of rocks, his gaze moving unceasingly.

Crack.

The rock inches from his head splintered. He ducked.

Crack.

Shit. He was pinned down. The shooter was probably trying to buy himself time to get back to a vehicle. He couldn't still think he could get by Adam to her – unless he hadn't seen that Adam was carrying.

He weighed the possibility of hunkering down with the idea of ambushing the asshole, but he didn't like how blind he was here.

He belly-crawled a few yards and risked taking a look. Nothing, nothing…*there.* A shift that suggested movement. Tan, brown. Then nothing again. The guy had disappeared behind a low-growing evergreen. Still out of Adam's range. He took a chance and bolted for the next excuse for cover, a couple of madrone trees contorted to grow sideways.

Another flash.

Crack.

This shot hadn't come anywhere near him. He had to trust Naomi had obeyed him and stayed flat behind the low ridge of volcanic rock. He crouched low, peering around the red tree trunks with peeling bark.

The next flash was metallic. Vehicle door. An engine started up. Adam ran full out, but too late. The sound of the engine had receded long before he reached the highway. He thought it had headed north rather than back toward Cape Trouble, but wasn't positive.

He kicked a broken branch in frustration, then holstered his weapon and raced back the way he'd come, jumping obstacles. All he could think about now was the blood.

Shouldn't somebody have heard the shots by now and called 911? Or had the fog muffled sound down below? Hell, maybe this was hunting season around here and nobody had paid any attention; he had no idea, only knew he heard no sirens to suggest help was on its way.

She hadn't moved. He felt cold for an instant, thinking she'd lost consciousness. What if she'd been hit twice— But then he realized she was looking right at him.

"The shooter took off," he said.

She nodded and rolled to a sitting position. She was bleeding, but not enough to be life-threatening. Adam yanked his shirt over his head, squatted in front of her and said, "Let me see."

Without a word, Naomi took her bloody hand away from her upper arm. He ripped the blood-soaked tear wider open, then held her by the elbow and gently wiped with one sleeve of his shirt until he could see that the wound was a furrow rather than an in-and-out. He didn't think the bullet had splintered bone, but the wound would hurt like hell nonetheless. He used the other sleeve of his cotton tee to wrap it snugly. She cooperated by clutching the body of the shirt to her chest. Not until he was done did he let himself meet her stare.

"You're a police officer."

"Yes."

"Why didn't you say?"

"I usually don't." Which was honest; women in particular reacted in several predictable ways, and he didn't like any of them. "Can you walk?" he asked. "I could call for an aide car, but it would be a wait. Or I can carry you."

She looked at him like he was crazy. "Of course I can walk."

"If we head for the highway, we could probably catch a ride, but it's uphill getting there."

"And who is going to stop for a half-naked guy and a bloody woman?" She shook her head. "The trail is fine."

It wasn't fine. She swayed when she first stood and her eyes did a whirlygig. He caught her as her knees buckled.

*****

The wave of dizziness subsided. Naomi found herself held tight against a hard male chest that happened to be naked. Adam's heart slammed beneath her ear. As her eyes regained focus, the first thing she saw was the scattering of dark hair over very nice muscles – and the thin line of hair leading down his flat belly.

She closed her eyes. Gathered herself, and straightened. Not waiting for him, she turned and began to walk. She was *not* letting him sling her over his shoulder and carry her down, playing hero.

She cradled her arm with the other one. The fierce burning helped keep at bay the other pain – the feeling of betrayal cramping beneath her breastbone.

Without asking whether she wanted help or not, Adam wrapped an arm around her waist. She didn't lean at all. In fact, she did her best to pretend he wasn't there. At the same time, she wouldn't be childish and slap him away. It would be stupid to fall when she didn't need to.

They dropped over the edge of the promontory and started toward the first sharp turn of the switchback.

"You came looking for me, didn't you?"

He cut a glance at her. "I did."

Her feet skidded on pebbles but he caught her weight and held her until she was able to resume walking.

"Why?"

"Because I don't think you were honest with investigators. I think you know a lot more than you said."

She didn't fire back a denial. If he'd found her, he likely wasn't the only one who had. So the mugger wasn't a mugger. He was…somebody trying to find her insurance policy. Or, more accurately, where she'd emailed or stored that insurance policy. Which a semi-skilled IT person probably could, given unlimited access to her computer. She'd done her best, but— Oh, face it. The average twelve-year-old could find what she'd tried to hide.

Her mind wasn't working right. It was hard to think beyond putting each foot in front of the other. The fog had engulfed Jasper Beach, giving the eerie illusion that she and Adam were on an island floating in the grey sea. But they were about to descend into it, which would make visibility poor. She was already chilled, and mist beaded on Adam's sleek bare shoulders and dark hair. She hoped he hadn't noticed she was shivering.

Pure determination kept her plodding on.

He'd lied to her. It was all lies.

Naomi didn't know she'd said that aloud until he said, "Not all."

She snorted. "You mean, you like my French toast."

His arm around her tightened as they reached a couple of natural steps of basalt, made treacherous by loose pebbles and dirt.

Treachery everywhere.

"Careful here." His arm was a solid bar, his voice gentle in her ear.

She would never run this trail again.

No, she realized; she would never see this trail again. Now she had no choice. Two choices: show him the video, or take off. Of course, she had to slip away from Adam Rostov before she could flee.

Her forehead crinkled. Funny, he wasn't one of the detectives who'd talked to her back then. She'd have remembered *that* face. Maybe the death of Santa Lucia Detective Frank Donahue had become a cold case being stirred, like the politician's murder was.

The pain kept expanding. From both sources, arm and heart. Maybe at first she'd been numb.

Surprised to discover she was walking on pavement, Naomi lifted her head. Fog swirled around them. Houses formed indistinct shapes in the gray.

"Here we are." Relief infused Adam's voice. Had he thought she wouldn't make it?

Here seemed to be his Tahoe. She tried to keep plodding, but he stopped her, unlocking with his free hand and opening the passenger door.

"Upsy daisy."

"I'm going home."

"Sorry. Hospital first." His expression was utterly inflexible.

"But then I'll have to…" She trailed off.

"Report this to the police?" His voice dripped irony and what might be anger. "Seems like the logical thing to do. Somebody *shot* you, Naomi. It is the law."

She nodded dully and allowed herself to be boosted up into the seat. Had she really thought she could escape him this quickly?

He told her he had to grab his wallet, and she nodded, not moving. He'd be keeping an eye out the window. Besides, the way she felt, she wouldn't get far. He was right; she did need to go to the hospital before anything else.

The short wait for him gave her time to think, as much as she could through the burning pain and the muffling effect of what might be shock.

He knew who she was, so continuing to lie, to say, *I have no idea what this could be about*, was pretty much a no go.

Given the name Naomi Varner, anyone doing a quick internet search would learn too much about her.

She closed her eyes. She should have gone with her instincts and taken off several days ago, instead of willfully blinding herself and going on a date with a man who had been too interested in her. How stupid had she been to believe this extraordinary looking guy, who just happened to be here on vacation, had been blitzed by his attraction to *her*? After years spent in the land of the beautiful, she knew what she wasn't.

She kept her eyes closed when he got in, started the engine and backed out of the short driveway. Panic drummed in her. Run, or trust him and Daniel enough to tell them what happened and show them the video?

"You with me?" he said finally, after a minute.

"I haven't passed out, if that's what you mean."

The hum of the engine told her when he accelerated onto the highway.

"You don't have to be afraid of me," he said quietly.

"Right. You came to Cape Trouble to ask me a few friendly questions. Which is why you introduced yourself right off the bat, explained what you needed." Her eyes popped open and her heart constricted. "*You* searched my house. Oh, God. Was the whole mugging thing faked to give you an in? And I tenderly patched you up," she said acidly.

His fingers were so tight on the steering wheel, the knuckles showed white. She heard his teeth grind together. At least his torso wasn't bare anymore; he'd thrown on a T-shirt while grabbing his wallet. "No. I didn't search your house, and the mugging wasn't faked. Give me some credit."

"Why would I?" She turned her face away. She couldn't bear to look at him again.

A couple more turns, and they pulled into the parking lot of the small hospital Cape Trouble was lucky to have. He, of course, rolled to a stop directly in front of the E.R. By the time he set the brake and got out, two people had emerged pushing a gurney. Adam spoke briefly to them, then opened her door.

"I can walk," she insisted, and kept insisting as Adam swung her out of his SUV and onto the damn gurney, where he flattened a hand on her stomach and scowled at her when she tried to sit up. With the other hand, he lifted his phone to his ear.

If she'd thought she was having panic attacks before this, Naomi discovered those were *nothing*.

*****

The second worst day of her life only got worse. Okay, maybe third worse day, although she'd been young enough when her father died, the impact had faded.

Once her arm had been stitched and dressed, the doctor released her. Tempting though it was to call someone else – Anita, maybe, or Hannah, or Monica – and ask for a ride home, Naomi suspected she wouldn't get away with it. Not given that two cops now hovered in the waiting room.

Both turned to look at her when she appeared in a wheelchair – no, she wasn't to be allowed to walk out, any more than they'd let her walk in. From their faces, she couldn't tell whether the two men had achieved an understanding while they waited together or not.

"I'll get the car," Adam said.

Naomi opened her mouth…and closed it. This time, he'd probably saved her life, risking his own.

When he went out, she looked at Daniel Colburn. "So, how much did he tell you?"

"Enough to raise some questions." He didn't look hostile, but he didn't give off an 'I'm on your side, come what may' vibe, either.

Naomi wondered if she wasn't a little bit stoned on the pain medication.

A minute later, the black Tahoe appeared at the curb outside the glass doors. Adam once again tossed her in. Daniel said he'd follow them, and walked away.

"What did the doctor say?" Adam asked.

She shrugged, then wished she hadn't. "I'll have a scar. Big deal. Come back if I develop a fever."

"He should have kept you overnight."

"It's a flesh wound." Who knew she'd ever be able to say that?

She did feel peculiar. Flippancy wasn't her style. She couldn't help appreciating how intensely irritating Adam seemed to find every word she said, though.

"Is that even your name?"

He scowled at her. "Unlike you, I use my own name."

"Just asking." She closed her eyes and let herself drift, so familiar with the route, each time he braked or accelerated she knew exactly where they were.

She'd been half afraid he'd try to take her back to his cottage instead of hers, but he stopped in front of hers.

"Wait until I come around," he ordered.

By the time he did, a slightly smaller SUV, also black, had pulled up behind the Tahoe. She'd seen Daniel's Honda Pilot before. Looked like black was the color of choice for cops, she thought, then remembered Adam's was actually a rental. Maybe whatever was in his garage at home was bright red…but, picturing his wardrobe, she knew better. Had to be black.

Regrettably, she felt wobbly enough she had to accept Adam's help descending from the ridiculously high seat, and even let him bear a little of her weight on the way to the door. She hated how desperately she wanted to let herself lean and trust the arm he had around her.

He took her key from her and unlocked. He and Daniel followed her in. Naomi went straight to the sofa even though bed sounded better. Ignoring the two men, she was able to loosen the laces on her Nikes with her good hand – her right, thank God – and kick them off, tuck her feet up under her and pull a fleece throw over herself.

She heard water running in the kitchen. Adam called, "Tea? Coffee? Cocoa?"

"Tea."

Would he leave her alone tonight? Her heart squeezed. God, if she showed them the video, would he arrest her and drag her back to California? What she'd be admitting to was obstruction, at the least. Even though the video involved a different crime than the one he'd come here investigating.

Would Daniel agree to lock her in one of his two cells for the night?

The teapot whistled, and a minute later Adam set a steaming mug down on the coffee table in front of her. Both men had mugs in their hands, too, presumably coffee since neither had the string with a tag dangling from it like hers did.

She looked at Adam. "I want to see your I.D." It came out loud and belligerent. She didn't care.

He raised his eyebrows, but dug a badge out of his back pocket and handed it to her. She studied it, then lifted her head in astonishment. "You're with Santa Lucia P.D."

"That's right." His expression was wary.

"No wonder you weren't one of the investigators I talked to. You don't have any jurisdiction over what happened at my restaurant!"

She was vaguely aware of the way Daniel looked at him.

"No, I don't," he admitted.

"Then…I don't understand. What are you doing here?"

"You know Frank Donahue was a detective with S.L.P.D." He glanced at Daniel. "He's the cop who was murdered in Ms. Varner's restaurant." He leaned a little on her last name before meeting her eyes again, those gray eyes implacable. "Frank was my partner."

It was all she could do not to moan. *Worse* just kept accelerating. She stamped out the tiny flicker of thought she'd had of telling him everything. If she did, she really would find herself hustled back to Santa Monica and put straight behind bars.

"I don't understand why you're so sure I know more than I told investigators."

"They didn't seem to clue in that you were Greg Cobb's girlfriend. Seems like you and he both failed to mention that little fact."

She had, and had been surprised Greg did, too.

"I wasn't his girlfriend," she objected, knowing how weak her argument was. "We'd dated a few times, that's all."

"Right. It was just *business* that had you letting him use your restaurant for after-hours meetings," he said cynically.

She raised her chin at that. "It was. He paid, just like anyone else. When the restaurant was closed, we rented it out for all kinds of events. Bar Mitzvahs, bridal showers, engagement parties…"

"And organized crime get-togethers."

She glared at him. "That's not fair. I didn't know."

"Uh huh."

Seeing the hostility on his face made her heart hurt. She'd wanted so much to trust him, had come as close as she had with anybody in the last two years. She'd let herself *feel* something for him.

Daniel cleared his throat.

"Naomi, let's start with the name change. Are you using fake I.D.?"

His expression was guarded, but still kind, she thought. She looked at him instead of at Adam.

"Not exactly. My birth name is Naomi Kendrick."

Adam made a scoffing noise in his throat that had her flashing another glare at him before she turned back to Daniel.

"My father died when I was a child. When my mother remarried, my stepfather adopted me. I used my birth certificate to go back to Kendrick, that's all."

"Did you get a new social security number?" Daniel asked.

"Um…yes."

"How?"

She focused on the steam rising from the cup rather than their faces. "I have a friend who is good on computers and a graphic artist besides. She…tinkered with my birth certificate, changing a couple of little things. And, you know, they don't really look that closely when you go into the Social Security office. I said I'd been raised abroad, that my parents were missionaries. I do a good South African accent."

One more illegality, but who was counting?

They both stared at her.

"What difference does it make?" she cried. Her throat seemed to be swelling. For the first time since she'd been shot, she felt like crying. Not that she would. She shrugged and looked down at her lap. "I was scared." It came out so small, she felt small. And for good reason.

"Why?" Adam asked softly.

She didn't mistake the quiet way he asked for sympathy. Oh, no. It was, of course, the million dollar question. *Behind Door Number Two…* After admitting that she was scared, she pretty much now had to answer his question, unless she was to hire a lawyer and refuse to incriminate herself, which she couldn't do because she'd broken so many laws they'd get her on *something*.

And…hadn't she felt guilty every day, every hour, for these past two years because she *hadn't* shared what she knew? Now was her chance. And if it turned out Adam was corrupt like his partner, well…she'd always known someone would catch up with her sooner or later. Although if he was, why hadn't he just let the gunman kill her today?

"I heard something I wasn't supposed to," she said dully.

Daniel didn't move. Adam leaned forward, elbows braced on his knees, eyes intense. "You were there when Frank was killed."

She could not tell him. She couldn't.

"It's not that. It was the meeting."

The intensity didn't abate. "What did you hear, Naomi? And how do you know you weren't supposed to hear it?"

She bit her lip. "Greg had always asked me to stay in the kitchen. I…put out coffee in an urn beforehand, but he said these were private deals. He didn't want anyone getting skittish before everybody's names were on the bottom line. I protested and said I knew how to keep my mouth shut. He said he knew he could trust me, but the people he was negotiating with wouldn't." She gave a broken laugh. "I always sat in the kitchen and worked out a new menu, that kind of thing, until he came to say everyone was gone."

"What was different that last time?"

"His meeting dragged on and on. I was tired and I wanted to go home. And…I suppose I was being nosy." She would wish quite desperately she hadn't, except she might have kept dating Greg. Even slept with him. Imagine having to live with *that*. "He had an off-duty police officer wandering the restaurant outside the private room where he was holding the meeting. I stuck my head out of the kitchen to ask the guy if he knew when they'd be done, only I saw him down the hall just going into the men's restroom. So, um, I sort of tiptoed toward the private room, thinking maybe I'd hear them breaking up or something…" Naomi looked down to see that she was wringing her hands. When she raised her head again, both men were looking at her hands, too. No mistaking that she was cool and collected here.

"Wasn't the door closed?" Adam prompted, his gaze lifting again to hers.

"It was open, I don't know, just a couple of inches. And…I heard Greg saying, 'A hit like this, I do it my way. Not yours. You know your business, I know mine.'"

Adam's expression changed. "A hit."

"I stood there totally frozen, thinking, hit? What's he talking about? Only, the other guy said, 'There can't be any connection to me. You understand that? I need to be able to go on TV and express my deep condolences to the widow, my outrage that the political process can be subverted this way.'"

"Jesus." He straightened, understanding transforming his expression. "Not James Heath…?"

Naomi nodded.

"Who's Heath?" Daniel put in, then said, "Wait. I think I read about that."

Frowning at Naomi, Adam said, "He was a California state senator, running for U.S. Congress. He was shot and killed. To appearances, he'd hired a prostitute and things went wrong. It looked sleazy."

"That was…one of the other things Greg said. That he'd make sure there was a scandal to blacken Heath's name, too."

Adam shook his head, scrubbed his fingers through his hair, and said in disbelief, "So you just stood there eavesdropping."

"No." She took a deep breath. "I did something way more stupid. I had my phone in my hand. I thought about taking a picture, but I don't know how to turn off the flash."

If she hadn't had their complete attention, she did now. One way to rivet an audience.

"But I can shoot a video with no flash. So that's what I did. It's only like a minute long. I was in a total panic, watching the bathroom door for that guy to come out and praying nobody in the room saw the phone hovering there. But it was kind of dim in the hall – most of the lights were out, so I thought I could do it."

"Why aren't you dead?" Adam asked bluntly.

Because I killed a man to save myself. "It turned out Greg suspected something. I made a deal. I'd keep what I knew to myself if he let me go."

Contempt flashed on his face. "Heath might still be alive if you'd gone to authorities."

"I warned him." Tears burned in her eyes as she held her chin up in defiance. "I did. But I couldn't tell him who I was and I don't think he believed me."

"His murder happened in Compton," Adam said slowly. "I heard his campaign manager claiming someone had called to say a hit had been ordered on him."

"Why didn't he hire bodyguards?" She was begging for answers. "Why did he let himself be caught alone?"

"His campaign manager and his wife both said they got so many threats and warnings, they had to shrug them off. 'You can't let the crazies keep you from living your life.'" The last was obviously a quote.

"God." Naomi buried her face in her hands.

"It was Greer who ordered the hit." He sounded stunned, but not as if he didn't believe her.

She swiped at her cheeks with a corner of the fleece throw and raised her head. "Yes. That's why I took the video. I didn't think anyone would believe me."

"The video you never shared with anybody." His eyes glittered. With rage, she realized. "Why?"

"Because a man was killed in my kitchen that night. A police officer. Because another off-duty police officer worked for Greg, and I think a second one was waiting outside. He hadn't bothered to shut the door. They weren't the only ones. I'd seen others. They had to know what his business was. Because—" She closed her eyes and swallowed before she could go on. "Because there was a third man at the table. He said he was an FBI agent. He showed his badge. Greer nodded and knew who he was." Her voice had been rising. She couldn't help it. "Because I didn't have any idea who I could trust." Her hands might be trembling again, but she hid them in the folds of the throw as she stared her defiance at *this* police officer and delivered the *coup de grace*. "And I still don't."

CHAPTER SIX

Trying to get a grip before he said something he shouldn't, Adam ground his teeth together. "There are some insults I'll take. That isn't one. I saved your life today."

For a minute, it was as if Police Chief Daniel Colburn wasn't even there. Adam and she stared at each other, her eyes turbulent with emotions, his…probably the same.

Abruptly she ducked her head. "I know you did. You're right."

He exhaled, so on edge it was no wonder he'd overreacted. She could have died today. She hadn't, but he was still shaken, more than he should have been. And then, God damn it, to find out what she'd been hiding…

"Why?" he said in honest bewilderment. "You could have emailed the video to Heath's people."

Naomi shook her head hard. With her shoulders rounded and her head bent, she looked small. Vulnerable. She was biting her lip, he saw, hard enough he frowned and leaned forward.

Just as she looked up. This time her eyes were dark with guilt and grief…and her tongue caught a drop of blood on her lip. "No, she said in a pained voice. "I risked my life for nothing. It's…really poor quality. It's too dark, and the sound quality sucks. I used its existence as a bluff. But that's all it's good for."

He shook his head. Unbelievable. She'd held a cold-blooded killer off for two years by convincing him she had something she didn't? The fact that she was still alive was a freaking miracle.

He said the obvious. "That's why the guy grabbed your bag. He needs your computer."

"I suppose so," she said miserably. "But…if he searched my house, why did he do things like look under shelf paper?"

"Because they suspect you might have copies on thumb drives? Or a letter with still pictures printed and stashed away? Something you can use as a threat even if they get your computer?"

Daniel spoke for the first time in a while. "Will you show it to us, Naomi? Let us judge."

Her laugh was broken. “Sure. Why not?” She struggled to rise. “I’ll go get my computer.”

Adam stood. “Let me get it.”

“No, it’s hidden.”

How successfully, in a place this size? He followed her into her bedroom, which had just been a bedroom the first time he’d swept her house. This time he was more aware of details, because she was with him.

The décor was as unexpected as what she’d worn to dinner last night. A flannel duvet cover had ranks of stylized elephants in a very African print. An African mask carved from a very dark wood dominated one wall. On other walls were vintage flower prints, framed in simple dark woods that meshed although he didn’t know why. An antique dresser held a colorful collection of old bottles. On a small bedside table stood a funky lamp, probably artisan made, combining a green glass magnum wine bottle with twists of wrought iron that reminded him of the earrings she’d worn the day before. The only other furnishing was a rocking chair upholstered in a bold yellow and white print that looked ethnic. African, too?

She’d said she could do a South African accent.

His gaze went back to the bed. The last damn thing he should be thinking about was sharing that bed with this woman.

He shifted uncomfortably and had to tear his eyes away.

She stopped in front of a crude closet formed of cedar slats that walled off a corner of the room. Adam remembered ones like it in the cabins at a rustic resort in the Sierra Nevada Mountains his family had gone to summers, when he was a kid. Before their lives went wrong. Naomi opened the door then looked over her shoulder. Evidently she hadn’t heard him following her, because she froze at the sight of him.

He propped a shoulder against the door jamb, crossed his arms and raised his eyebrows.

In response, she glared with impotent anger he understood. After a moment, she pushed aside the hanging clothes, bent over and fiddled with something at the back, then struggled to lift out a square formed out of the same old cedar slats. Adam stepped forward.

“Let me.”

She didn’t want to let him do anything, that was obvious enough. So was the fact that she hurt. Then she nodded curtly and moved aside. Adam found himself peering into a sizable space that held one suitcase…and her canvas messenger bag.

He grabbed it and slung the strap over his shoulder, then nodded at the suitcase. "That all you left California with? What you could get in one suitcase?"

She shrugged. "And a couple of cardboard boxes. I brought some of my cookbooks and a few things I loved."

"The mask." No reason he should be sure of that, but he was.

"Yes." Her voice was tight, but at least she was talking to him. "In college, I did a year abroad in South Africa. I still have some of the things I brought home. That was one of them."

He looked around again. "I like the room."

Under the circumstances, it was a stupid damn thing to say, and he felt his cheeks heat at her astonishment. Without another word, he walked into the living room.

He set the bag on the coffee table but let her unzip it, remove the laptop and open and fire it up.

"You'd better both come and sit here." Naomi's gaze shied from his. "Or maybe we should do this at the kitchen table."

"No, this is fine." Colburn sounded kindly, and she gave him a grateful smile that irritated Adam. He was the enemy, Daniel Colburn her friend.

A friend who had a fiancée, he reminded himself, without feeling any better.

He watched as she went online.

"It's not stored on your computer at all?" he said thoughtfully.

Naomi shook her head. "If my laptop was stolen, I didn't want anyone to be able to find it too easily. Because if they did, they'd know it doesn't matter what other copies exist."

"What other copies do exist?"

"Well… I have a couple of different cloud accounts and I sent it to an attorney who was a roommate of mine in college."

"'If I die under suspicious circumstances, watch this?'"

"Something like that."

She sat back when the video flickered to life. Both men leaned forward, eyes intent on the screen.

She was right; the scene was murky. Because he'd seen photos of Greg Cobb and expected to see him, Adam could tell that was Cobb sitting off to the right. To the left…shit, the camera – or the door – cut off all but a man's hands, folded on the table. Nearly facing the smart phone camera she'd used was a third man, but he was a little farther away and grainy. And, damn it, the whole thing wobbled.

Her hand had been shaking, Adam realized, shocked by a vicious explosion of anger and fear as he imagined this small woman having the guts to lurk outside that room trying to film this unholy conversation.

Pay attention.

The voices were mostly indistinguishable mumbles. A word or two came through.

"…sure?"

A sharp, "Not until…"

The man at the head of the table made a slashing gesture. If Cobb's expression changed even once, Adam couldn't tell.

"…week." Or was it weeks, plural?

The screen abruptly went black.

Naomi chewed on her lower lip again and eyed them. "You see?"

"Did you try to get this cleaned up?" Colburn asked.

"No, I… It's so bad, I didn't think it could be. I'm not very technological. Do you think it can be?"

"Yeah, let me think about this."

Shock followed by some intense emotion crossed her face. Adam had to label it as anguish. What was she thinking? That she could have prevented Heath's death and hadn't?

Apparently oblivious to her shock, Colburn rambled on, "I'm reluctant to go to a private lab. If they do clean it up and hear what's said—" The local cop looked at her. "Can you tell us what is said?"

She'd blanked whatever she felt. "More or less. I told you some of what I heard. In here, they were arguing about payment. They agreed on three hundred thousand dollars, half in advance, the other half once it was done."

If they could sharpen this video enough to get a warrant, then they could follow the money. Suddenly Adam re-ran what she'd said.

"Is that what Greer said?" he asked. "It? He wasn't more specific?"

She seemed unwilling to meet his eyes, but did. "I don't think so, not then, but he did say, 'You know how close the primary is. You have two weeks.' And Greg said—" Her voice wobbled and she stopped, but gathered herself. "'I can accept a two week deadline. Heath will be singing in the heavenly choir, but his earthly reputation won't be so saintly anymore.'"

"And this is all on there?"

She recoiled from whatever she saw on his face. "Yes. I think so. I guess I might have cut off something at the end."

"Why did you stop filming when you did?" Colburn asked. "Did you think you'd been seen?"

"No. I mean, I don't know. Because I was standing out of sight. You know. All I could see was what showed on my phone, and it was really dim in the hall, and… Mostly, I was craning my neck to see the door to the men's room, and I was so nervous I guess I just chickened out."

Chickened out. Adam shook his head. She'd only been videotaping a contract killer as he scheduled a hit.

"What were you thinking? You wanted to commit suicide?"

"I thought I had to have proof!" she yelled. Tears shimmered in her eyes, shaming him. Then, softer, she said, "I wasn't thinking. I just…did it. Afterwards—" She looked at Daniel again, not at Adam. "—I hurried back to the kitchen. The whole way, I had my head turned. Just as I was going in the kitchen, I saw the bathroom door start to swing open. If I'd waited, like, five more seconds…" She shivered.

"You'd have been seen."

"Yes." She pressed her lips together. "But Greg did see me. Or enough to make him suspicious, anyway."

"Or Greer or the other man saw movement and told him."

Her lashes fluttered. "I…suppose so."

Adam was having one hell of a hard time holding it together, but he had to do his job. "You say you made a deal." He managed to sound almost calm. "That night?"

Naomi shook her head. "I was… Once I got in the kitchen, I was shaking all over, totally freaked. I'm thinking the meeting has to end any minute, and then he'll come in the kitchen, and he'll know the minute he sees me, standing there quaking. I wanted to run. Just go out the back door. But I'd noticed before that he has another off-duty police officer patrolling outside during his meetings."

"And it didn't once cross your mind that meant he might be bad news?" Too sharp – Adam didn't turn his head, but he knew Colburn was studying him.

"No!" She yanked the fleece throw up to her neck and clutched it protectively with a fisted hand. "They were police officers. We used off-duty officers ourselves for traffic control when we had something big going on and everybody arrived or left at the same time. Greg dressed really well, and he drove a Bugatti sports car. I looked it up and they're ridiculously expensive."

Greg Cobb owned half a dozen cars. Adam, too, had looked up the Buggatti Veyron 16.4 that Cobb owned, and knew the price tag topped $1.5 million dollars.

"I thought he was really rich, and that he hired bodyguards because he had to worry about kidnapping."

"Is that why you dated him? Because he's rich?"

Given his hostile tone, her glare was fully justified. "No! He's handsome and charming. I only went out with him a few times. I don't think it would have gone anywhere. That last night—" She didn't seem to want to go on.

Colburn cut an irritated glance at Adam and intervened. "Let's get back to that last night. Did he come into the kitchen while you were still shaking?"

"Yes. Well, I'd started pulling myself together. I mean, as much as I could. I dropped my phone into my bag, so at least I wasn't clutching it. I told myself I could act. Five minutes, tops. Smile, say I hoped his meeting was successful. Only, he noticed right away that I was agitated." The way she was staring, expression stark, Adam could tell she was seeing that night instead of the present. "I told him I'd just discovered I was missing some ingredients I needed for the next day and I was mad at staff. I said I had to stay, fire off some emails." She blinked, as if summoning herself back to the here and now. "I had a small office off the kitchen."

Colburn nodded. Adam sat frozen.

"I thought I'd pulled it off. Only then he stopped me and—" This shudder was visible even under the blanket. "He was going to kiss me. I jerked away."

Adam closed his eyes. “And he knew.”

“Yes. I mean, I didn’t know then for sure. He just kind of shook his head and said, ‘Naomi,’ as if he was disappointed in me. He said goodnight and left, but nothing about calling me or anything. So I thought—” She made a face. After that, her voice sounded tight. “I waited a few minutes, in case he was watching, then left.”

“The next time you heard from him?” Colburn asked, in that same patient, soothing way Adam couldn’t have summoned right now to save his life.

“After—” She sneaked a quick look at him. “I almost always opened the restaurant myself. I was sort of a workaholic.”

He made himself nod his understanding.

“But when I opened the next day, there was this dead man in my restaurant. He was, um, lying on his side so I could see the knife sticking out of him. A big handgun lay on the floor and I saw that he had a badge on his belt. You know. S.L.P.D.”

Adam had seen the crime scene photos. For all that he worked homicide himself, it was different when the victim was someone you knew well. Sometimes the faces were contorted, sometimes slack. Frank’s had been like that – vacant.

“Your restaurant wasn’t in Santa Lucia,” Colburn said.

“No, Santa Monica. That’s who came when I called 911. They grilled me, because my fingerprints were on the knife, of course.”

“Just yours?”

Adam knew this, and wanted to see how honest she was. This was one of the things that had bothered him.

“Yes. That particular set of knives was mine. Others did use them, but would usually be wearing gloves. I usually wore gloves, too. So there were also all kinds of smudges from when I or someone else had handled it with gloves on.”

“The knives didn’t go through a dishwasher?”

She looked shocked. “That would be like driving the Bugatti through the car wash behind the Shell station.”

He almost cracked a smile.

“So,” she went on, “I helped schedule and oversee interviews of all my staff, too.” She seemed to be gaining confidence, as if this part wasn’t so bad. “A couple of them had keys.”

“Who?” Adam asked.

"I had a front of the house manager. She scheduled waitstaff, bookings, did some of the marketing. My sous chef – assistant chef – had a key, too, obviously. He had to open when I took a day off, or if I couldn't for some reason."

"They were the only two people."

"Yes."

"So when did you hear from Cobb again? Or did you call him?"

"Call *him*?" Her incredulity had to be real. "Are you kidding?"

"All right. He called you. Or did you see him?"

"No, he called. He said, 'I like you, Naomi, but you listened to a conversation you shouldn't have.' I thought about pretending, but…" She grimaced again, an unnatural expression on her pixie face. "I told him I'd not only listened, I'd used my phone to shoot video. I said I had him and Senator Greer in living color *and* audio. *He* said, 'That's a problem, Naomi. I can't let that go.'"

It was Colburn who nudged her. "And?"

"I threatened to go to the police. He laughed. He said he had connections everywhere. And…I knew that was true. I told him I could find someone. ATF, DEA, someone, somewhere. Because it wouldn't be just my word. But if he would leave me alone, I'd close the restaurant, move away and keep my mouth shut. I claimed I'd already emailed copies to several people, just in case. The last thing he said was, 'If you break your word, I'll find you, Naomi. You'll never make a promise again. Or break one." Now her voice shook, and those caramel eyes were haunted. She turned them on Adam. "He's found me, hasn't he?"

"Yes. That's how *I* found you."

Naomi stared. "What do you mean?"

He didn't want to name Sam. "I have a friend in the Los Angeles office of the FBI. Awhile back, aware of my interest, he let me know they had a wiretap on Gregory Cobb's phone. Or, I should say, phones. He changes mobile phones the way most of us change our socks. He's careful, and so is everyone who works for him. But last week, he didn't throw away the latest phone quick enough. The task force was listening to calls to and from that number. My friend said another man called Cobb to say he'd found the chef. The conversation didn't include your new name, but the guy did say you were in Cape Trouble. I caught a flight the next morning, drove straight over from Portland."

"Was that…the same day I thought my house was searched?"

Adam nodded.

Colburn leaned forward. "Play it again, Naomi."

She did, then sat back, letting the two men all but press their noses to the screen.

"The guy we can't see on the left. That's the FBI agent?" Colburn asked. "Did you get a look at him?"

"Sort of. A quick one."

"Enough to identify him if you met him face to face?" Adam asked.

"I don't know. I don't think so. He was looking at Senator Greer, so I saw his face partially turned away. He had brown hair and…I don't know. There wasn't anything special about him."

"Big guy? Small?"

She bit her lip. "Sort of…medium, I think. It's hard to tell when someone is sitting, you know."

Yeah, it was. Adam pictured those hands, utterly relaxed, and thought, *Scum-sucking son of a bitch.*

"Do you know a lab that would handle this confidentially?" Colburn asked him.

"No." Adam thought it was time for some honesty of his own. "My lieutenant doesn't know I'm here. He started to get annoyed at my interest in the investigation into Frank's murder. Told me to drop it. Threatened me with a suspension if I wouldn't."

"Maybe *he's* on Greg's payroll," Naomi suggested, calm as you please. Still huddled behind her fleece barricade, though.

He had to consider the possibility coldly, blocking any emotional filter. More honesty: "I don't know. I do know I can't go around him, and convincing him to pursue this…" He shook his head.

Daniel stood, stretched, and moved to sit on a chair on the other side of the coffee table from Naomi and Adam, leaving a cushion between them. "I still have connections in San Francisco, but anybody there would recognize Dominic Greer and we'd lose control of this." He sounded thoughtful. "I have an idea, though. We have to report today's shooting to the sheriff's department, if someone from the hospital already hasn't. I trust Sheriff Mackay. He came from Portland P.D. He might have the right connection for us. I think we need to bring him in anyway."

Adam didn't like bringing in anyone he didn't know, but he also recognized that he needed allies. So far, his impressions of Daniel Colburn were all positive, however irked he was to see that Naomi apparently already trusted him.

"Let's not lose sight of our main problem," Colburn added. "Who tried to kill Naomi today?"

She laughed. She actually laughed. It was a moment before Adam realized there was some hysteria in the sound. "*Our* problem? Don't you mean, *my* problem?"

"My job is to protect the people in my community," the police chief said. "That includes you."

"Except I don't live in Cape Trouble."

"You work in my town. One of the assaults took place in Cape Trouble. You're…a friend, Naomi."

She swallowed. "Okay." Then she turned a fierce stare on Adam. "What's in it for you?"

"I still think you can help me figure out who killed Frank." He frowned. "I'd protect a woman I saw being assaulted no matter what. And now I know you."

"Plus, think what a coup it would be if you could be responsible for arresting Greg Cobb for murder."

He controlled his flare of temper. He'd lied to her. More than that – he'd kissed her. He deserved the blazing anger directed at him, as it wasn't at Daniel Colburn who was also pushing for action.

"I wouldn't be making that arrest," he said slowly. "You know that. Whatever my motives, keeping you safe is my first priority." He was disturbed to discover how truthful that was, despite the contempt he'd held her in for so long.

She didn't say anything, but her expression spoke for her. *Yeah, sure*, it said, and he had to wonder if she didn't still suspect he'd set her up for one or the other of these attacks.

"I think we might have two separate interested parties here in Cape Trouble," he said. "Three, counting me."

"What?" She stared at him in shock.

Colburn looked less surprised. This was where he'd been going with his question.

"Someone searched your place."

"Maybe," she objected.

"I'm going to say probably, given what happened the next day."

After a moment she gave a reluctant nod.

"He didn't find what he was looking for in your house, so he waited in the alley for you and grabbed the bag that held your computer and phone. His intent was frustrated again. I think Greg Cobb sent this guy. His orders are to find the video, figure out where you have it stored, who else might have seen it. How bad it is." He frowned. "It would be interesting to know what spurred Cobb to hunt for you now."

"What do you mean? Maybe it took this long for him to find me!"

"If he'd tried very hard early on, he'd have found you," Adam said flatly. As if there was no doubt.

She didn't like that. "What makes you say that?"

"You continued the same profession. You didn't move far enough away. Somebody who did their research would have found the adoption decree and your birth name, then the new social using that name." His eyes narrowed. "Unless you tinkered with the name?"

"Only my middle initial. That's all I have, an initial. Mom meant to name me Naomi Helena, but it was just H. My friend changed it to R. Oh, and the year I was born."

"Clever, but not good enough."

"Why not? You couldn't find me without help."

"I wasn't looking real hard. As you've pointed out, the investigation isn't mine."

Colburn cleared his throat. "This isn't getting us anywhere."

She ignored him, all that hostility still trained on Adam. "Maybe *you* led the sniper to me. Did you ever think of that?"

"Why would anybody have been paying attention to me? I'm not one of the investigators. I'd followed up with Santa Monica detectives a few times. That's all. Nobody had any reason to think I'd go haring off after you the minute I learned where you were."

He braced himself for one of them to say, *Yeah, and why did you?* Loyalty to Frank, dissatisfaction with the investigation going cold, only went so far. But neither asked. Daniel Colburn may have understood the agony he'd felt when he heard Frank had been killed. His partner. That counted, but it wasn't the whole explanation, either. It was his own history that left him feeling raw when he heard the whispers about Frank.

Naomi's blanket had dropped enough, he could see her shoulders sag. "If the same guy didn't shoot me, who did?"

Adam rubbed the taut muscles at the back of his neck. He wanted to pace, but her house was so small. "There are two other obvious possibilities. Someone from Greer's camp, and the third man sitting at that table."

"But…" The one word was almost silent, her eyes huge and dark. "Would Greg have told anyone else that I'd eavesdropped? Or that I'd taken a video?"

He'd been thinking about that. "Probably not, unless he wasn't the one who saw you in the first place. Greer was damn near facing the door. What if it was him who saw you? Cobb might have promised to deal with you, then had to give updates."

She searched his eyes. "Is that what you think?"

"No. I think the shooter is the FBI agent sitting at that table."

Her chin shot up, defying the fear in her eyes. "Why didn't *he* find me sooner, if I was so incompetent at hiding?"

"Because he didn't see you. The camera didn't catch his face, which means he wouldn't have been able to see it, either. He knew you owned the restaurant and that you found the body when you came to open up the next morning. But later… The L.A. office isn't so huge he might not have heard talk about the wiretap. It's even possible he's involved in the operation to bring down Cobb – if he's on Cobb's payroll, maybe has been sabotaging it – so he had reason to hear the bit about finding the chef. Big shock there."

"Alternatively," Colburn suggested, "he and maybe Greer knew Naomi might have heard something. Like you said, one of them saw her. But way back when, Cobb assured them he'd take care of you. Voila! You disappeared. They're happy, assuming you're six feet under. As you say, he didn't tell them what you were holding over him. It would make him look incompetent."

Adam took up the narrative. "But something stirs up Cobb, who does find you. Hearing what was said during that call, the FBI agent goes to Cobb, who says yeah, you overheard some of the conversation but don't worry, I'm taking care of her. He maybe admits you've got something on him, so he has to move carefully. The guy is left with a cold chill. Did you hear his name? See him? He thinks, to hell with Cobb. He'll take care of this problem personally. Thanks to Cobb, he knows where to find you."

She'd been shrinking in her corner of the sofa. He felt cruel, seeing her diminished by each blunt hammer blow, but also believing she had to fully understand the danger she was in.

"You don't think he sent somebody else?" she asked, sounding steadier than he would have expected.

Adam shook his head. "Who? I doubt the L.A. office is rife with corruption. No, our guy is doing a little moonlighting. Maybe not happy with his salary, or he made a mistake that Cobb is blackmailing him with. He's got the skill set to do the job himself besides."

She met his eyes again. "So does Greg."

"That's true." He gentled his voice. "But we're positing two people here with different agendas. One wants to find the video before taking any other action. The other is a sniper whose goal is a lot simpler: to kill you."

"How far away was he set up?" Daniel asked, sounding professionally interested. "Could you tell?"

"Two to three hundred yards. He didn't make a kill shot, but he hit her. That's impressive shooting. He saw her go down." Adam, too, had reverted to thinking like a cop, forgetting that Naomi was listening. "If I hadn't come over the rise, he could have trotted along to where she fell and finished the job."

She flung the fleece throw at him and stumbled to her feet. "I have to disappear. I should have done it days ago." She looked wildly around, as if already deciding what to take or searching for a hole to bolt into. "I'll email the link to both of you. Just give me your addresses. But then I need to go."

Adam rose to his feet slowly. She backed away, shaking. Scared of *him*.

Looking perturbed, Colburn said, "Your testimony would be critical, Naomi."

She hugged herself, still inching toward her bedroom. "If Greg was the only one who wanted me dead, I might be safe once he's been arrested. But he isn't, is he? You've just spent half an hour convincing me he isn't! So I will never be safe if I don't succeed in disappearing once and for all."

Adam didn't make the mistake of pursuing her. Right this minute, she couldn't go. All she wore were the tight running pants and a scrub top she'd been given at the hospital to replace the shirt they'd cut off her. Her shoes lay on the floor by the sofa.

"I've protected you so far," he said quietly.

She turned one furious, despairing look at him. "For three whole days? Anyway, I got *shot* today."

"Because you didn't wait for me. What were you thinking?" Damn it, had he just yelled at her?

Yeah.

"Nobody had tried to hurt me." Tears clogged her voice. She'd reached the doorway into her bedroom. "Anyway, he'd have still had a shot even if you'd been right behind me."

"He'd have been less likely to take it."

"I need to clean up. Change clothes." She scooted back into the bedroom and shut the door.

"How big is the window?" Colburn asked in a low voice.

"Little as she is, she could probably get out, but would she try to run without her computer?"

The police chief spread his hands. *Who knows?* "We'd hear her."

Now that he was on his feet anyway, Adam prowled the small living room, listening for the scrape of the painted wood window frame being pushed up. "When she uses her head, she'll realize she needs help," he growled.

"I don't know about that. She might have always been a loner. If not, she's learned to be one. First time I set eyes on her, I guessed she was running from something." Frustration or something more creased Daniel Colburn's forehead. "I figured it was a stalker of some kind. That she'd come to me if she needed me, but I don't think she would have. If not for you, she'd already be gone."

Adam thought so, too. He grunted. "Maybe I should help her vanish. If she's willing to show up and testify when the time comes…"

"She goes, and you know the bad guys here in town will creep back under their rocks." The other man's steady blue eyes met his. "And we both know how hard it is to really disappear with any success. You going to dump her somewhere and be confident she's safe? Or that she'll stay put?"

Crap. "She wouldn't stay."

"That's my take."

They were both silent, their gazes trained on her closed door.

They heard nothing until the door suddenly opened and she reappeared, having changed to jeans, a baggy sweatshirt and fuzzy slippers. She stalked back into the living room, raising her eyebrows at Colburn.

"Isn't Sophie wondering where you are about now?"

Colburn glanced down at his phone, expression guilty.

"And you." She fixed a hostile look on Adam. "Why don't you go back to lurking? You've obviously been watching me. Feel free. Just do it from somewhere else."

He shook his head. "Nope. I'm not leaving, Naomi." He turned to Colburn. "Can you stay long enough for me to grab my stuff?"

"You bet."

She looked from one to the other of them. "I have no say in this?"

Adam shook his head in disgust. "What, you have a death wish?"

Anger glittered in her eyes, almost disguising the fear. "Maybe what I don't like is being staked out as bait."

He gritted his teeth, even though in a way she was right. Hadn't he and Colburn tiptoed around saying just that?

"I'll be back," he said, and went out the front door.

CHAPTER SEVEN

He'd have to leave her alone sometime. Sleep.

The voice in Naomi's head wasn't murmuring anymore, it was screaming. *Run.*

She should have gone days ago, she knew now. Except…she had lived with a crushing sense of guilt. She'd saved herself at the expense of a man who might have been a politician but who also, so far as she knew, lived by his principles. A decent man. She could have prevented his death. She'd told herself she had done everything she could, but that wasn't true. It especially wasn't true if it turned out the video would have been persuasive after all.

Now, at least, she had handed it over to someone else and it was possible that justice would be served. If the dross she'd filmed really could be transmuted into gold, James Heath's wife and family would soon know the truth. His reputation, at least, could be salvaged. For his wife, simple grief had to be better than believing he'd died betraying her.

And Dominic Greer would no longer be able to enjoy the fruits of evil. Which sounded stupidly melodramatic, but that's what Naomi thought every time she saw a photograph of his smug face. Had a sitting United States Congressman ever been arrested for murder? Naomi had no idea, but she hoped whoever arrested him did so in the most public way possible. In the hallowed halls of Congress, if possible. She wanted him to suffer all the humiliation he'd heaped on Heath's family.

But she also knew that neither Daniel nor Adam were really thinking about her testimony, required on some far-off occasion. Pure and simple, they wanted her to keep wearing a huge target on her back. And maybe the world would be a better place if she did what they were asking, if a corrupt FBI agent was arrested, too, but the chances were a whole lot greater that he'd succeed and she'd be dead. And maybe he'd be stopped then, but she would still be dead. If there was one thing Naomi had learned about herself two years ago, it was that her instinct for self-preservation was powerful.

And now it said, *Run.*

This time, she was going to obey.

She sat on her sofa, staring straight ahead. Her arm throbbed in time with her heartbeat. She wanted to take a pain pill, but didn't dare dull herself, not if she was to out-smart two intelligent men who already suspected she intended to take off.

Daniel Colburn sat in the same easy chair, his very blue eyes on her. She'd swear he hadn't looked away since Adam had left. They hadn't talked, either, not until now.

"If it makes you feel any better," he said, sounding awkward, "I did some research on Rostov. There's no question he is who he says he is. I found a decent photo taken at a crime scene."

Naomi shrugged. She overcame the temptation to be childish and refuse to say another word. "I told you. Greg Cobb had, I don't know, half a dozen cops working for him. The one—" Shock buffeted her. Oh, dear God, she'd almost made a gargantuan mistake and said, *The one in the kitchen.* Throat dry, she swallowed. "The one who was in the bathroom – you know – wore a Santa Monica P.D. uniform. I saw the patch clearly. Another time it was a Los Angeles County Sheriff's Deputy. I told you the dead man was with Santa Lucia P.D. Adam is sure he was a good guy, but I'm not buying that."

"If he wasn't, why was he killed?"

The question was mild, his eyes keen. Her heartbeat fluttered. Had he guessed—? No, how could he?

"He wanted out? He tried to blackmail Greg? How am I supposed to know?" She knew her antagonism was only ramping up his curiosity, but couldn't seem to help herself. "If he was a good guy, how did he get into my restaurant when it was closed and locked? Why wouldn't he have had a warrant, or at least backup? Why didn't even his own partner know he had a lead on Greg Cobb? Tell me that."

He inclined his head but remained watchful. "I don't know. But how did his killer get in? Did you walk through before you left?"

"No. For the first time in my life, I didn't. I scuttled out the back, made sure that door was locked, and drove home terrified someone was following me."

"That's understandable, Naomi."

It was even the truth. She was just neglecting to mention a missing chapter of the story.

"All I'm saying is, Detective Rostov shows up out of the blue and claims to be my saviour, and I'm supposed to buy it? I don't!" She sounded hysterical. *Gee, I wonder why?*

"But he has jumped in to protect you twice. Tell me why he'd do that if he works for Cobb?"

"Because he's trying to worm his way into my confidence to get the video, which I just handed him." With horror, she realized how plausible that actually was.

"Do you distrust me?"

She didn't even have to hesitate. "No."

"Unless he plans to knock me off, too, and do it before I get a chance to talk to Alex Mackay, he can't run to Cobb with it."

"What if he comes back and guns us both down?" Now she *really* sounded hysterical.

His mouth quirked. "There's a witness. Your next door neighbor was watching when we arrived from the hospital. Maybe he shrugged after that and turned on the TV, but I'm thinking we're more interesting than re-runs. He's gonna still be watching."

Yes. Bless Arthur and his incessant nosiness. Of course he was stationed right by the window.

"He's probably not alone, you know," Daniel continued, his tone kind. "Not in this neighborhood."

"Yes, but…does anybody but you know who Adam is?"

"Sure. I filled out a report about him rescuing your bag. Elias Burton and Ms. Sanchez both heard his name. I made my officers all aware of him. And don't forget, he came out in a big way at the hospital today, too. He's not trying to hide who he is."

"He lied to me for days," she said stubbornly.

"You mean, he didn't tell you what he did for a living."

"Or that he'd come to Cape Trouble specifically to track me down."

Daniel nodded. "I don't blame you for being mad about that. But he didn't know you. Under the circumstances, I might have done the same thing."

She opened her mouth to ask if he would have passionately kissed a woman while still lying to her, but a curdling sense of shame stopped her.

Plus, she heard his SUV outside.

"He's parking here?" She jumped up. "You know what the neighbors will think!"

Daniel chuckled. "Having his vehicle sitting outside your house will also protect you. It's like posting a sign warning that you have an alarm system."

She looked out the front window and, fuming, realized he hadn't parked at the curb. Oh, no, he'd pulled into her driveway, where his gigantic SUV blocked her from getting out in her car. He'd done that on purpose.

She turned to Daniel. "You won't help me get away?" She knew it was hopeless, but had to try.

"I might, if I thought you could pull off a vanishing act." His pragmatism didn't hide the pity he felt. "But it's next to impossible these days. Realistically, your best chance is to let us handle this and keep you safe."

"Why don't you say what you really mean? You'll *try* to keep me safe."

Duffel slung over his shoulder, Adam walked in the front door while she and Daniel were still staring at each other. She had to still be vibrating with hostility, which alternated with terror as her go-to emotion today.

His eyebrows rose. "Everything okay?"

"Wonderful. Couldn't be better." She went to her bedroom and, with great restraint, closed the door carefully instead of slamming it.

For a moment, only silence came from the living room.

She flung herself into her chair and began rocking, desperate for some comfort.

The low sound of their voices came through the door. She could just imagine what they were saying.

She loved this chair. She'd had it upholstered with fabric she'd brought back from Africa. *I'll have to leave it behind*, she realized. In fact, this time she'd have to leave behind everything she couldn't slip into her messenger bag. Naomi was surprised at the way her heart cramped as she looked around at the objects she'd collected. They meant more than she'd understood. The few she'd been able to bring along gave her a sense of continuity, a sort of reassurance that she was still the same person she'd been. The bits and pieces she'd acquired since had given her the sense of home she so desperately needed. This time, she couldn't take anything.

My cookbooks!

She hugged herself. Most could be replaced. And…she'd learned an important lesson. Whatever she did with her life after this would not involve cooking. Apparently that had been her biggest mistake. She wouldn't make it again.

I don't know how to do anything else.

Sure she did. She could type or answer a phone. If undocumented aliens cleaned hotel rooms, that meant a lot of hotels paid under the table. She could do that, too. Heck, she could *wait* tables. She could set up a housecleaning business. Go back to school, once she had a new identity. She'd find something.

Worry about that later.

The voices diminished, and she knew Daniel Colburn was leaving, abandoning her to Adam Rostov. Who made her heart race and her blood thicken. Who'd made her trust him, when all the time he was deceiving her because he suspected her of murdering his partner.

Which she had.

For now, she'd distracted him, but she knew that wouldn't last. He, too, would want to know how Frank Donahue *and* his killer came to be in her closed restaurant.

Naomi squeezed her eyes shut and then opened them quickly, shuddering, when all she saw on the back of her eyelids was the change to that weary, regretful face in the split second when he knew he was dying. She'd never actually seen anyone die before, and hoped she never did again.

A knock on her bedroom door had her stiffening.

"Naomi?" His gritty voice was both matter-of-fact and gentle. "I'm going to make something to eat. Are you hungry?"

Her stomach growled. She didn't want to sit down with him for a meal, but she had to eat. Pretending to cooperate would be smart anyway. She called, "I'll be out."

He must have stood there for a minute, but finally she heard his footsteps recede. With a sigh, she stood and followed him to the kitchen.

"I can cook," she said to his back. He'd found a frying pan and set it on the stove.

He glanced at her, shook his head and reached into one of half a dozen grocery bags that had appeared on her counter. "You're hurt. Sit. I can do hamburgers and baked beans. I even have buns."

It actually sounded good. "You brought your own groceries."

"No sense in letting the food I bought go to waste." He poked in several bags. "Damn it, I know I have an onion."

"If not, I do, in the bottom drawer."

He gave up on his bags and took one of her onions. A minute later he had canned baked beans warming in a saucepan and hamburgers sizzling on the burner. He sliced the onion and a tomato, tore lettuce and set out a small jar of mustard. "No catsup, unless you have some."

"No."

He'd changed from sweatpants to faded jeans, but still wore the same long-sleeve black T-shirt. Black…suited him, she thought, remembering the comparison with Elias Burton, whom she'd always imagined as an archangel. So golden, and almost too beautiful to look at. And yet, she'd often thought, his paintings gave away how much darkness he carried inside. With Adam, she couldn't tell. He was too guarded. She knew now that the times she'd thought he was being open, he'd been lying.

For all her anger, she couldn't seem to look away from him, lean, strong, with a leashed grace in his movements that made her wonder if he did martial arts. Dark stubble emphasized the hollows beneath his cheekbones and made her realize he'd shaved a second time the night they went out to dinner. She had laid her hand on that hard jaw when he kissed her—

"What would you like to drink?" he asked, jarring her from a memory that was both erotic and painful.

Bastard.

"Just water."

She turned her head and fixed her gaze on the Chamber of Commerce calendar that hung at the end of the wall-hung cabinets. November featured a photo of the sand dunes across Mist River from town. Naomi was startled to realize she should have flipped the page – it was December now.

Didn't matter; she wouldn't make any of the appointments scribbled in the little squares.

He dropped some ice cubes in her water and poured milk for himself. In a matter of minutes, he was setting plates on the table. Her mouth watered as she inhaled.

"You seem to know what you're doing in the kitchen," she said stiffly.

"Eating out all the time gets old. I can do the basics. I'd rather eat almost anything you cooked, though."

Why she felt compelled to make stilted conversation, Naomi had no idea, but she said, "Almost anything?"

"I've never much liked seafood. Fish of any kind. Or cooked cabbage or spinach." He took a bite of his burger and appeared to mull over his tastes as he chewed. "I'm afraid I'm a traditionalist. I like knowing what's in anything I put in my mouth."

Under other circumstances, she might have smiled. "You're one of those people who's happy to see macaroni and cheese on the menu."

The corner of his mouth curled, although his eyes remained watchful. "Yeah. I admit it."

"I…don't do much with fish myself."

"I noticed."

She bet he'd noticed a whole lot.

She set down her own burger. "Why are you so sure your partner wasn't on Greg's payroll?"

Anger flashed in his eyes. "Because I knew Frank. We'd worked together for almost three years. He never let me down."

She studied her food instead of him. "Was he married?"

"Yeah," Adam said gruffly. "Three kids. Two still in college."

She didn't say anything.

"He grumbled about how much it cost." He knew what she was thinking. "But Frank, sell out so he didn't have to borrow money? That's bullshit!"

She nodded, even though he was wrong. Frank Donahue had been willing to kill an innocent woman in cold blood for money. What other explanation was there?

What if I was wrong? What if—? But she wasn't wrong. He'd regretted what he was going to do, but he had every intention of doing it anyway.

"What I can't understand is why he went after Cobb on his own." Adam almost sounded as if he was talking to himself.

Repeating a conversation he'd had over and over. "Why didn't he call me? After I heard, I checked my phone. No messages, no missed calls." The pain in his gritty voice brought her head up. "He had to know I'd come."

"Had…you ever investigated Greg? I mean, how would Frank even have known about him?"

The pain was in his eyes, too, along with dark fury. "Cobb has come close to being arrested half a dozen times. If he doesn't have an unbeatable alibi, witnesses recant. Every cop in southern California knows who he is."

"I really was a fool then." She'd only taken a few bites, and was losing her appetite.

He hesitated. "Journalists have been careful. I don't know if they're scared of him, or just of lawsuits. Even if you'd done a search, you wouldn't have come up with much."

She might have been comforted had it not been for that hesitation. The one that said, *Hell, yes, you were a fool.* Plus, there was what he'd said earlier: *It didn't once cross your mind that meant he might be bad news?*

It should have crossed her mind. Greg had been too vague about what his business was. She'd let herself get sucked in by how flatteringly interested he was in *her* business. About his tales of international travel. He'd been charmingly self-deprecating even though he exuded arrogance.

She'd been stupid. Call a spade a spade.

"How long had you been seeing him?"

"I told you. He'd been dining at my restaurant for a year or more. He'd brought women he was seeing or entertained what I assumed were other businessmen. When he found out the restaurant was available for private parties, he booked that same room four or five times, maybe. But he asked me out the first time only about a month before that night. I worked almost every day, and supposedly he was out of town for a week in there. We'd gone out only a few times. Dinner, when I was off. He thought I'd like to try other restaurants."

Adam's eyes flickered. Both of them were remembering that he'd suggested the same thing when he asked her out.

"Once he took me to his house at Malibu. It was right on the beach. We bodysurfed, then his housekeeper laid out a really lavish lunch."

"After which she made herself scarce." His tone was dry.

This was none of his business, but for some reason she told him anyway. "Yes, but I'd gotten sunburned. I burn easily. Even if I'd wanted to, there was no way."

"Did you want to?"

"What difference does it make to you?" Naomi cried. He was the one who didn't say anything this time, but he didn't look away, either. It was her who finally did.

"No," she said softly. "I was glad to have an excuse. I…couldn't figure out why I— I mean, he really is good looking. Athletic, smart. He can talk about anything. He was openly interested in me but also…patient. I kept making excuses, even to myself."

"You wondered what was under the surface."

She hadn't thought of it that way, but it was true that she never felt as if she really knew him. She remembered that night thinking how cold and flat his eyes were. *The windows to the soul.* She'd never seen his soul.

"He claimed his father was an international businessman, and that he'd grown up around the world. He said he spoke half a dozen languages. He had that confidence. Was any of it true?"

"To some degree. His father owns a couple of import-export stores, and he takes buying trips. He's pretty small time, though. Greg and his mother probably went with him on occasion, but mostly he grew up in Akron, Ohio. Dad's stores are in Cleveland and Akron. Greg was smart, won a National Merit Scholarship. He went to Ohio State, where he majored in business. He ended up with an MBA."

"He did say he had an MBA."

"Did he tell you he was on the pistol target shooting team at Ohio State, too? Won a lot of medals." Cynicism and rage burned in Adam's gray eyes. "He got a useful education in more than one way."

"You really think he killed your partner. But he was stabbed, not shot." *With my knife. The one that had my fingerprints on it.*

"I doubt Cobb himself killed Frank. I suspect he kills only when he earns a great deal of money to pull the trigger himself. Even then, he may not do it himself anymore. Most contract killers are loners. They either live like ghosts, or they have a boring, everyday identity. Cobb's different. He has employees. According to my FBI friend, he's got his fingers in the drug trade now."

No wonder Adam had been disgusted with her. What universe had she lived in, dating the head of a drug cartel? "And I thought I could hold him off with my little video," she murmured. "I bargained with him. How funny is that?"

"*Funny* is not the word that comes to mind."

"No." Naomi shook her head, more to clear it than in denial. "So...you don't think he killed James Heath himself?"

"A high profile client like that? Yeah, I think he might have offered personal service. So to speak."

Naomi pushed her plate away. Adam looked at it, then at her, expression regretful.

"We shouldn't have talked about this while we were eating. I'm sorry."

Her stomach turned over. Frank Donahue had regretted what he felt he had to do, too. And maybe Adam's motives were pure, but she had no doubt he would be as ruthless in his own way. He was consumed by his quest. If she got trampled underfoot, he might be *regretful*, but he wasn't about to let any danger to her divert him.

I'm pretending to be cooperative, remember?

"We'd have both been thinking about it. I'm not a big eater, anyway."

"So you said."

"I hardly ever sit down to a real meal, like I did—" She stopped. *With you.* "Mostly I taste when I'm cooking, and that's enough."

"All right." He sounded unexpectedly kind.

I can't do this anymore. She stood and carried her plate to the sink, awkwardly scraping the leftovers into the trash, then rinsing it. When she started out of the kitchen, he said, "Don't go yet."

"Why?"

"There are things I want to say."

She stopped to gather herself, then turned. "Things."

"Yeah." Color rose to his cheeks, unless she was imagining it.

All she wanted was to get away, but she almost had to go back to the table and sit down.

His eyes narrowed. "You hurt."

"I was going to take one of the pills and go to bed." Which was the truth. Escape wasn't happening tonight, and maybe the pain pill would help her sleep. It would help to be well-rested when the chance came to run.

With chagrin, she knew that, pills or no, she wouldn't have slept at all if he hadn't been here. Even though he was a threat to her in one way, he also made her feel safe.

"I'll get you one." He stood. "Where are they?"

"In the bathroom."

He returned a moment later with the bottle and shook a pill out into her hand. She swallowed it, using the glass of water she'd hardly touched.

Resuming his seat, Adam frowned down at his plate. "You accused me of lying to you. I did lie about one thing."

"What was that?"

The eyes that met hers were wary. "My parents. The way I grew up."

"Why would you lie about them?" she asked in astonishment.

"I was trying to give us something in common."

"The constant moves."

"Yeah." He grimaced. "I'm sorry."

"You made that all up." *I am so gullible.* She'd lashed out at him without really believing he'd lied about everything.

"No, I borrowed. Juan Ramirez is a good friend of mine. He's with S.L.P.D. too. I've been lucky because his parents have sort of adopted me. I was talking about them."

"The aphids."

His mouth twisted. "Yeah."

She wouldn't ask him about his parents. He and she weren't friends.

"My dad was a cop," he said abruptly. "L.A.P.D. When I was eight or nine, he lost his job. He'd been accused of being on the take. He denied it. Said he was a scapegoat, or he'd been chosen as cover for guys who really were dirty. We ended up moving to this dusty, nothing town almost on the Mexican border where he got hired as sheriff." Adam told the story in a near-monotone, but she heard the perplexed, scared boy he'd been. "He was bitter, started boozing. A familiar story. Mom got quieter and quieter. I tried to find places to be besides home." He fell silent, expression brooding.

Finally, Naomi couldn't help herself. "What happened?"

He met her gaze. "When I was fourteen, he killed himself." His jaw muscles flexed. "The bastards who blackened his name killed him."

Connecting the dots, Naomi wanted to bang her head on the table. *I am doomed.* She *knew*, but asked anyway. "Why are you telling me this?"

"Because you told me about a tough childhood, and I lied. I didn't feel good about it." His jaw tightened again, before he finished. "There's been talk about Frank. I won't see Frank's family go through what we did."

It was almost funny. She'd think the perfect storm that was her life couldn't get worse, and it did. Now she knew: Adam really was on a crusade, with Frank standing in for his father.

Tasting bitterness, she said, "So you want to prove I'm guilty of something horrible so you can clear your partner of suspicion. But being a stand-up guy yourself, you'd like to think you've been completely honest while you're going about it." She rose to her feet, furious and exhausted and feeling hopeless all at the same time. She let her lip curl. "God forbid *you* should have anything to feel guilty about." Then she walked out, hearing nothing but silence behind her.

*****

Shaken by the expression on Naomi's face right before she left the kitchen, Adam didn't move for a long time. What he didn't like was the knowledge that she was right; he'd wanted her to be… How had he labeled her? An amoral bitch. Yeah, he'd convinced himself that's what she was, because it was the easiest answer. He couldn't get to Greg Cobb, but he could get to Naomi Varner slash Kendrick.

Oh, yeah, he thought, *I got to her all right.* What he'd done was lie, and then kiss her as if he hadn't been able to help himself. As if he'd needed to kiss her more than he needed to eat or sleep or breathe.

And now he was more confused than he'd ever been in his life. She was nothing like he'd assumed. What he'd found was a complex, vulnerable, courageous, proud woman who, against all evidence, he believed.

For two years, she had defied Greg Cobb and gotten away with it. That was miraculous. She'd have lost eventually, of course; in fact, one thing he *hadn't* lied about was his conviction that she'd already be dead if he hadn't followed her when she set off on that run.

He knew something else: she hated him, and for good reason. He had lied, if mostly by omission, he'd manipulated her, and he did want to use her as bait.

He was also determined to keep her safe, whatever it took, but he doubted she believed that, and he couldn't blame her.

He swore aloud. Viciously, but also quietly.

Was there another way?

Frowning, he gazed at the doorway to the living room without seeing it.

Sure there was. He could set her free. He remembered the earrings she'd worn that night, with the tiny birds taking flight. He could help her assume another identity, as she'd begged him to do. He at least knew how to avoid some of the pitfalls. She'd given them enough, they might be able to bring down Cobb and Greer without her.

But not the third man at that table, the one the edge of the door had cut off. And Colburn was right. Once she was settled into that new life, she'd be completely on her own. Any small slip, and she'd be found again.

And if she never made that slip?

The burning sensation beneath his breastbone didn't surprise him as much as it should have. He knew what was bothering him.

She'd be on her own – and so would he. He'd never see her again.

A matter of days ago, he'd despised her. He still couldn't claim to really know her. He felt sure she was still holding back. Thinking about it, he realized she'd dodged talking about Frank's death. But he believed what she'd told them about that night. He believed she hadn't been Cobb's girlfriend.

And the idea of never seeing her again was…unacceptable.

He groaned and thought, *So who's the fool?*

CHAPTER EIGHT

Accepting the set of car keys, Naomi slung her bag over her shoulder and said, “I won’t be gone long. Twenty minutes, tops. Hold down the fort.”

“Of course I will,” Anita said.

On impulse, Naomi gave her waitress a quick hug, something she never did. Looking startled, Anita had no chance to make the embrace reciprocal. Motherly. Naomi didn’t dare give her that chance, or she would have been crying. Instead, ignoring the sting in her eyes, she slipped through the kitchen and opened the back door, taking an even more than usually cautious look up and down the alley.

Nothing moved.

Of course, anybody could be behind either of the two big dumpsters, or crouched behind the cars and SUVs parked back here.

Taking a deep breath, clutching the borrowed keys tight in her hand, she hurried toward Anita’s almost new and treasured green Subaru Forester, parked on the other side of the dumpster from her own spot. Which was vacant today, because of course Adam had insisted on driving her, no doubt congratulating himself on having her safely trapped in the café for the day while he went about his business.

Poor Anita, facing the lunch rush and no chef. No food to serve. She’d be alarmed at first when Naomi failed to reappear, then scared. For me. How long it would take her to realize that her boss wasn’t coming back? That The Sea Watch Café was no more? That her job was no more?

That I stole her car.

Not stole. Borrowed. She’d get it back. *Once I’m safely away, I’ll call and let her know where to find it.*

Naomi unlocked and slung her bag across to the passenger seat. Please God, Adam didn’t decide to come back for lunch. He’d had breakfast at the café, but she knew he and Daniel intended to get together and plot. Probably by this time they were meeting with the county sheriff. Adam had made her promise not to set foot out of the restaurant until he was there to get her. So, sue her. She'd lied.

That gave her at least three hours, unless Anita got worried enough to call Daniel. No matter what, Naomi should have time to get as far as Lincoln City. Once he found out she was gone, Adam would likely assume she'd gone north instead, the logical route to Portland. South would delay his pursuit, if only briefly. There was a branch of her bank in Lincoln City, too, where she could withdraw every penny she had. Plus, Lincoln City was larger than Cannon Beach to the north. She could park Anita's Subaru somewhere it wouldn't be spotted too soon, and with luck find a cheap secondhand car to buy quickly. Which she'd trade the minute she reached Salem, where she'd either catch a bus or find another car or…

Maybe she should keep going south and *not* turn inland, she thought. Unpredictable might trump convenience.

Think about the next step, she counseled herself, *not two or three steps away.*

As always, she locked the minute she was in, letting go of the extra tension that had gripped her as she scurried across the alley. The engine started immediately, and she released the emergency brake. Her hand shook and she was breathless. Her heart was racing, that's why. *Déjà vu.* For a moment, she tightened her hands on the steering wheel, closed her eyes and did some deep breathing.

I've done it before, I can do it again.

Last time she hadn't stolen a car.

Borrowed. I'm only borrowing.

Anita would have loaned it to her without a second thought, if Naomi had been able to tell her what she was doing and why.

Don't waste time. Go.

She opened her eyes, saw a dark figure in the side mirror and screamed. She thrust the gear into reverse and stepped on the gas.

Instead of jumping back, Adam leaped behind the rear bumper so she'd have to hit him to keep going. Naomi slammed on the brakes and sat there, shaking like a leaf. He'd been out here all this time, waiting for her to try to make a getaway.

A hand slapped the window inches from her head. She flinched, refusing to look at him, but even through the glass she heard his bellow.

"Open the damn door, Naomi!"

She controlled the shakes enough to push the button so the window glided down a couple of inches.

"You promised," he snarled.

"You're not the only one who can lie."

"God damn it! You think that creep out there isn't waiting to catch you alone? Is this glass bullet-proof? Tell me that!" His voice boiled with fury.

She pressed her lips together.

"Open. The. Door."

At that moment, she hated him. She'd have run him over if it would have done any good, but it wouldn't. She'd be pulled over within the first five minutes. Daniel undoubtedly knew where Adam was and why. Humiliated, she realized they'd both guessed what she would do.

After a minute, she shifted to drive and eased the Forester back into place, set the emergency brake, grabbed her bag and got out. Adam reached for her arm and she jumped back.

"Don't touch me!" she spat.

He leaned toward her, his face taut with that same rage. "What the hell was this about? How far did you think you'd get?"

"Far enough to walk into a crowd and disappear." Instead of letting herself shrink back, she thrust out her chin. "What the *hell* this was about is staying alive. You'll get over it if I die for a good cause, but *I won't*. And I don't want to die." She was mad to hear the tremor in her voice, but couldn't help it. Wouldn't let herself see the pity or contempt in his eyes, so she pushed past him and ran for the restaurant door.

She had almost reached it when Adam grabbed her good shoulder and wheeled her around. "Oh, no," he said, low and angry. "We're not done."

"Gosh. I thought it wasn't safe to stand out here in the open."

She saw the jolt before his head turned sharply to scan each way. "Inside, then," he said, from between gritted teeth.

She managed to unlock, then tried to close the door in his face. Of course she failed; he was stronger than her, pushing her back and grabbing one of her hands before she could race for the front. In the confined space, he loomed over her, making her bitterly aware of how easily he could dominate her physically.

"Is that you, Naomi?" Anita called. "Did you decide not to go after all?"

"No, I ran into Mr. Rostov. He distracted me."

"Who?" The comfortably plump waitress appeared in the kitchen and her eyes widened at the sight of Adam. "Oh! Oh, my. I suppose after the shooting…."

He smiled at her with deliberate charm. "I convinced her I'd stop with her to do any errands later. I don't want her running around by herself until Chief Colburn figures out who fired those shots."

Like everyone else, Anita assumed Naomi had been shot by a careless hunter. Although everybody professed to be puzzled by why anyone had been firing a rifle out on the point.

She'd shaken her head that morning and said, "So close to the highway. It's crazy."

Crazy wasn't quite the right word, Naomi had thought then and now. *Cold-blooded* was closer.

She handed back the keys, thanked Anita again, and said, "I'd better get started on lunch. Adam can chew me out while I'm slicing and dicing."

Anita chuckled comfortably. "I'll finish setting the tables and then come back to help."

Adam erased any hint of charm the moment she was out of sight. "So now I have to watch you non-stop," he said, a scornful curl to his lip. "There are more useful things I could have been doing."

"Like what?" Refusing to let him see how she'd shriveled inside, she hung her coat and muffler on a hook by the door and stowed her bag in a cupboard, then went to the sink to wash her hands.

"Like check out everyone who arrived in town within the right time frame."

For some reason that surprised her. "You don't think he's here under his own name?"

"No, but neither of these guys is likely to have a wife in tow. If we identify the single men, we can run background checks. Maybe come up with some possibles to watch."

She thought of all those single men who had made her uneasy. "He wouldn't have come into the café to eat, would he?"

"Probably not. He can't be sure you wouldn't recognize him, for one thing. Unless he's someone Greer hired, but I really don't see that as a likely possibility."

She looked down at the Yukon Gold potatoes she'd heaped in front of her. Her potato chowder was easy and popular. Given that she hadn't expected to be here to prepare any soup, easy was a necessity.

"I'll stay put," she said tightly. "I swear."

Adam leaned back against the door, his arms crossed, his expression still dark with anger. "Turns out you lie."

"I give up." She snapped on plastic gloves. Hands almost steady, she picked up the peeler. Golden curls flew. "I wouldn't get far enough to do any good."

"No. You wouldn't."

"Why didn't you just have one of Daniel's officers pull me over? Why the big scene?"

"Because I wasn't the only one who might have been waiting in that alley, Naomi. Did *that* occur to you? Did you think about what happened to you the last time you went to your car when it was parked there?"

She looked at the potato in her hand. "Yes."

"That's it? Yes?"

Even knowing tears glittered in her eyes, Naomi glared at him. "Yes. *Yes!* I was scared, okay? Does that make you happy to hear? But I'm more scared of being staked out like…like that goat in Jurassic Park. Because I don't think you can keep me safe." She finished bitterly, "I don't even think that's a priority for you."

Shock wiped out the anger. "You really believe that."

"Why wouldn't I? Oh, damn." She turned her back on him and snatched a paper towel to swipe furiously at her cheeks and blow her nose. And that meant tearing off her gloves and donning clean ones before she picked up the peeler and the next potato. "Go do what you have to do. I've conceded."

"What you said. That's crap. I wouldn't—"

"Here I am," Anita declared cheerfully. "What do you want me to start with?"

Adam said something foul under his breath that, thankfully, Anita apparently didn't hear.

"Go," Naomi ordered him. "You're in the way."

"You'll be here when I get back." Tamped frustration sounded like gravel in his voice.

"Apparently I don't have a choice."

His teeth showed, but he turned and opened the door.

Naomi bleated like a goat. Well, a sheep, anyway. Her "Baa-a" earned her one last, savage look before he left, ordering, "Lock behind me."

After a stunned moment, Anita said, "Oh, my. Is he *mad* at you?"

*****

Adam made it back to the police station to find a sheriff's department car parked in the small lot and Sheriff Alex Mackay already seated in the police chief's office. The man rose stiffly and held out a hand.

They shook, Adam recognizing stoicism and catching a glimpse of old scarring showing above the collar of the guy's shirt. Mackay looked to be in his forties, although the effect of chronic pain might have aged him past his actual years. Silver threaded brown hair, but he was a big guy who was somehow maintaining his conditioning, because a powerful build showed no sign of softening.

"Daniel's been telling me about you. And about Naomi's problem. I've never met her, but I eat at her café when I get the chance. She's talented in the kitchen."

"Yeah, she is," he said grumpily, aware Daniel was watching him. "Not so good at using her head in other ways."

"You were right, then?" Daniel asked.

"Oh, yeah. She tried to make a getaway. Apparently she was 'borrowing' her waitress's car. I should have let her get a block away and had you arrest her. We could have kept her safe in jail." He raised his eyebrows. "If you have one?"

"Couple of temporary holding cells. Otherwise, we contract with the county."

"Our jail isn't very big, either." Mackay had just as stiffly resumed his seat. "Not real suitable for keeping women long-term."

Adam looked at the one empty chair, straight-backed and not meant for lingering, longed to pace and sat anyway, exhaling a frustrated breath. "This time she swears she'll stay put."

"You think she means it?" Daniel asked.

"Yeah," he muttered. "She's convinced we plan to stake her out."

"I can see why it seems that way to her," the police chief said. "Not sure that isn't what we are doing. Except I don't see a good alternative."

"You going to show me this video?" Mackay intervened. Evidently he'd had most of the story from Daniel Colburn already.

"She did email the link to you?" Adam asked.

"Yep."

Despite the piss poor quality, Adam was as riveted by the short video as he'd been every other time he watched. He still couldn't believe she'd taken it at all. The way the image vibrated made his gut clench.

Feeling…protective, he guessed that was part of his nature. Maybe it was the same for most cops. He never liked seeing fear or suffering, especially when it was on a kid's or woman's face. He had never before felt anything like he did now, though. Never wanted so desperately to go back in time and change the unchangeable. Never wanted to kill for a woman's sake.

Never felt so goddamn much for a woman who clearly hated him and hadn't hesitated to look right at him and lie.

He could only imagine how he'd have felt a few hours from now if he'd trusted her and then discovered she was gone.

Mackay sat frowning at the now black screen of Daniel's desktop. "I've seen miracles accomplished on photographs. A face or a license plate brought out, crystal clear, when I'd have sworn they weren't there. I suspect this won't be much of a challenge to someone with the right software who knows what he's doing."

"You have the right someone in mind?" Daniel asked.

"I think so. There's a guy at the lab in Portland. It was thanks to him we recovered a little girl snatched by a serial pedophile and murderer because a teenager across the street had her cell phone in her hand and snapped a picture. It was so bad, I didn't think it would be any help, but it only took this guy minutes. We had an Amber Alert and a BOLO out before he got a mile away."

Daniel looked at Adam. "Your call."

"Do it." He grimaced. "You happen to have any job openings if I get fired?" He was mostly kidding.

"I think you're over-qualified for my department."

Mackay chuckled, a rusty sound. "Me, I almost always have an opening in the detective division. Feel free to give me a call."

"I might be doing that," Adam said ruefully.

He had a disconcerting thought. What if they pulled this off? Proved Congressman Greer had wanted to win the election so bad he'd hired Greg Cobb to kill his opponent? Caught the fed in the act of trying to silence Naomi? Arrested all three of them, which meant she was safe to return to her life. Which life would she choose? The one she'd fled two years ago – or the one she'd built here in Cape Trouble?

He had an uneasy recollection of how he'd felt at the idea of her taking on a new identity. Was he really going to wish her well, pack up and go back to California?

Why not? He'd lost any chance he might have had with her when he'd lied to her. When he'd kissed her under false pretences.

Yeah, and he couldn't forget that he'd met her only days ago, and he'd been singing a different tune then. It was still possible she was conning him. Sure he wanted her. So what? He'd wanted other women before. He'd get over it.

Crap.

"You started on calling hotels?" he asked.

Apparently they were going to have to visit each individually, which he'd expected. There was a Forest Service campground and a KOA campground, too, nearby enough to be worth checking. Unfortunately, it was just as likely that either or both of their targets had set up camp somewhere along the miles of deserted shoreline or tucked into the dense Northwest forest. He'd glimpsed a few tents or campfires during his drive along the coast. If he wanted to be as close to invisible as possible, that's what he'd do. He held onto some hope because most southern Californians would find unthinkable the concept of camping out in the cold and wet, having to crap bare-assed amidst the ferns.

"What about that new resort under construction?" Mackay asked. "You can't tell me all the hiring was local."

"No, and Randall Bresler, the guy behind it, signed three to six month leases on several houses in town to bunk workers. I think it's damned unlikely that anyone after Naomi knew about the employment opportunity, went through the hoops to get hired and is showing up for work every day, though."

"No," Adam agreed, "unless Cobb's people had located her sooner than we think."

"There's no chance he has the means to find a local with a gambling problem and major debts, say, who'd be subject to pressure?"

Now, there was an unwelcome idea. Outsiders would be easier to identify.

"I know he's into drugs," Adam told them. "That might give him some connections up this way."

"That's one problem we don't have much in this county," the sheriff observed. "Possession, sure, but we don't have enough population to provide a worthwhile marketplace."

"We'll assume outsiders for the moment." Daniel was frowning, too, though. "He – either he – could be bedding down anywhere up to an hour away, though. Doesn't have to be here in town."

"And, assuming you're right and there are two of them around, does the guy trying to get his hands on Naomi's computer know the sniper is here in town, too?" Mackay threw out. "And vice versa?"

"Her having to go to the hospital with a GSW probably gave the sniper away," Adam pointed out. "If the sniper is who I'm thinking he is, he had to assume someone from Cobb's organization was after her, too."

Daniel muttered something obscene.

Adam told them about Sam Weismann and their shirt-tail relationship. "I trust him as much as I do anyone. He's in a position to take a look at agents who just happen to be on vacation right now, or doing unspecified field work that can't quite be pinned down," he said.

They felt some of the same hesitations he did, but finally agreed that the advantages outweighed the possibility of word getting back to the dirty agent that questions were being asked.

In the end, they decided that Adam would be tied up with the protection detail, Daniel would investigate room or tent site-by-the-night possibilities in Cape Trouble and Jasper Beach, and Alex Mackay would cover the rest of the county as much as possible. He was going to call one of his detectives during the drive back to North Fork and assign the job.

"Call me paranoid," Adam said, remembering the way his hackles had lifted as he watched Detective Payne scrutinize the street, "but I was a little bothered that one of your detectives was close enough to respond almost immediately to her 911 call when she suspected the break-in."

The sheriff, already in the doorway, turned back to look at him. "Who was it?"

Daniel said, "I checked. Ah…something Payne."

"Jason." Mackay seemed to mull it over. "I don't know anything bad about him, but he hasn't been with the department very long. Came from Eugene or Corvallis, someplace like that. I think there were family reasons. His responding to the call the way he did was entirely appropriate if he happened to be right by Jasper Beach."

"How long is not long?" Adam asked.

"I'll have to look. Three or four months." He frowned. "I had in mind to call Sean Holbeck. Daniel has worked with him."

"He seemed to know his job," Daniel concurred.

The other men promised to stay in touch and, reassured, Adam left. A glance at his watch told him he'd be in time to get lunch at the café, assuming the chef hadn't crossed her fingers behind her back when she swore she'd stay put, and tried for another getaway.

*****

Naomi twisted in the car seat to stare at Adam in alarm. "*You* may trust this FBI agent friend, but why should I?"

"Sam is…" He started to say, more than a friend, but calling him friend wasn't right, either. It wasn't as if they socialized except when they were dragged into it by their respective siblings. "He's kind of family," he finally said. His gaze flicked between rear-view and side mirrors and straight ahead. No tail that he could see, but why would anybody bother? Everyone concerned knew where Naomi lived.

"*Kind* of family?" She had a death grip on the seatbelt where it crossed her chest. "What's that mean?"

"Sam's brother is married to my sister. When Ellen got married, I gave her away and Sam was best man. To their kids, I'm Uncle Adam, he's Uncle Sam."

She blinked at that. "How long have you known him?"

"Uh…" He had to think. "Ellen and Ben are coming up on their ten year anniversary."

"You're *positive* about this guy."

"Yes," he said, a little surprised how sure he was. "I can also tell you, if he'd been the man you saw that night, you would have remembered his face."

"Why?" she said suspiciously.

He smiled as he put on the signal for the turn into Jasper Beach. "Big nose. Really big nose."

Out of the corner of his eye, he caught her trying not to smile.

"Really ought to make an appointment with a plastic surgeon big?"

"Oh, yeah." Now he grinned. "His wife says it's sexy. Big hands, big nose, big…" He let it trail off, warmed by the tiny giggle he heard. "Sam blushed. I didn't know he could."

"Does he have children, too?"

"Two. Teenagers. He's older than Ben."

Naomi averted her face again until they reached her driveway. Then she agreed suddenly, "Okay. You're right. I'd remember a big nose."

"I wish we had a forensic artist. A good one might be able to pull more out of you than you think you remember."

"That sounds painful. What do they do, squeeze your brain like a toothpaste tube?"

He'd turned off the engine and remove the key, but she hadn't moved. The way she was eyeing her small house gave Adam the idea that she wasn't eager to go in.

He chuckled at her imagery. "Never seen one work," he said. "The one my department uses won't let anyone watch. She closets herself with the witness, and next thing we know she's drawn a face that nine times out of ten proves to be amazingly like the scumbag we end up arresting."

"Do you think of everyone you arrest as scum?" Now she did look at him, her gaze unexpectedly intense. "Don't you ever have doubts? Or…or understand why they might have done what they did?"

"Do you *understand* why our friend up on the bluff tried to take you out with a bullet?" he asked harshly.

Naomi winced and looked away. "No," she said in a small voice. "Of course not." As if galvanized, she unclipped the seatbelt, grabbed her bag and opened her door.

"Just a minute. Let me get around there."

Her surprised face turned to him, but she did wait. He used his body to screen hers from the likeliest direction a shot could come and hustled her inside, his head turning the whole way. "I wish we had some Kevlar for you to wear."

"Some what?"

"A vest. Bullet-proof."

"Oh. Do you have one?"

"In California. The sheriff is going to rustle one up for me and see what he can find that might fit you, too. He doesn't think they have any sized for a woman, though."

She rolled her eyes. "Doesn't that figure."

"Do they have any women deputies?"

"I'm sure I've seen a couple of different ones." She walked through to the living room and set her bag onto the coffee table.

He hovered in the doorway between the kitchen and living room, not wanting to crowd Naomi.

Or maybe the trouble was that he did. The last thing he should do was make any kind of move on her. Aside from ethical considerations, he felt sure it wouldn't be well received. He watched with some chagrin as she cradled her injured arm with her other hand now that it was free. Her face was drawn, making him freshly aware of how fine-boned she was, how small. How vulnerable, for all her defiance.

"You hurt," he said, straightening.

She offered a one-shouldered shrug. "I'm lucky it was my left arm. But I can't cook very well with one hand, and I wasn't about to have the café closed another day when it was supposed to be open."

He couldn't help raising his eyebrows. "Yeah? Didn't look to me like lunch was ready to be served when you pulled your little stunt."

"Fine." She looked at him with dislike. "You're right. It would have been closed forever if I'd had my way." She snatched up her bag again and started toward the bedroom. "I'm going to lie down."

"That's probably a good idea." With a closed door between them, his head would clear. By the time she reappeared, he could be dispassionate again.

And if he believed that, next thing he knew he'd be whipping out his checkbook to buy one of those sea stacks along this stretch of coast, one that supported a couple of spindly trees on top and was no earthly good to anybody except as a backdrop in a scenic photograph.

He told himself he was trailing her through the small house to make sure she actually went *into* her bedroom and not out the front door. But just before she closed yet another door in his face, he heard himself say, sounding pissed, "Why am I the bad guy here, Naomi?"

She swung around, glower in place. "You're kidding."

"No." Okay, now he was crowding her, but she wasn't backing away, either. He inhaled the scent of her, woman and a hint of ripe peach. So little to arouse him. "I'm trying to keep you safe. I'm trying to figure out who killed a good man. Get the evidence to convict the guys who killed another good man. Why does any of this make me a bug you want to squash?"

"Because you could have just asked!" she yelled. "You didn't have to lie. You didn't have to—"

"Kiss you?" He leaned in even closer. "Is that what I didn't have to do that makes you so mad?"

"Yes!"

"I didn't do it because I had to. You know that, don't you, Naomi? I kissed you because I—" *Had to.* God help him. Just not the kind of 'had to' she'd meant. "I want you," he said hoarsely. "I've wanted you since I set eyes on you. Does that make me the enemy?"

She stared at him, seemingly speechless.

He groaned and reached for her.

CHAPTER NINE

On a surge of need she couldn't combat, Naomi rose on tiptoe and flung her arms around his neck. She didn't allow herself to think; didn't want to think, because if she did she'd be afraid.

His mouth was hot and hard and hungry. The kiss was almost angry. He resented her as much as he wanted her. He resented her *because* he wanted her. She felt the same, but right this minute she didn't care. If she'd ever been driven by this wild need to merge with another human being, she couldn't remember it.

He devoured her mouth, his tongue driving deep. One big hand wrapped the back of her head so he could adjust the angle to please him. His other hand gripped her hip and buttock so tight she'd probably find fingerprints later. He lifted her and pulled her so close his heat burned her through their clothing and she felt every hard inch of him.

Naomi was mindless, ravenous, melting down and yet buzzing with energy all at once. She wanted to climb higher on his body, get closer, explore him, but she'd have to free one of her hands to wrench his shirt up, and she was already savoring the feel of his bare skin and the taut muscles of his neck, the thick silk of his dark hair. She heard herself making little noises, answered by rumbles from him. His hips rocked, and she wanted nothing more than to wrap her legs around him and take him inside. Let him fill her, make her forget—

"Damn," he groaned, lifting his head to look down at her with burning eyes. "Naomi—"

Sex is just sex, remember? whispered a voice in her head. *Is that* really *what you want?*

"Oh, my God." She went rigid in his arms, then lurched back. What had she been *thinking*?

That was the trouble. She'd been trying not to think, and look where that had gotten her.

He didn't try to come after her. His expression changed slowly, the lust that burnished his cheeks fading into shock.

"I didn't mean—" He stopped and shook his head, as if he was trying to get a defunct appliance to start. His brain. If it was slow responding, that was probably because his blood had all gone south. The thick ridge under his zipper wasn't subsiding.

A longing cramp deep inside made her wish she hadn't looked. She folded her arms tightly over her breasts. "What didn't you mean?"

For a moment he tipped his head back and looked up at the ceiling. Then his eyes met hers with painful honesty. "I meant to kiss you. But…not to take it as far as I did. Neither of us is quite ready for where we were going."

"I thought men were always ready." She sounded both belligerent and hurt, a mix that made her cringe.

"This wasn't like that."

"What was it like?"

"My body has been ready from the beginning. I think you knew that."

She gave a little shrug. *Her* body had been ready since she set eyes on him, too. There'd been that burst of adrenaline and fear, both because he might be the enemy and because she couldn't afford to fall for a man.

"But I haven't known how far I can trust you," he said. "I'm pretty sure I want more than a couple of nights in your bed, Naomi. What I want…takes trust. On both sides."

This longing cramp was centered under her breastbone. She had to ignore it, too. "Then you shouldn't have started anything. I don't think I know how to trust. It's…never worked out that well for me." She hated knowing how pathetic she sounded., but she'd already told him too much about herself the other night.

"I don't believe that," he said softly, his gaze laser sharp now. "I think you're scared *because* you trust me."

It was like a hard smack that spun her head to one side. Yes. She wanted to.

I do, she thought hopelessly. *I trust him to follow his convictions and to hold onto his loyalties.* One of the most powerful of which was to Frank Donahue, because Frank had come to stand in for Adam's father. He couldn't salvage his father's reputation, change what he and his mother and sister had suffered because of his father's disgrace, but he thought he could salvage Frank's for the sake of his wife and kids. Naomi had no idea if he understood how deep his identification with Frank's family went.

Admitting Frank had been been on Greg Cobb's payroll and willing to commit a cold-blooded murder would mean more than accepting his partner's weakness and guilt; it also meant facing the possibility his father hadn't been wronged at all, that he'd been on the take. Adam wanted to believe in his father. And he'd worked day in and day out for three years with Frank. Her, he'd known a few days.

If she were to trust him, that meant she had to tell him. And she already knew his trust wouldn't extend far enough to allow him to believe her.

So…it was a really good thing they were standing several feet apart now, because she had been about to make another huge mistake.

"I hope you mean it about keeping me alive," she said. "But, see, I'm not even so sure you do. So, trust? It's not happening."

He studied her for a long time. Her skin crawled, because she could swear he knew what she'd been thinking. But finally he dipped his head and one side of his mouth lifted.

"Okay, Naomi. We'll stick with keeping you alive for now."

"Good idea," she said sharply.

"I had a question." It almost sounded casual. "Once when we were talking, you said something about your restaurant. You said 'we' offered lunch and dinner. Did that mean you had a partner or investor?"

She blinked in surprise. Whatever she'd expected, this wasn't it. "No. The money was all mine, mine was the only name on the loan application, and I told you I like to be in control. That kind of business is a team effort, though. With the café, I come closer to managing on my own, but I still can't. If you'd asked about it, I'd have told you 'we' offer breakfast and lunch."

"Okay. Just curious."

Right. "You thought Greg was a silent partner which is why he could do whatever he wanted at the restaurant."

Adam frowned. "The thought crossed my mind back when you said that. I've…come to know you well enough to doubt it could be true, but I needed to ask."

"Well, now you know." Thank goodness, she'd donned hostility again as if it was a protective garment – Kevlar, she thought. And, oh, she needed it. "And if you don't mind, I'd like to lie down. So…"

His eyes narrowed, but he also gave something like a bow that was just a little bit mocking before he backed out of her bedroom doorway, letting her – finally! – close him out and be alone.

And then she didn't move, just kept standing there staring at the door and wishing for things she couldn't have. For too much.

*****

When he reached Sam, Adam said, "Any chance you can call me back?"

The small silence told him Sam understood what he was asking. "Sure, give me a few minutes. I'm tied up right now."

His usual restless self, Adam prowled through Naomi's small house. When he was a kid, a teacher had been convinced he was hyperactive and he'd been tested. The conclusion was that his powers of concentration were just fine; his problem was keeping his butt in the chair. That hadn't changed, although he'd learned to channel his inability to stay still for any length of time.

What he wanted to do was walk the perimeter, but not when he was distracted by waiting for a phone call. Instead, he eased a curtain aside a couple of times just enough to peer out. Her cottage was situated a few blocks from the highway. From here, he couldn't see the few small stores and the gas station. This was the quietest damn neighborhood he'd ever seen. He assumed that would change when the new resort opened. Naomi had told him a couple of artists had studios here at Jasper Beach, but if so they hardly ever emerged, either. He'd seen other curtains twitch up and down the street, though, so he knew the unusual action at Naomi's place had been closely observed.

When his phone vibrated, he saw with satisfaction that the number was unfamiliar. "Rostov," he said.

"This better be good," Sam grumbled. "I cut a meeting short."

"You're not in the office?"

"No, I went out to my car."

"Good. This is going to interest you."

Sam listened in grim silence. "Damn," he said finally. "Congressman Greer?"

"The shit will hit the fan."

"You believe her?"

"Yes. If the video shows what she says it does, Greer doesn't have a defense."

"Unless he comes right out and says kill James Heath for me, he'll think of a story to explain anything he said."

"That'll be made tougher by the fact that he's sitting at the table with Greg Cobb at all."

"He can claim he thought Cobb was a businessman interested in supporting him."

"I don't think that'll wash if he says what I think he will."

"Damn," Sam said again.

Then, of course, he challenged Naomi's belief that the third guy at the table was FBI. Easy to *say*, but wasn't it likelier that Greer had wanted reassurance and Cobb had provided it?

"I can't deny that's possible. Naomi did see the guy show identification, though. She also had the impression Greer had heard of the guy at the very least, maybe had dealings with him before but this was the first face to face. Also, her current problems are suggestive."

Sam wasn't much for swearing, but he let an obscenity slip. "She can't describe him at all?"

"He was sitting, remember, but she thinks medium height. Brown hair. Nothing memorable. She barely saw his face in profile." Adam coughed. "I told her I could guarantee it wasn't you."

"Yeah, yeah," Sam growled. "Me, I'm distinctive. That's what Gail says."

"Distinctive. Right."

"Damn." Sam seemed stuck on the word, which sounded more heartfelt each time he said it. The brief hint of amusement was gone. "There's not much to go on."

"Either he's on the in enough to have heard the conversation about the chef, or else someone told him. I'm assuming there isn't a lot of gossip around your office."

Sam grunted. "Cobb could have told him."

"But why would he?" He gave Sam a moment to process that before saying, in a harder voice, "Something else to go on. He's here. He's been here since mid-day yesterday at a minimum, and probably at least a day longer than that."

"Why longer?"

"He'd already found out where she worked, at a minimum. It's conceivable he followed us from there, kept an eye on her house and saw her set off for the run, then drove up the highway to set up for the shot. There are quite a few restaurants in town, though, and I doubt he wanted to ask for her by name, because somebody might remember. I think it would have taken him another day to chat up locals until someone mentioned her name without him asking for it."

"You went straight to her café."

"Yeah, but I did ask. Said somebody had recommended this place to eat, that I couldn't remember what it was called, but I thought the cook was a Naomi something. I didn't want her to know who I was right off the bat, but later…" He shrugged. "No big deal. I wasn't planning a crime."

That earned him another grunt of concession.

"One other thing," Adam said. "The guy shot her from close to two hundred yards out. I don't know about your snipers, but ours train at shorter distances than that."

"We have agents who do, but it's rare. Usually they're ex-military."

"You can eliminate anyone who is female or black, six foot four and blond, redheaded or balding—"

"Or has a big nose," Sam said blandly.

"Or has a big nose. Then look at who can shoot like that, would have been in a position to hear about Naomi, and just happens to be out of town right now."

"And if I don't come up with anyone? Or a too long list of possibles?"

"We worry about it then. In the meantime, I'm trying to keep her alive. Ellen won't forgive you if anything happens to me."

"Sure, lay that one on me." Sam sighed. "Okay. This number should be safe for now. Stay safe."

"Will do."

He went back to his restless pacing, interrupted when a tan SUV he didn't recognize pulled into the driveway. He did recognize the man who got out and came to the side of the house, arms full.

Adam opened the door. "Sheriff. I didn't expect you."

Alex Mackay's smile momentarily lessened the somber look in his eyes. "It happens that I live in Cape Trouble. It's a lot prettier than North Fork, and worth the commute. I figured I could handle this errand myself."

Adam stood back. "Come on in."

Mackay did, his gaze sweeping the interior the way Adam's did every time he entered a room. "I had a thought," he said after a minute. "The intruder didn't find anything when he searched, but what if he left something?"

An electronic bug.

"Seems unlikely. He didn't know about me, then, and it's pretty damn unlikely Naomi was going to talk to herself about where she'd hidden her insurance packet."

Mackay shrugged his acknowledgement as he set two vests on the table.

"I don't have the electronic equipment to be positive, but I've searched as well as I can. It's not a very big house. I didn't find anything." And hadn't mentioned that search to Naomi.

"Just wanted to be sure you'd thought about it." He nodded at the Kevlar he'd brought. "My negotiator is a woman, and of course she was fitted for a vest. She's a lot taller than Ms. Kendrick, but lean. She doesn't wear it day to day, and is happy to lend it."

"You get much use out of her training?" Adam asked, curious.

Mackay smiled again. "You'd be surprised. Most of the time we call for her in domestic situations, but every so often something else comes up. Did Daniel tell you about the bank robbery this summer?"

"In Cape Trouble?" Adam said incredulously.

The sheriff chuckled. "You wouldn't think, would you? A drugged out idiot thought the teller would hand over a little money, no problem, only it just happened that a Cape Trouble officer took a break to deposit his check. The idiot flipped out when he saw the uniform, took a potshot and then some hostages. As it happens, my negotiator, Rebecca, didn't get there until it was all over. Daniel talked the fool out on his own."

Laughing, Adam said, "And aren't we lucky so many of them are idiots."

"You can say that again." Between one blink and the next, Mackay's face became more guarded. "Ms. Kendrick."

Adam half-turned, bothered that he hadn't heard her coming.

The sheriff introduced himself and expressed his regret for her "troubles." It sounded downright courtly.

She thanked him and said she was about to put dinner on and would he like to stay? "I can have it on the table in less than half an hour," she coaxed.

Not happy with the way she was avoiding his gaze, Adam said nothing.

Mackay surrendered without a fight. He didn't wear a wedding ring, and apparently had no one waiting at home, because he didn't reach for his phone.

As she worked, Naomi was subdued but pleasant, even friendly. Call him a jackass, but Adam didn't like seeing her cordiality to another man when she apparently wasn't speaking to him.

After a few minutes Mackay excused himself to use the john, however, and Naomi turned from her cutting board to look at Adam. "I was really bitchy earlier. What happened was…two-sided, but it scared me and I wanted to blame you. I'm sorry," she said simply.

"I'm the one who started it," he admitted.

She offered him a small, twisted smile. "It's my fault you were mad. The rest of what I said, though, is still true. This…isn't a good time."

No, it wasn't, but he had a bad feeling this was the only time they'd have. What he felt for her was a first for him, and it was powerful. If they could learn to trust each other, he could see them having a stab at a future together. Adam found he really wanted the chance to find out if that was possible, but he heard Mackay coming and could only nod.

Appearing relieved, she went back to dicing tomatoes. She already had hot water on to boil and a frying pan heating. His stomach growled as he wondered what she was making. It was bound to be good.

He wondered if she'd have come out of her bedroom and offered to cook if she hadn't heard that someone else was here.

Even given what she'd said, he was surprised she could get a meal on the table so quickly. Sautéed vegetables that seemed to include squash as well as bell peppers in a couple of colors and those diced stewed tomatoes were stirred into whole wheat rotini, with a sauce that included cheese she'd grated and evaporated milk and who knew what else. Fortunately, she'd made a mountain, because he and Mackay both had seconds followed by thirds.

"Ah-h," the sheriff finally breathed, leaning back in his chair. "That was fantastic."

She smiled at him, her face momentarily more relaxed and happier than Adam had seen it since the night he took her out. "Probably better than whatever microwave dinner you planned," she teased.

Mackay grinned. "Frozen burritos."

"I baked cookies the other night. So many I had to freeze most of them." She made an apologetic face. "If anybody's interested, I'm defrosting some."

Adam, for one, had been acutely aware of the plastic container of cookies on the counter.

"I cook when I get stressed," she explained. "These are white chocolate and pecan. Not creative but good."

She used the microwave to warm a plateful and brought them to the table. Somehow he found room for several, as did Mackay. Naomi nibbled at one, more to keep them from noticing how little she'd eaten than because she wanted one, at a guess.

When the sheriff finally rose, a take-home container of more cookies in his hand, Adam said, "I'll walk you out," and under Naomi's alarmed gaze strapped on the tactical vest and grabbed his flashlight. He hoped she hadn't noticed that he was always armed these days. "Thought I'd take a look around," he said.

Outside, Mackay leaned against the still closed driver side door. "I'll wait."

Nights here were uncommonly dark to Adam's eyes, because he was used to city lights that stretched for so many miles, stars were dimly seen at best. Or, hell, maybe smog had something to do with the lack of clarity of the night sky in southern California.

He hadn't seen a lot of stars since he'd reached the Oregon coast, though, and he wouldn't be seeing any tonight. He'd been stunned when he read that the annual rainfall on this stretch of coast was seventy-two inches a year – and that somewhere between eleven and twelve of those inches fell in November. That figure for one month alone was damn near the rainfall for an entire *year* in L.A. He'd heard the patter start on the roof not long after he and Naomi had gotten home, and it was coming down hard now. Made him think he'd been lucky with the weather since he got here. It had drizzled a lot, but not poured until now.

Nonetheless, he circled her house, half wishing any part of her yard had been fenced to make the sightline more difficult for a shooter, but few yards in Jasper Beach were fenced, and those were mostly low ones that confined yappy little dogs as elderly as their owners. He'd have been a lot happier if Naomi had had an attached garage, too, but would have settled for a solid back to the carport. Instead, a sort of shed that probably held the lawn mower formed one corner, leaving a ten foot or wider opening into her back yard, which was open to the yards on the street backing hers.

A few porch lights tried to penetrate the sheets of rain. Adam was already soaked in the five minutes it took him to make the full circle and return to where the sheriff waited, gaze roving.

"Maybe you and she both should decamp," he said. "Could she find someone to fill in at the restaurant?"

He only had the same thoughts ten times a day. In the end, it always came down to the same conclusion. "What good is a temporary fix?"

Mackay made a rumbly sound Adam took for agreement and swung himself behind the wheel in his SUV. Watching him, Adam winced in sympathy. He wondered if the guy was still healing from whatever had happened, or if this was as good as it was going to be. If so, that must be hard to accept.

Once the visitor had backed out, he let himself back in the house, to find Naomi washing dishes at a furious rate, her body language tense. At the sound of the door, she turned and took in his soggy state.

"I'll get you a towel. No, forget that. I'll grab some dry clothes from your duffel, too, if you don't mind me poking in it. No point in you dripping your way through the house. The washer and dryer are right there. I'll put a load in as soon as you change."

He looked down at himself ruefully. "Good idea." He hadn't anticipated getting sopping wet so fast.

She dried her hands, then left the kitchen long enough to produce a towel, dry chinos, knit boxer shorts and a sweatshirt from his duffel. "Here," she said, thrusting the pile at him. Then she turned her back on him and plunged her hands into the dishwater again.

The utility area was barely an alcove. Adam hesitated and stepped behind the washer. The vest, flashlight and handgun he laid atop the dryer. The vest had kept his shirt from being as soaked as his pants, which landed with a wet splat when he dropped them onto the floor. Goosebumps rose from the chill. He'd already had a suspicion the cottage wasn't well insulated. A cold draft from around the door motivated him to towel himself dry briskly.

Instead of getting dressed, he wrapped the towel around his hips. "You mind if I take a shower?"

"Feel free," she said, without so much as glancing over her shoulder.

Maybe just as well. He couldn't help wondering if she'd like what she saw if she did, though. Leaving the flashlight and vest where they were, he took his weapon and the clothes and started through the kitchen, passing not three feet behind her. He'd reached the doorway when the back of his neck tingled and he quit feeling cold. His body stirring, he came to a sudden stop and turned to find her stealing a look at him. Half-turned from the sink, she stood absolutely still, her gaze traveling slowly upwards over his body until it locked with his. Soapy water dripped unheeded from her hand to the floor. Her eyes were dilated, dark with panic…and need.

Just like that, he couldn't find enough oxygen to take his next breath. She didn't seem to be breathing, either.

They stared at each other for a long, hungry moment, before a stricken expression came over her face and she whirled to face the sink again.

"Please go," she said in a choked voice.

He had to do what she asked.

*****

After having driven around a couple of blocks, his searching gaze sweeping yards and rooftops and shrubbery, Adam finally pulled into Naomi's driveway. It had only taken three days of having an around-the-clock bodyguard for the routine to become familiar. She knew better than to leap out before he came around to protect her with his body for the short distance into the house.

As he reached for his door handle, Naomi burst out, "Why hasn't anything *happened*?" She sounded like a fretful child and didn't care.

Two more days had come and gone since she agreed not to run. Two more evenings spent shut in the small cottage with *him*. Now she was facing a third, and she didn't know if she could stand it.

Adam's swift look was inscrutable. "He'll make a mistake."

She nodded, because that's what he wanted. All she could think was, *Mistake*? Which *he* will make one? And what kind of mistake?

Gee, what if *Adam* was the one to make the mistake?

What if he made that mistake, and he was killed because of her? How would she live with that?

Apparently satisfied he'd settled her and obviously unaware of the path her too vivid imagination had taken, he got out and walked around the back of the Tahoe. Once she slid to the ground, he slammed the door, wrapped an arm securely around her and hustled her the fifteen feet to the house, his free hand on the butt of his gun. He let her unlock and open the door while he stood behind her, head turning unceasingly.

She knew the routine inside, too. They stepped in together, after which he pushed her gently to one side by the washer and dryer, locked the door behind them and then walked through the house. She waited frozen in place, irrationally infuriated when he returned smiling. "All clear."

Only then did he let her go to her bedroom to remove the Kevlar vest, which was miserable to wear. She was afraid it was going to stink when she returned it to the sheriff's department negotiator, Rebecca Walker. Adam didn't want her taking it off even when she was back in the kitchen at the café.

"Someone could trick you into opening the back door, or rush the front. The vest could save you."

Fine, but she sweated like a pig in it, and it was heavy, and…she was being petulant. She knew that, but she had now spent forty-eight plus hours wanting to scream, and only half the reason was the bone deep terror because somebody wanted to kill her.

The other half was Adam Rostov.

The night she saw him walk through her kitchen wearing nothing but a towel slung around his waist, his dark hair standing on end after being roughly dried, water still beaded on his shoulders and back and tanned, muscular calves, she had waited only until he was in the shower to race for her bedroom and shut herself in. And stay there.

But she couldn't huddle behind a closed door every day for hours on end. So the next day she'd resolved to play it casually, as if they were friendly acquaintances who happened to be stuck with each other for a while.

It was good that he cooperated, of course, but the result was that they hung out talking, her actually forgetting for long stretches why he was really here and believing he was just a guy on vacation who liked her. She wanted to know him, and there was at least the illusion that he felt that same hunger.

Ditto night two, during which topics inevitably became more personal. Instead of favorite bands, they got around to talking about why they felt strongly about some issues. Adam dwelled on the battered women and rape victims he saw, and the ways the process increased their trauma, but also his frustration with women who balked at testifying and then went back for more. Naomi told him about her own fundraising focus on an L.A. battered women's shelter and also the fight against breast cancer. A close friend of hers had died of breast cancer when she was only thirty-one.

The worst part was the heat she saw in his eyes, reminding her of the desire she did believe he felt. In the two evenings, he hadn't made a move, respecting her expressed wishes, but he definitely looked. Unfortunately, she looked, too, when she thought he wouldn't notice, and, damn it, she was in a seemingly permanent state of frustrated arousal that she could never satisfy.

Yesterday evening, she'd worked out a new recipe while he alternated sitting at her table, pacing through the house and an occasional check of the 'perimeter'. Naomi hated it every time he went outside. That's when she thought about the vest beneath his denim shirt and why he wore it. Unlike her, he didn't take his off when they got home. He might have thought she hadn't noticed the big black handgun he carried all the time, but she had. Every single time he went outside, she'd stand very still and wait for the sound of a gunshot. She'd have to look away when he came in so he didn't see her bottomless relief. Having him go out to hunt for a killer…that didn't become routine.

And then there was her confusion. He wasn't the enemy, she did believe that, but he was still a threat to her. More of a threat than ever, as her feelings for him weakened her.

She kept wondering why he hadn't asked more about his partner's death or what investigators told her or even what she suspected. Instead, he talked about everything *but*. Each time she let herself believe, even for a minute, that one topic was flowing naturally into another, she'd realizing that even when he smiled, he was also watching her. Waiting.

Her own tension cranked up until she didn't know if she could stand it.

This afternoon, when she came back to the kitchen after stripping off the wretched vest, he offered to make dinner.

"You've been cooking all day."

"I told you I made a bunch of stuff when I was stressed. I experimented with different cheeses on a vegetarian lasagna. I can defrost it in the microwave."

"Lasagna?" He sounded so hopeful she laughed and got it out of the freezer.

She'd almost have rather cooked from scratch – God knows she could use some comfort cooking – but she was tired, too. Between listening for every sound in the night and thinking about the man on the couch in her living room, she'd been doing a lot more tossing and turning than sleeping.

A glance at the clock told her it was only four-thirty, technically too early for dinner, but she'd barely had a bite since leaving the house this morning, and she'd discovered that Adam was always hungry. As lean as he stayed, he must burn calories at a phenomenal pace. That probably had to do with the fact that he didn't stay still long, and didn't sleep much. If she got up to use the bathroom during the night, the lamp was almost always on in the living room and he'd look up from a book or his laptop and quietly ask if she was all right.

Maybe this wasn't normal for him. She knew he was on edge because of the threat to her, but he had to relax sometimes, didn't he? She tried to picture him sprawled in bed, sound asleep. Or satiated after amazing sex.

She almost moaned, imagining it, and had to sternly remind herself why making love with him was a really terrible idea. If nothing else, he'd soon be gone from her life. Best possibility, they'd triumph, and he'd go away. Or this would drag on until even he admitted that her disappearing was the best plan.

He'd find out she'd killed his partner and arrest her.

Or, her personal favorite, she'd be dead. That was a possibility, too. One she absolutely refused to dwell on, even though, come to think of it, she wasn't sure she wouldn't rather die than go on trial for murder.

Most of the time, he was so damn confident, she almost believed she'd somehow survive. And then she'd remember her real role here and know better.

Ba-aa.

She was ripping lettuce for a salad when he asked, "Was your mother a cook, too?"

Of course he'd guess that much. Her hands barely faltered. "Yes. A really good one. When I remember her, we're always in the kitchen." It had to be the stress that caused her eyes to sting. "She liked to eat a whole lot more than I do, though. Mom was short but plump."

He came to lean against the counter only a few feet away. Too close. "Mine is, too. Now." He frowned. "Those years before Dad died, she got skinnier and skinnier."

"Unhappy."

"I always thought she was trying to disappear," he said slowly. "It scared me." His gaze traveled over her body. "Did you used to eat better than you do now?"

Had she? "I was always little and scrawny for my age. Everyone worried I didn't eat enough, but I've just never been interested."

"And yet you cook extraordinary food for everyone else."

She peeled cucumber. "Feeding people is satisfying."

"Did your stepfather like your mom's cooking?"

Damn him. "Yes."

He didn't say anything else, although he kept watching her. And she thought, *Yes. Yes, Mom cooked to divert him, please him, protect herself and me.*

Even then, she'd known that.

So why do I cook? Because I learned it as a coping mechanism?

I don't know.

"Your family," she heard herself say. "Before your dad was fired. Were you happy?"

"Yeah." His voice became even huskier than usual. "Mom smiled all the time. Dad seemed larger than life to me. Soccer came later for me. Back then, I played baseball, because that's what he'd played. He was always willing to pitch, or catch so I could practice my pitching. He'd take Mom out dancing, or just put on a record and they'd slow dance in the living room. He liked to make us happy. He was always bringing presents home to Mom, or he'd come in the door and say, 'I've got tickets to tomorrow's Dodgers game. Who wants to go?' He could produce tickets to anything. Man, my sister wanted to see Duran Duran, and somehow Dad scored her a pair of tickets. I could never figure out how—"

If she hadn't been looking, she wouldn't have seen the stunned expression on his face as he broke off mid-sentence. He was good at covering what he didn't want her to see. This time, it was too late.

Heart pounding, she whispered, "Adam?"

He pushed away from the cabinet. "I'm going to take a look outside," he said, sounding angry.

She'd have reminded him he had come in only a few minutes ago, but he was already gone. Getting away from her.

The microwave beeped and she went mechanically on with the meal preparations, wondering if there was any chance at all he could let himself accept the dark knowledge that had been inside him all along, or if, while he circled her house, he would succeed in burying it deep again. Leaving him able to believe his father had been both innocent and wronged.

Like Frank Donahue, she thought bleakly, and was afraid she knew the answer.

CHAPTER TEN

Son of a bitch. Had he actually let himself entertain, even for an instant, the possibility that his father *had* been on the take?

Yes.

Shaken to his core, Adam took a quick look around, then folded to sit on the single step leading up to the side door into Naomi's cottage. He couldn't focus well enough to patrol. Here, he knew she was only a few feet away and safe for the moment.

Why now? he asked himself, half in anguish, half in genuine puzzlement. It wasn't as if he'd forgotten that his father had liked to do things for his family, had had a gift for coming up with those ultra-desirable tickets that made Adam's friends green with envy. He'd partly remembered the flowers and pieces of jewelry Dad brought home for Mom because he quit bringing them after he lost his job. Adam had believed his father was so consumed by his own bitterness, he hadn't thought of doing things like that anymore. And yeah, of course money must have been tight. He'd probably lost his pension, too. But he had found a job only a couple of months later, and it wasn't the value of the things he brought home to Mom that mattered, it was the thought.

He remembered the worry and tension that filled the house in those years, Mom shushing Adam and Ellen where once both his parents had encouraged exuberance. Her glow had taken time to fade. She'd believed in her husband, Adam thought. Had complete faith. It was his anger that had done so much damage to all of them, not the accusations.

Hadn't Mom ever wondered how he afforded all those little extras? Adam had to ask himself now. She'd never worked, and cops' salaries were notoriously stingy. Then, Adam hadn't really known how steep the price of concert tickets was. Sure, they were cheaper then – but salaries were lower, too. A lot lower. And the pretty pieces of jewelry had later been sold, because some of them had had diamonds set in gold. Dad shouldn't have been able to afford the frequent dinners out, either. The pickup truck his friends envied, which he'd supposedly gotten for a song because he knew how to play hardball.

"They knew I meant it when I started to walk out," he'd bragged.

Oh, yeah, Adam thought now, he played hardball all right.

My father was on the take. Guilty as sin.

After he got fired, was he genuinely bitter because his buddies all did it, too, and he felt unjustly singled out? Or were the angry protestations of innocence cover for the humiliation that had destroyed the father Adam remembered, like termites hidden within the walls that turned a solid wood structure to sawdust?

My father, the crook.

He heard himself give an incredulous laugh. Man, did he know how to bury his head in the sand or what?

And he knew why the light bulb had flashed on now: because he'd let himself talk to Naomi as he hadn't to anyone else, ever. The only friend of his who knew about his father's history was Juan Ramirez, and him only the bare bones. Adam had told the story created by Dad to protect himself, and perpetuated by his family who hadn't wanted to admit the possibility that he'd taken bribes.

Naomi was sharp enough to have understood what he was really saying before he did. He didn't know how he felt about the swift compassion on her face or the soft way she said his name. He could trust her to keep what she knew to herself, but he had to wonder if the new knowledge would change how she saw him. Maybe that compassion was really pity, because she guessed how willfully he'd blinded himself.

He bent forward and drove his fingers into his hair, yanking hard. Could she be in there right now thinking he'd known all along and lied to her? What if it crossed her mind that, if his father had been a dirty cop, he might be, too?

God knows, she'd been suspicious all along. And how could he blame her, given her experience with Cobb's staff of part-time, off-duty cops?

Was Dad's worst sin taking handouts to turn an occasional blind eye? Or did he do more?

Adam searched his memory. Dad had done outside gigs, he remembered that much. Directed traffic after big games, things like that, or so Adam had believed. Mom, too, he thought; she'd always been pleased, because it meant extra money. Keeping two kids in decent clothes and sports equipment cost. She had talked hopefully about starting college funds for Adam and Ellen.

Maybe some of those gigs hadn't been so innocent.

Another memory slid into his mind: Frank bitching about what it was going to cost to put his kids through college. Enraged at what he was presumed to be able to come up with. His face had turned purple. "Who the fuck are they kidding? On what I take home?"

But Adam slammed that door shut. No. Just…no.

Frank talked about taking some of those off-duty jobs, but had been pissed because of the long hours the two of them already worked. It wasn't as if they were eight to five.

Adam clenched his teeth. He wasn't going there. His father might not have been the man Adam had believed him to be, but there was no reason to let that new and painful knowledge cast a shadow on Frank. Damn it, they'd worked closely together! Adam hadn't been a kid anymore, one who'd desperately wanted to believe in his daddy.

Did his mother know?

Will I ever say anything to her?

Hell, no. He might talk to Ellen about it one of these days, though. She was a couple years older than him. She might have seen more than he did, might even have been keeping her mouth shut to protect his memories of their father.

Yeah, I'll do that, he thought, relieved at the reminder he had someone he could really talk to. Opening up too much with Naomi was…high risk. Best to drop the subject.

Hard, when what he wanted to do was go right back in there and rip himself open for her benefit – after telling her that, whatever she feared, she could trust him.

Whether he could trust her, though, that was another story. She swore this time she wouldn't run…but she'd promised before, too. And no, that wasn't a personal betrayal – she was scared, and for good reason – but it *felt* personal, damn it.

Disconcerted by how much he did want her to trust him, to believe he'd never let her down, he finally groaned and got to his feet. The sky had darkened appreciably just while he sat here. In fall and winter, night came way earlier this far north than in southern California. When the sky was overcast like today, though, the change was subtle. No spectacular sunset over the ocean gave warning of nightfall.

He moved quietly between houses, checking out the black silhouettes of rooftops. Naomi's house was mid-neighborhood, too far from the higher ground of the promontories encircling Jasper Beach to allow for a sniper to set up with that advantage, thank God.

He could see in windows at neighbors puttering in their kitchens or chatting on phones, completely unaware of him slipping through their yards. The beanpole tall, painfully skinny guy next door – Arthur – was already at his table eating a microwave dinner right out of the container. At least he had a real dessert to look forward to; yesterday Naomi had sent Adam over to deliver a plateful of cookies to the old guy.

Calmer when he let himself back into the house, he found her setting the lasagna on a hot pad on the table. He inhaled, and his mouth started to water.

"Dinner's ready," she said brightly and unnecessarily.

Adam shook droplets of drizzle from his hair. "Does it ever snow around here, or does it do nothing but rain all winter long?"

"It mostly rains." She added a salad and then couple of different dressings. And – damn – garlic bread, too. Adam had never eaten so well.

He just wished Naomi would eat a little more. She might claim she never did much but nibble, but he'd swear she was losing weight in the short time since he'd first set eyes on her. Then he'd thought *pixie*; right now, he was thinking more *waif.*

He hoped like hell it wasn't a conscious decision, a way of saying, *If you won't let me disappear the way I want, I'll do it the only way left to me.*

As dark as his mood was, it improved as he ate. He couldn't have had a better meal in the finest Italian restaurant in L.A.

"Your talents are wasted in this burg," he finally said, wiping his mouth and trying to decide if he could possibly stuff in a third helping.

"I'm happy here." A tiny crinkle between her eyebrows suggested some inner perturbation.

'Happy' wasn't a word he mostly associated with her. More often than he liked, Adam found himself remembering their one dinner date and the way her face had lit with smiles he hadn't seen since.

"There are some good people here," he conceded. He had been unexpectedly impressed with both Daniel Colburn and Alex Mackay, men he thought he could call friends if he were to stick around long enough.

As if she'd read his mind, Naomi asked, "You haven't said when you're expected back to work."

Yeah, that was a problem, one he'd been blocking out. He had something like six weeks of vacation unused, but he'd only asked for two, expecting it to be enough to find out what the chef really knew. Unfortunately, his absence left the detective squad short-handed. The lieutenant would not be thrilled if he were to call and say, "I'm having such a good time, I think I'll stay another few weeks." No, he'd be ordered to get his ass back to work.

"I won't abandon you," he said, disturbed by what he was really saying. If he had to quit his job, that's what he'd do. For a woman he hadn't met ten days ago.

For a moment, she looked deep, something he didn't understand on her face. Hope? Or was it despair?

But all she did then was nod and go back to pushing food around on her plate.

"You're scaring me," he said gruffly.

Her head came back up, her eyes startled. "What?"

"Please eat."

"Oh," she said after a moment, very softly. "You're thinking about your mother."

His mother? Then he remembered what he'd said, about thinking Mom had been trying to disappear.

"No." He frowned at her. "It's you I'm thinking about."

"Oh," she repeated, even more quietly, before taking a bite. Under his gaze, she made some inroads on the small servings she'd given herself. Then she looked up with a tiny flicker of a smile. "Are you satisfied?"

God, no, was all he could think, trying not to let his gaze drop from her face to that delicate, utterly feminine body he craved. Apparently he didn't hide his powerful response well enough, though, because he saw first shock on her face, then the same helpless desire he felt before she looked away.

"We still have cookies," she offered, in a small, husky voice.

"Thank you," he managed, hearing the roughness in his voice. He'd have stood to fetch the damn cookies instead of acting as if he expected to be waited on, except then he wouldn't have been able to hide how hard he'd gotten with so little excuse.

Crap, he thought. How much longer could they go on like this? He didn't recall ever *hoping* someone would shoot at him before, but there was a first time for everything.

Surreptitiously, he rapped his knuckles against the table edge. If shots were fired, he wouldn't be the target; Naomi would. He couldn't wish for that.

After dinner he talked to Sam, who called once he got home from work, and then Daniel, who did the same. Daniel and the detective Adam hadn't met, Sean Holbeck, had come up with a fairly lengthy list of apparently single men staying at lodging in the area or registered at a campground. By running names, they'd eliminated some as unlikely, but were left with too many.

"Do you know how many men have brown hair?" Daniel grumbled.

What could Adam say? He and Daniel both could be said to meet Naomi's vague description, although Adam's hair was dark enough to be almost black. Trouble was, they couldn't rule out the possibility that the guy had changed his appearance.

Sam said something similar, and reported on how goddamn difficult it was to nail down the whereabouts of anyone without giving away why he was looking and what he suspected. Upside, so far nobody appeared to have noticed his peculiar interest. When pressed, he admitted he'd come up with a handful of names of agents who seemed most likely.

"She sure she didn't hear the name?" he asked.

"I'll grill her some more," Adam said, and looked up to see Naomi hovering in the living room doorway. She'd gone to take her shower, and he hadn't heard her come out. "I'll check in tomorrow," he said, and ended the call.

"Grill me?"

He grimaced. "Sam's frustrated you can't give him a name."

"I think Greg did say it," she said slowly. "But I really didn't care who else was there, because I'd just recognized Dominic Greer from an article in the paper the day before, and I was thinking, hey, cool. And then I heard FBI."

"Followed by something about a hit."

She nodded.

"Would you be able to pick out the name from a list?"

"I really don't think so," she said apologetically. "I truly wasn't paying any attention, and I didn't hear it clearly."

He grunted.

"I'm sorry."

"No, don't be."

"Any word on the video?"

"Mackay called the guy and he said he'd try to get to it tomorrow."

Naomi nodded again, still hovering. "I think if it's okay, I'm going to do some cooking."

"We just ate."

"Maybe some desserts I can serve at lunch tomorrow."

"Okay." He sounded as gentle as he could with his sandpaper voice. She appeared grateful for his understanding, which filled him with a complicated stew of emotions. Chronic state, he thought. He even summoned a hopeful smile. "You need a taste tester, I'm available."

He won an answering smile that fell short of merry, but tried. "I'll keep that in mind," she said.

He stayed where he was for a few minutes, listening to the sounds coming from the kitchen: cupboard doors and drawers opening and closing, refrigerator door, soft bumps and bangs, a crunching sound he thought was eggs being cracked into a bowl.

Comfort cooking. Had anyone ever offered her a different brand of comfort? Say, held her while she talked out her troubles or even cried? Kissed her until she forgot her troubles? Rocked her to sleep in the most elemental way possible?

It was awhile before he was sure enough of his self-control to follow her to the kitchen, where he had no doubt seemingly idle conversation would end up with him rolling over and baring some other vulnerability to her.

*****

Come morning, Naomi was grumpy and exhausted, and Adam didn't look as if he felt any better. His light had been out when she got up to go to the bathroom at two a.m., but his voice had immediately come from the darkness asking if she was okay.

It annoyed her unreasonably that she had to pee during the night and he never seemed to. He ate and drank way more than she did! Where was the justice?

She winced at the sight of herself in the mirror. If she'd been going anywhere people would see her, she'd have had to trowel on the makeup. As it was, Anita must be getting used to her looking like hell, and Adam—

It didn't matter what he thought.

Nice try.

He looked terrible, too, though, his eyes sunken and the lines in his face deeper than usual. He had a crease down one cheek, which suggested he *had* slept some. Oh, God, she thought guiltily; the sofa, bought at a garage sale, had to be hideously uncomfortable even aside from not being long enough for someone a whole lot taller than her. Would he take her up on it if she offered to switch?

No.

"I'm sorry," she mumbled as they prepared to leave.

He gave her an irritable look. "For what?"

She opened her mouth then closed it. "For everything" was what she'd have said, but really he was the one making her hang around with a target painted on her back, so why should she apologize?

He switched off the kitchen light and then the porch light, too, before stepping outside first. "Damn, it's dark," he growled. "You have your vest on?"

"Yes. I'm not an idiot."

Grunt.

Naomi wished she wasn't able to interpret his nonverbal sounds so accurately.

"Watch your step."

He said that every morning as she squeezed by him, presumably under the belief that if he didn't, she'd surely trip and fall flat on her face. She knew he wasn't very happy about the fact that they had to leave for work when it was still pitch dark. The roads between here and the café were always deserted this early. Probably the only people in town awake at this hour were cooks at various restaurants that served breakfast, some hospital employees and a few patrol officers.

"*Wait*," he said with sudden urgency, and Naomi realized she'd been tired enough to disregard their now-standard procedure. She was already plodding toward his Tahoe, her hand out to feel her way past her own car, while Adam was still locking the back door.

Alarm zinged through her and she came abruptly awake. Even as dark as it was, she felt horribly exposed and swung around to rush back to him.

She was still using touch to guide her, but suddenly the car window beneath her fingertips just…crumbled. In her bewilderment, Naomi almost turned around again, but Adam came flying at her, his big body surrounding her and crushing her against the side of the car.

He jerked, hard, and then bore her to the concrete slab of her carport.

One more sharp, pinging sound, metal on metal, and Adam, snarling under his breath, shoved her forward, crawling on top of her, until they inched around in front of her car. Grit scraped her hands and her knees hurt and she didn't understand what was happening.

But then he had his phone out and talked in a low, tense voice, "Shots are being fired, 322 Madrona Street."

Shots? But…why hadn't she heard them?

Oh my God. He – whichever he – had used a silencer. Death could come like that, in a near-complete absence of sound.

And, in shock, she realized something else – one of those shots had hit Adam. She'd felt the impact just before they went down.

"Don't move," he growled, when she started to lift herself, desperate to see that he was all right. He put pressure on her head, so that her cheek pressed the rough surface. Now that her eyes had begun adjusting to the dark, she saw the big gun in his hand. He had her completely covered, so if another shot connected it would hit him and not her.

She cried out in involuntary protest.

"Hush," he murmured into her ear.

The sound of a siren came, far off, as lonely as a train whistle in the night. But as they waited, his body hard and tense above her, the siren grew louder, and she knew when the squad car turned into Jasper Beach.

Not a minute later, it came flying into her driveway. Another siren sounded, too, somewhere out on the highway.

"We're behind the small car," Adam called. "I'm putting my weapon down."

"You the caller?" The voice was a man's, but it sounded a little high, as if he was scared.

"Yes. I'm Detective Rostov," Adam said calmly. "Sheriff Mackay and Chief Colburn both know who I am."

"Ms. Kendrick with you?"

"Yes."

"Are either of you injured?"

He raised a little higher off her. "Naomi?"

"I'm okay."

After a pause, Adam cleared his throat. "I don't think so. Can we get up? I'd like to get her safely in the house and then look for the piece of shit who just tried to kill us."

The other siren came screaming down their street.

"He'll be long gone," Adam said for her ears only, as he pushed himself up to a kneeling position. "But stay close anyway."

Naomi nodded shakily, although in the dark he probably couldn't see her anyway.

She hadn't been entirely honest. Getting slammed to the concrete by someone who outweighed her by eighty pounds or so hadn't felt good. She stifled a moan as she picked herself up.

"You were shot," she said.

"Yeah. And, goddamnit, it hurts." His tone was more grumpy than anything. "Here." Rising to his feet, he hoisted her to hers and gently pushed her toward the steps to her side door. He swore a couple times, something about having dropped the keys, then evidently discovered he'd left the house key inserted in the lock.

Naomi let him boost her up the steps and inside, where he flipped on the porch and inside lights. She blinked at what felt like starbursts in front of her eyes and tried to figure out why she felt so dazed.

She should be getting used to being assaulted and shot at, shouldn't she?

A second voice in the driveway she recognized as Daniel's. How had he gotten here so fast? She heard him giving orders and realized a couple more vehicles had pulled up.

As if none of that was happening, Adam said, "Sit," and she obeyed, her knees happy to give out and drop her onto one of the kitchen chairs.

A man filled the doorway. Daniel, apparently satisfied that his orders were being carried out. "You two okay?"

"I'm trying to find out." Adam crouched in front of her, his face creased with worry. "Talk to me, Naomi."

"You're the one who was hurt." She gripped his T-shirt and tried to pull it up. "Are you bleeding?" Tears that hadn't fallen somehow clogged her voice. "You took a bullet that was aimed at me."

"That's what the vests are for, Naomi. I'll have a bruise. That's all."

She sat there shaking, the fabric of his T-shirt wadded in two fists, the hard muscles of his belly beneath her knuckles. She knew on one level that they had an audience, but all she really saw was Adam, the sharp lines of his cheekbones never more evident. As if they were alone in a bubble, he never looked away from her.

"I don't want to do this anymore," she whimpered. "I don't want you to die for me. You shouldn't do that. Throw yourself in front of me."

"It's all right, sweetheart." His voice was impossibly tender. "I know what I'm doing."

"If the bullet had gone higher or lower—" She couldn't finish.

"Most shooters aim for the torso."

Her teeth chattered. Ashamed of herself, she tried to turn her face away. Adam caught her chin so she couldn't hide from him.

"You're in shock. And I did hurt you. Your cheek and hands are both scraped, if nothing else. We can go by the E.R…"

Try for some dignity, she told herself, took a deep breath and said, "Don't be ridiculous. Go do whatever you have to do."

He frowned at her.

She caught sight of the clock behind him and gasped. "Oh, no! The café! I need to get there."

Adam said something obscene about the café.

"No, I'm okay. I can work," she insisted, wishing her voice sounded sturdier, hoping she'd actually be able to stand up if he gave her permission.

"Now you're being ridiculous." He rose to his feet and scowled down at her. "Why don't you go take a hot shower? Then we can put ointment on anyplace that's raw, ice on any significant bruising."

She bit her lip, remembering him sitting in this very chair as she cleaned his scrapes up and dabbed on ointment.

"Where was he?" she asked in a small voice.

"Close." His jaw muscles spasmed. "Between your cottage and Arthur's. Those shots were fired by a handgun with a suppressor." He glanced toward Daniel when he said that. "We know he has sniper training. I expected him to keep his distance."

Gripping the doorframe, Daniel leaned back to talk to someone outside. After a moment he straightened, shook his head and looked back at Adam and Naomi.

"No surprise, we're not finding hide nor hair of him. You didn't hear a vehicle?"

Naomi shook her head, but she'd been so stunned by then she wasn't sure she would have.

"No," Adam said. "He'd planned where to go. Are there any empty houses? Or, damn, he could have been parked out on the highway a little to the north. It's so goddamn dark out there, it wouldn't have been hard for him to slip away." He made a rough sound in his throat. "Naomi is right. Unless we can think of a way to set up a foolproof trap, we need to get her safely away from here."

Wonderful moment to discover how very much she didn't want to have to start all over again, create a new life alone. How much she didn't want to leave Adam. There was probably some kind of biological imperative, she thought; what woman wouldn't want to keep a man who'd taken a bullet for her?

Of course, she had no idea if he'd been operating on instinct because he was a police officer and that's what he did…or whether, maybe, he felt something for her.

Think about this. Don't be stupid.

"I'm going to take a shower," she announced, and managed to get to her feet without having to clutch him for support. Both men looked surprised as she walked away.

*****

Adam could not believe he'd been so careless, let her get what could have been a fatal few steps ahead of him.

"You got here fast," he said, turning back to Colburn, who was watching him with a shrewd gaze Adam feared saw more than he had meant to expose.

"I asked dispatch to let me know immediately about any calls to this address or from you or Naomi. I threw on some clothes and ran." One corner of his mouth turned up. "Think I'll go home and put on underwear and socks before I start the rest of my day."

Adam cracked a smile despite his generally grim mood. "Cup of coffee?"

"I won't say no, but let me talk to the officers first."

"You also told dispatch to send Cape Trouble officers, didn't you?"

"Yeah, but the second responder is a sheriff's deputy. We got lucky and he wasn't far away."

"I think the fact that real live shots had been fired scared the shit out of the first guy."

Daniel grunted a laugh. "Most of my officers are kids. I have only one guy with any experience."

"The kid didn't do anything wrong. I could tell, that's all."

Daniel left for a few minutes. Adam stared at the coffeemaker, willing it to drip faster, and listened to the sound of the shower.

If I'd been a step slower, she'd be dead.

Not necessarily. She was wearing a vest, too, he reminded himself.

Yeah, but the shot had hit him high. The punch had been over his shoulder blade, which hurt like a son of a bitch now that he thought about it. Naomi was easily six inches shorter than he was. Which meant she'd have been struck in the neck or even head, depending on her stance.

Adam closed his eyes. Somehow the shooter had known, or at least guessed, that she was wearing a vest.

Or he'd felt rushed when the first shot missed. The one taking out the side window of her little car had been aimed at her torso.

Why it made him feel better to think the guy hadn't specifically been trying to blow her head off, Adam didn't know.

If she hadn't turned back when she did, if he'd been a step slower…

A raw sound escaped him. *I was so sure I could keep her safe.*

He willed his body to absorb the adrenaline. As it was, he desperately needed action, and there wasn't a goddamn useful thing he could do.

The shower had gone silent. Listening for her, he poured two cups of coffee. He hadn't taken more than a couple sips when he heard Naomi's soft footsteps.

"I've been thinking," she said.

He turned slowly. The strain showed on her face, and he hated seeing the raw scrape he'd put there, but otherwise what he mostly saw was a steely resolve that made him understand how she'd survived this past two years.

"Thinking what?" he asked.

"That I should call Greg."

CHAPTER ELEVEN

Naomi sat stiffly in the front seat of Adam's Tahoe, staring at the number she had just typed into her phone, but hesitating before she made the final commitment.

She didn't have to do this.

Yes, I do.

Although she didn't look at him, she was very aware of the man waiting patiently beside her. In the driver's seat, of course, even though they weren't going anywhere.

His initial reaction to her suggestion hadn't been positive. Even after thinking through the ramifications, he remained unhappy. Allowing her to confront a professional killer, albeit long distance, apparently violated his most primitive sense of what was right. What she couldn't quite tell was whether that was because she was a woman, or only because she was a civilian.

Or...because it was her, Naomi. Because she wasn't just someone he could use anymore.

Did his reasons matter?

What would he say if she chickened out? Nothing, she guessed. His feelings were too mixed about what she was doing. *As if any of my options are good*, she thought miserably.

She bit her lip hard enough to sting, slid her thumb across the screen and pushed 'send'.

They were out here in his SUV because they'd agreed to wait until she took a break between breakfast and lunch to make the call. Adam had finally, reluctantly, delivered her to the café, late enough the breakfast menu had of necessity been somewhat abbreviated. It didn't turn out to be one of their busier mornings, fortunately, and Anita reported that diners seemed understanding of the limited choices.

Adam had refused to leave her alone even for a minute. If there'd been more prep areas, Naomi would have put him to work, but as it was, what she'd done was introduce a brooding, somehow dangerous presence into her kitchen. He remained unmoving except for that restless gaze. Impossible to ignore however hard she tried.

She was still annoyed because he had also refused to take off his vest to allow either her or Daniel look at his back. "If I had a broken bone, I'd know it," he said stubbornly.

So not only had he been there, hovering in her kitchen, he probably hurt like hell the whole time. But, of course, he was too tough a guy to be anything but completely stoic.

Ring.

She'd have stiffened if she hadn't already been rigid. Maybe Greg wouldn't answer.

Ring.

Naomi gripped the phone tight, mentally rehearsing what she'd say if she had to leave a message.

Halfway through the third ring, he answered brusquely. "Cobb."

She wouldn't have sworn she'd know his voice, but she did, so well that she shuddered. She looked wildly at Adam and was steadied by his intense gray eyes.

"Hello, Greg," she said, going for cool and not sure she was achieving it. "This is Naomi."

Adam nodded as if to say, *You're doing fine.*

"Naomi," Greg repeated, sounding…she couldn't decide. Wary?

"Varner. Remember me? Videographer?"

"How did you get this number?" Greg asked sharply.

"Oh, I have connections." She paused to let him think about that, then hardened her voice. "You've violated our agreement, Greg."

"What are you talking about?"

"Give me a break." *She* sounded sharp this time. Even disgusted. "I'm not stupid. But just in case you're not the one trying to kill me, you might want to know that someone else is. Who else is aware I was listening that night?"

"Nobody."

"Uh huh. See, here's the problem. If I die, my little video will be seen 'round the world, starting with several law enforcement agencies. You do remember that I made provisions."

"I remember," he said tersely.

"Somebody shot me a few days ago. Local police say he must have trained as a sniper, because he'd set up almost two hundred yards out. Fortunately I was only hit in the arm, and I wasn't alone. This morning, somebody tried again and came really, really close. I can't help thinking I know a guy who *specializes* in this kind of thing. And you're telling me you know nothing about it."

"I have nothing to do with it, Naomi."

"But, see, I've been living such a peaceful life since the last time I saw you. So I have to believe there are only three people who want me dead enough to send someone to kill me. That would be you, a client of yours who shall remain nameless, and the third party at that meeting."

She gave him a minute to think both about what she'd said, and about the wiretap that he must fear was in place and allowing others to listen in. Unlike him, she was in a position to know that the FBI had only learned in the past twenty-four hours about this particular number and wasn't yet listening. According to Adam, Sam had almost balked about supplying the number. He could be in deep shit over this. For all her inner terror, Naomi loved knowing how frantic Greg must be, trying to figure out how she'd acquired the number.

Time to finish this. "I'm guessing you can figure out who's causing my problem," she said. "Let me repeat: if I'm killed, *you* have a problem. A really visual one."

She closed the connection before he could say another word.

"Perfect," Adam said, his voice warm. And then, "Damn, Naomi," and his strong arms came around her. That was when she realized she had begun to shake, as if she'd had another near-death experience.

*****

Her breakdown was brief. So brief, Adam was awed. Damn it, watching her threaten Greg Cobb, cool as could be no matter how scared she really was, had shaken *him.*

Now all Naomi did was lean against him and quake for maybe a minute, her face pressed against his neck. No tears, and she didn't say a word. Then came a few shuddering breaths, and finally she straightened.

"I need to get started on lunch."

Reluctantly, he let her go. He understood how much she needed to focus on the routine of her everyday life, believe that upholding the reputation of The Sea Watch Café mattered. "You're okay?" he asked, doubting she'd be honest if she wasn't.

"Yes." She'd composed herself, but the turmoil in her eyes gave her away. Looking into them was enough to make him feel as if that damn bullet had hit his chest instead of his back. "Do you think this did any good?" she asked after a moment, very softly.

"I think you scared him," he said honestly. "We know from the way he discards cell phones that he's aware he's been listened to, or at least that he's paranoid about that possibility. He's going to make the same leap we did. An FBI agent could have found you through him. Greer, though, is another story."

"But…what will he do about it?"

Adam only shook his head. He knew she hoped Gregory Cobb would go turncoat to save his own ass. Sell out the former ally/employee, even though if word got out he had, it would damage his reputation. Who'd sign on with him if he couldn't be trusted?

Adam didn't want to say what he really thought would happen: the hunter would shortly find himself hunted, and no one would ever know for sure who was responsible.

And Adam felt no pity at all.

"It'll be interesting to find out," he said, voice neutral. "Whatever he does, I hope it's quick."

After checking out the alley, he rushed her back into the restaurant and locked the door behind them, then took up his station as she went straight to the sink to wash her hands. He admired her ability to compartmentalize; she was already thinking about food, at least on one level.

Him, he settled into plotting how he could get her away from Cape Trouble unseen. There'd been two attempts on her life. Three struck him as an unlucky number in this context. Maybe she did need to go on the run again.

Her own attempt last week to take off had been doomed even if he hadn't stopped her. He wasn't the only watcher waiting for her to do something like slip out the back door and run for it. The strange vehicle had been a good thought, but wouldn't have saved her.

If a policewoman could be substituted for Naomi, though, so Adam could be seen hustling her out of the restaurant and taking her home like he did every day, while really she'd left earlier out the front door, disguised…

His main objection to that plan was that he'd be trusting someone else with her safety.

Yeah, and chances are you'll never see her again. That's what you like least of all.

Wrong, he thought grimly. What he'd like least of all was to see her go down. If she was killed on his watch, he'd never get over it.

Spoon in hand, she turned to look at him, making him wonder what sound he'd made. He shook his head slightly, Naomi searched his face and finally went back to work.

Anita kept hanging new orders on the carousel, keeping Naomi busy. That was good for her. The stress was less evident on her face now.

Adam's back hurt enough he finally consented to half-sit on a tall stool.

Anita had just called, "We're closed," when Adam's phone rang. Daniel's number.

"Mackay's guy came through," he said. "Naomi's video is damn near Oscar quality. Slam dunk for a jury."

"I want to see it."

"You heading back to the house? I can bring it."

Adam covered his phone to ask Naomi how close she was to being ready to go, then said, "Half an hour."

"Good, I'll be right behind you."

Adam stowed his phone. "Colburn says the video cleaned up nicely." He heard how coldly satisfied his voice was. "He's bringing it over for us to see."

Shock and something else slid across her face, a shadow that left him wondering.

All she said was "Oh" before she turned away quickly, plunging her hands back into soapy water. He watched her, but didn't ask questions. He would, but later.

Anita, as cheerful as ever despite her curiosity about his presence, departed out the front. He left Naomi long enough to prowl the alley, checking behind dumpsters and parked vehicles, then moved his rental SUV close to the back door. Even then, he did his best to shield her as she locked and hopped in. He wished again for bullet-resistant glass.

He drove straight to her cottage, a little surprised to see two marked police cars in front, one Cape Trouble and one county. Both Daniel and Alex Mackay walked around the corner of the carport as Adam pulled in.

After greeting the sheriff, Naomi joked that only the best was good enough for her. Adam appreciated her attempt at humor, able to see how hard she was working to hide how she really felt.

Mackay went straight in with them while Daniel retrieved his laptop from his car. Naomi's gaze flicked to it, then rose to his face, her eyes desperate. "You can really see the men? And…and hear what they were saying?"

"Yes." He sounded gentle. "It's a shocker. Everything you hoped for."

She swung away and pressed her hand to her mouth, but not in time to entirely silence the sob that tore through her.

"Naomi." Adam moved between her and the other men, his hands resting on her shoulders..

"No. I won't cry. I just—" She turned to face him, naked misery in her brown eyes again. "If only I'd gone to the police in the first place—"

"Unless you'd gone to the wrong person." He shook his head. "You had good reason to be afraid. Don't second-guess yourself, Naomi."

"I have to!" she cried. "A man *died* because I didn't do enough."

It was as if they were completely alone. All he saw was her face, made stark by guilt. Not pretty right now.

"You might not have prevented it no matter what. You could have been unlucky and spoken to someone on Cobb's payroll. Even if you'd talked to the investigating officers and they were honest, would they have believed you?"

"I had the video."

"Which was lousy. It wouldn't have gone to the lab if they hadn't believed what you said. And then, who knows, it might have taken days, weeks. Depends how backed up they were, how much of a rush was put on it. Maybe Cobb would have told Greer sorry, forget it, but I can pretty well guarantee that if you'd stuck around, *you'd* be dead. He didn't know how much of the conversation you captured with your phone, but without your testimony? Odds are it wouldn't have been enough." This was truth, and he made his voice hard to emphasize it. "He couldn't afford for you to live to testify."

"That's not what you believed at first," Naomi whispered.

His hands still rested on her. His fingers tightened. "I hadn't had time to think it through. I came to Cape Trouble with some flawed preconceptions."

Something changed on her face. Suddenly, she withdrew from him, even before she physically backed away and then turned to the other two men.

"I want to see it."

Daniel nodded, set the laptop on the small kitchen table and opened it. Nobody said a word as they waited for it to come alive and for him to click on a desktop icon. As aware as he was of Naomi beside him, Adam couldn't look away from the computer.

The lighting was still dim, but the faces clear. The way the image wobbled – *because Naomi's hand was trembling in terror* – kept it from the Oscar quality Daniel had claimed. But…God damn. That was unmistakably U.S. Congressman Dominic Greer.

"You're sure you can get it done in time?"

Gregory Cobb leaned forward, his tone edgy. "I've already told you, not until I study my target. *I'll* pick the time." He sat back. "Once you've made the down payment."

"You think I'm going to pay a hundred and fifty thousand up front without knowing whether you can actually take care of Heath?" Scathing and angry, Greer slashed one hand through the air. He must be accustomed to instant compliance. "And you won't even agree to my timetable? You know when the primary is. If you drag your fucking feet, I'll be at risk because too many people will already have voted by mail. I'll pay you the other half if he's dead within a week. No later."

"Two—" Sound and picture both cut off.

"Unbelievable," Adam murmured. Then he gave a fierce grin and swung Naomi off her feet. "That was beautiful. You did it! We'll get them both."

She smiled, but he saw in her eyes how troubled she still was.

"No question," Mackay said, "but who do we go to?"

Adam set Naomi back on her feet. He had a little trouble convincing his hands to release her. "My friend in the FBI. He knows the story and is ready to move. He's high enough up to run with this."

"He'll want to talk to me." Sounding alarmed, Naomi crossed her arms protectively over her breasts.

What the hell? She was the one feeling guilty because she *hadn't* come forward. Here was her chance to exact justice.

"He will," Adam agreed.

"Will I…have to go down there?" She retreated a step, then another, as if driven by instinct. To run? "And what about all the laws I've broken?"

"What laws?"

She tore her gaze from Adam to look at Daniel, who'd spoken.

"I lied to investigators. Isn't that obstruction of justice, or something like that? I got a new social security number under false pretenses."

"So you could continue paying taxes. You were protecting yourself and trying to be honest, too. What's so bad about that?"

"Sam can guarantee you immunity against any charges," Adam put in. "That's pretty standard in a situation like this."

"Like this?"

"When a witness has been terrorized into silence." Adam heard the roughness in his voice. The idea of her fear had become increasingly unendurable for him.

She looked from one of them to the next as if seeking an escape. Alex Mackay still didn't say anything, although his expression was thoughtful. Daniel did bland but kind well. Adam had no idea what she saw on his face.

She closed her eyes, her arms tightening if anything, then nodded. "Of course I will," she said softly. "I can hardly live with myself for having run away. Now…at least I'll have the chance to do the right thing."

"We'll keep you safe," Adam said.

The look in her eyes sliced him to the bone. It said, *I don't believe you can.* And, after today's near miss, how could he blame her?

And maybe he was wrong about what she feared. The sense she still had secrets or fears he didn't understand stayed with him.

After the other two men left, he'd intended to call Sam immediately, but instead leaned a hip against the counter and watched Naomi, who still sat at the table looking lost.

"You're having trouble taking this all in," he said after a minute.

Her shoulders moved, but she didn't look at him. "It's…everything I wanted it to be, only it wasn't. And now someone waves a magic wand and it turns out I was wrong. Do you blame me for feeling dumb?"

"Dumb?"

Her eyes flashed quick anger. "I feel guilty, all right? You know that! Why do you keep making me say it?"

"Because you shouldn't. I'm a detective, and I understand why you made the choices you did. Those choices kept you alive."

"But if you'd been the detective who talked to me the morning after and I'd told you my story, you would have believed me enough to check it out, wouldn't you?"

He frowned. "Maybe. Yes. But I tend to be more open-minded than some. Flexible. And, yeah, honest. If you had a couple of long-timers…I don't know."

Naomi lifted her head and her eyes met his. No, more than that; she looked deep, making him uneasy. What was she searching for?

"But you came searching for me now, two years later, because you *didn't* believe I'd told the truth. So who knows?" She abruptly stood and said, "I need a shower," and hurried out of the kitchen, leaving him staring after her and thinking again about her hidden depths.

*****

Naomi felt like a coward lurking in her bedroom, but knew it wasn't that simple.

She craved his understanding, his belief in her, and desperately wanted to push it away, to tell him he was wrong about her.

Or maybe that he'd been right all along. Which he was.

She also wanted the comfort of his presence, the undeniable connection she felt to him, the weight of the air when they were alone in a room.

Soon, he would either learn the truth, or she'd have to start a new life far away. The idea that all her enemies would go away and she could placidly go on here in Cape Trouble seemed least likely, but that possibility, too, meant Adam would return home to his job and life. She didn't think he would have kissed her the way he had, looked at her the way he did, if he had a girlfriend waiting, but his extraordinary face, his lean, strong, quick body and the tension and sense of danger he exuded must be irresistible to woman. Look at her, drawn despite all common sense even when she hadn't known anything about him and should have been wary of too many coincidences. And the truth was, all that made her special in his eyes was what she'd done one night, a long time ago.

Both things she'd done that night: film two men making a diabolical bargain, and save herself by thrusting a knife beneath a man's ribs and wrenching it upwards. He only knew about one of those things, but if the second hadn't happened, too, he'd never have come to Cape Trouble searching for her.

If it hadn't happened, she'd be dead. *Remember?*

She clenched her teeth before they could chatter.

If Adam knew, he wouldn't want her. But right now, he did. And, oh, she wanted him.

Why couldn't she have him? It wasn't as if they didn't both know any hook-up would be temporary. Very temporary. Maybe very very, depending on what new and thrilling events tomorrow brought.

It would be harder to say goodbye if she did this.

Would it? she asked herself bleakly. She already felt more for him than she ever had for any other man. Saying goodbye would be bad no matter what.

I could love him. Maybe I already do.

Why not look at a night with him as a gift? Who ever regretted having an amazing experience? Swimming close enough to a sea turtle to look into his eyes and know he was looking back. Stand atop Mt. Rainier and see the world below you and rejoice because you'd been there without mourning because you'd never go back. She could think of making love with Adam Rostov like that.

Naomi took a deep breath and left the safety of her bedroom.

*****

"Naomi might be safer once you talk to her," Adam conceded, thinking it through.

"Or not," Sam said, dampening any optimism. "If you're right, and my, uh, co-worker catches a glimpse of me in Cape Trouble, his motivation to take care of her is going to rise exponentially."

Adam mumbled a profanity.

"Has to be done," his almost brother-in-law pointed out. "She is safer hunkered down where she is with you guarding her than she'd be during any attempt to get her out of town and to an airport. Unless we send in a National Guard helicopter to pick her up…" He seemed to mull over that possibility before discarding it. "We don't want to send up that kind of flare yet. No, I can fly into Portland relatively anonymously, rent a car and be over there by tomorrow afternoon or early evening."

They talked a minute more, but ended the call with Sam saying, "Count on seeing me tomorrow."

Sam had made the decision not to consult his superiors yet. He wanted the evidence in hand first – and admitted he'd begun to have his suspicions about the identity of the agent trying to assassinate Naomi. He wouldn't name him, not yet.

"I need something more than a suspicion," he said, sounding as unhappy as Adam would have been to learn someone he worked with and trusted had betrayed everything they stood for. It wouldn't be any different than him having to seriously consider whether Frank had been dirty. So damn unwelcome, the mind just shied away from it.

Setting his phone on the table, Adam closed his eyes and massaged his forehead with his fingertips, his thoughts reverting to what Sam had said about Naomi. Hell. *Safer?* Was she really safe at all, even with him here? Someone could shatter the glass in her bedroom window and pump bullets into her where she slept way quicker than Adam could get to his feet and rush in to protect her. This small cottage was far from impregnable. Locks were deadbolts, but the back door had a glass inset, for God's sake. Curtained, as were all the other windows, thanks, he felt sure, to the fear Naomi had lived with the entire time she'd been here. She'd chosen black-out curtains; he'd checked during his night-time prowls to be sure shadows of movement inside couldn't be seen. Even so, glass could be broken silently by someone with the right tool.

A soft whisper of sound had him half out of the chair in the split second before he saw that it was Naomi and began to relax.

"I'm sorry," she said. "I keep trying to hide my head in the sand."

"Can't blame you." He made himself resume his seat as she approached, looking shy, then pulled out the chair too close to him. The damn table was so small.

"Are you hungry yet?" she asked.

"I can eat if you want to, but I had lunch late."

She nodded. She'd fed him in the café kitchen and knew exactly when he ate. "Um…will you talk to me?" Definitely shy. "Tell me something about you?"

Something true, she meant. He remembered what he'd almost told her the night they went out like two normal people who were attracted to each other.

"Growing up, I wanted to be a fighter pilot. Navy, I thought, so I could land on aircraft carriers. That seemed the coolest to me."

She almost smiled at the hint of his boyish enthusiasm. "Did you join?"

"No. After Dad died, I changed my mind. Instead, I was going to be a crime-fighter extraordinaire, making everyone ashamed they'd ever suspected Dad of being on the take." His tone was wry, but not…pained. He was a little surprised at how easily he'd settled into acceptance of the knowledge that his father had taken bribes or pay-offs or just payment for turning his head or something worse. Which meant…he'd already known, somewhere deep inside?

Yeah, he concluded. That was exactly what it meant.

"I don't know how I deluded myself for so long," he said abruptly.

She touched the back of his hand, lying on the table. Then she curled her own into a fist and withdrew it. "We want to believe in our parents."

"I guess so." He wanted more touches. Those small, competent hands on him, but he also knew he couldn't ask. Not when she was utterly dependent on him. "You, too, huh?"

"Yes. I still don't understand…"

When she trailed off, he finished for her. "Why your mother put up with the abuse. Why she endangered you, too."

Naomi nodded.

"What's harder to understand is how you ended up so strong."

She blinked. "You think I am?"

"Don't you?"

Adam watched as she pondered that. The crinkles in her forehead smoothed.

"I suppose I do. I've done things—" She clearly thought better of what she'd come close to saying. "Things my mother wouldn't have been able to."

He smiled at her. "There you go."

She didn't smile back. Darkness seemed to shadow her most of the time, and never more than now. Adam wondered if it was a legacy of her painful childhood or of the past two terrifying years.

Although she'd wanted to talk, now she appeared to have run out of things to say. She peeked at him, then gazed at the uninteresting tabletop. He was surprised, given her mood, she didn't leap up to engage in comfort cooking.

Usually comfortable with silence, Adam found this one to be different. Tense. It left him free to look at her bent head, the delicate whorls of her ears, the curve of her jaw, the childlike texture of her skin. His heart clenched as he remembered her smiles that one evening, when he'd glimpsed the woman she had been before fear came to dominate her life.

He might have jumped up to pace or at least open some distance between them, except that studying her, thinking about her, had had the inevitable effect of arousing him. He was forced to continue sitting quietly in pretended relaxation.

"When you kissed me," she said suddenly, and he realized she was now looking at him, too. "Was that part of worming your way into my confidence?"

God, did she really think that?

"I don't do that." Maybe he should have been offended, but he couldn't blame her for her suspicions. "Naomi, I didn't intend to feel most of what I have for you. Not much that's happened between us was fake, and kissing you sure as hell wasn't. I wanted you the minute I saw you."

Her "oh" was almost soundless. Caramel, he thought again, looking into her eyes, but darker and richer than he remembered the color being.

“Then…will you make love with me?” Her breath hitched in what he thought was alarm. “I mean, not love, but—”

“Have sex?” The gravel in his voice had hardened into something with less give. Concrete. “No. But I can’t think of anything I want more than to make love with you.”

“Oh,” she said again.

“Why?” he made himself ask. “You’re still angry at me.”

Naomi shook her head. “I’m not. I was, because I came closer to trusting you than I usually let myself, and then to find out you’d been lying… But I do understand. And how can I be angry when you’ve done so much to protect me?”

He nodded. She wouldn’t go to bed with him to express gratitude, would she? But, damn, he wanted her, and his brain had quit working the way it should be.

Adam stood and held out his hand to her. *Damn, I hope she means it*, he thought, as he waited to see what she’d do.

CHAPTER TWELVE

He stood looking at the top of her head and the soft, feathery dark hair. *She* had to be at eye level with his erection, he realized. The sight had her cheeks pink by the time she lifted her gaze to his. She seemed…surprised. As if she hadn't believed he really wanted her? Or was she only surprised at herself? Either way, she laid her hand in his with an air of trust that squeezed his chest.

He tugged her to her feet and into his arms, surprised anew at how delicate she felt. She was fine porcelain instead of sturdy ceramic, although Adam knew in one way that wasn't true. He'd seen her in tight-fitting running clothes and knew her body was as strong as the determination that had kept her going despite the odds. But her bones were finely made. He wasn't a huge man, but his wrists were probably twice as thick as hers.

He ran his hands down her back and cupped her butt, squeezing and lifting her. Naomi lifted her arms around his neck and kissed his throat, pulling a groan from him.

The next second, his mouth found hers, and they were kissing deeply, passionately, as if taking up where they'd left off that first night, when he'd been so damn close to bearing her to the floor or pushing her up against a wall.

She kissed him back eagerly but still…not clumsily, that wasn't right, but as if she wasn't a hundred percent sure what she was doing. Maybe a woman forgot. He was willing to bet she hadn't let a man get this close to her since she fled L.A.

Since the last time she'd kissed Greg Cobb. The chill the thought gave him didn't last any longer than it took for him to lift his head and look at her face, even prettier softened and colored by desire.

He made a rough sound and kissed her again.

They managed to stumble through the house to her bedroom, bumping walls a few times, but he was fully aware when he had her backed up to the bed.

"Let me see you," he said.

Worry flared on her face. “I’m…not that…”

“Yeah, you are.” He tugged her shirt up and she cooperated by lifting her arms. Her bra was as dainty as she was, a virginal white without anything fancy about it, but his flesh surged anyway. He laid his hands over her breasts and gently rubbed.

Head tipped so she could watch, Naomi gave a tremulous sigh.

With a groan, he reached behind her to release the catch, then whisked the bra off to reveal small, perfect breasts. Her tight nipples were more pink than brown, to go with her very white skin. Adam picked her up and laid her on the bed so that he could follow her down, his mouth capturing one breast even before her back made contact with the coverlet.

He kissed and licked and sucked until he heard her saying insistently, “Please. Take this off,” and he remembered he still wore the damn vest.

Not to mention his Glock.

Separating himself from her was downright painful, but he reared up enough to rip off his denim shirt and fumble with the straps so that he could remove the vest and toss it aside. Once he set his weapon on the bedside table, she tugged at his T-shirt until he stripped that off, too, hiding his grimace at the pain from where the bullet had struck his back.

And then he had to groan again at the pleasure of – at last! – feeling her hands on him. She didn’t just stroke, she squeezed, even kneaded, and the strength of those hands was a major turn-on.

The part of his brain still functioning had the fleeting thought that he surely did hope she didn’t have only a one-off in mind, because he wasn’t going to last nearly long enough to enjoy her body and her touch as much as he wanted to.

But she seemed to feel the same urgency, because she unfastened his belt at the same time as he stripped her of jeans, panties and socks in one go.

For a minute he had to stare. She was slim and supple, her curves subtle but definitely there. Man, his hands were shaking as he finished undressing himself and grabbed a condom from his back pocket.

An expression of shock on her face gave him pause.

“I didn’t even think,” she whispered.

He grimaced. "I did. I bought these the morning after I kissed you for the first time."

"You…thought we'd get here?"

"No. I didn't know. I couldn't have made love with you until I'd told you the truth, but I wanted you. I…hoped."

She relaxed again, smiling. A tiny dimple flickered in her cheek. "I'm glad you had the foresight."

Yeah. He hadn't come to Cape Trouble with any expectation of having sex, that was for sure. What if she'd asked, and he'd had to say, *Love to, after I make a quick run to the pharmacy?*

And then they kissed and rolled and touched, Adam exploring her body as she explored his, until he couldn't wait another second and found his place between her legs. Sliding inside her was one of the best feelings of his life. From the astonishment on her face, he thought it might be the same for her.

They moved, sometimes coordinated, sometimes as if they were doing battle, but he'd been right – he couldn't last long. Fortunately, he didn't have to. She came around him with an exultant cry, and he let himself go, the pleasure roaring through him. He was unable to so much as say her name although it was there, in his throat, in his head.

Naomi.

*****

He crushed her into the mattress for a minute before seeming to heave himself off her and roll to his back. The air cold on her bare skin, Naomi suddenly felt vulnerable in a way that had panic swelling. She desperately wanted to burrow beneath the covers or leap up and get dressed. Instead she lay completely still, not wanting him to notice that she was freaking out.

Why had she thought this was a good idea? She'd wanted…she didn't even know. Comfort, satisfaction. Real closeness to another human being. Instead, she was terrified by more intimacy than she'd thought possible.

And *that* was why she felt so bare now.

His long arm came out and gathered her against him. "Damn, it's cold in here," he mumbled. Once he had her tucked close, his arm left her long enough to gather up her comforter and fling it partly over them. He must not know how he radiated heat. Naomi wasn't cold anymore, but she still did battle with the desire to separate herself from him, figure out how to pretend making love with Adam hadn't been so overwhelming.

That it was just sex.

"Are you all right?" he asked, voice still slurred, his head tilting as if he was trying to see her face.

No!

"Sure." She shrugged, as well as she could when half-draped over a hard, warm, male body.

His arm tightened around her. She expected him to say, *I don't believe you. Let's talk about it.* Instead, what came out was a drowsy, "Don't go anywhere. I need to sleep for a little while, and I don't want you even out in the kitchen without me."

And then, as far as she could tell, he dropped right off. His breathing deepened and his muscles went slack. Her mouth opened in outrage that she welcomed as a replacement for the irrational panic.

That was it? He couldn't say, *That was fabulous? Was it as good for you as it was for me*? Nope, he just took a *nap*?

But he didn't even know that she'd stiffened. And…she didn't actually want to get up and go into the living room or kitchen without him, not after what had happened this morning when she had almost gotten herself – or him – killed by not following his instructions.

In fairness, he had reason to be tired, too. She knew he wasn't sleeping much, and that was because he had dedicated himself to keeping her safe. Which meant she was being petty.

Once she gave up and let herself relax and even enjoy the sensation of lying half on top of his warm, strong body, some of the unnerving feeling of having her nerve-endings bared like electrical wires stripped of their plastic sheathing subsided. Her eyelids felt heavy, too. Her thoughts clouded.

*****

They made love twice more before finally agreeing they were starved and getting up, at which point he was careless enough to turn his back to her and she saw the bruise from the gunshot. He couldn't see it himself, but from her exclamations, it must be an ugly one.

Adam thought Naomi was incredibly cute in sacky sweatpants, a sweater that hung to mid-thigh, and thick, bright red fleece socks. With any other woman, he'd have suggested they settle for sandwiches, but Naomi put together a stir-fry almost as fast, and it was five-star restaurant fabulous. And then there were those cookies.

They didn't talk much over their meal, any more than they had in bed. Adam hadn't known what to say to her, and guessed she had the same problem. He shouldn't have made love to her, not yet; there was too much he didn't know about her, and one of the few things he felt sure of was that she still hadn't told him whatever secret she held knotted inside her.

He'd been coward enough not to press her so far. She had enough to deal with. Maybe they both did. And that was the other, flashing-in-neon-lights reason he shouldn't have so much as laid a hand on her: he couldn't afford to be distracted when his entire focus should be on guarding her.

It was natural to assume her silence might be partly uncertainty because he hadn't said anything about how he felt. He had the uneasy feeling, though, that she wouldn't have wanted to talk about feelings. He just hoped she wasn't conning him now while plotting an escape.

He finished his third cookie and took a swallow of coffee to wash it down. As far as he could tell, Naomi had mostly crumbled her cookie rather than taking even a bite.

"Sam plans to be here tomorrow afternoon," he said abruptly.

Her fingers went still and she stared at him. "He's coming *here*?"

"I told you he'd want to talk to you," he said, puzzled by her shock.

Naomi nodded, but looked dazed.

Adam reached for her hand, but she didn't return his clasp. Her fingers felt cold and unresponsive.

"Does he think he can tell if I lied to you?" she asked after a minute.

He frowned. "He wants to hear your story himself, that's all. This is big, Naomi. The FBI has been trying to nail Cobb for a long time. Arresting a U.S. Congressman for conspiracy to commit murder is even bigger. Won't happen without iron-clad evidence. To move ahead, *he* has to be sure. He might have questions I didn't think to ask. He wouldn't be coming if he didn't believe what I've told him."

She nodded again, but still uncertainly. "Is he, well, planning to stay? I mean, here?"

Adam tried to picture Sam bunking on the sofa and failed. Plus, he didn't much like the idea of him making any assumptions about Naomi because Adam was sleeping with her.

"No. He can have my rental house tomorrow night. I doubt he'll hang around any longer than that."

"Okay." She relaxed marginally, making him realize she'd had an attack of hostess anxiety, something he would never have expected of her. Although, come to think of it, owning a restaurant meant dedicating yourself to pleasing customers. He thought of Naomi's mother and the reason she'd worked at being a good cook. Yeah, being the best hostess possible was probably a need rooted in Naomi's deepest psyche.

"Sam's a good guy," he heard himself say.

"Are you friends?"

"Uh…" He had to think how to explain. "No. He has some of the attitude that always pisses off local cops who have to deal with feds. Mostly, though, except for the niece and nephew we share, the job is all we have in common. He's, I don't know, ten years older than I am? Has kids heading into their teenage years." Adam shrugged. "We get along. Respect each other."

Naomi nodded, and he saw how nervous she still was. "Him being FBI means he can overrule you, doesn't it? I mean, if he threatens me with jail time to compel my testimony, or something like that."

"No." He set down his coffee mug with a clunk. Making sure she saw that he meant every word, he said in a hard voice, "Nothing's going to happen I don't okay. I swear."

She went back to crumbling and squishing her cookie into nothingness. "How can you promise that?"

"If it comes to it, I'll help you disappear before I let him put you in jail. That is a promise, Naomi."

After a moment, she dipped her head. "Okay." She hesitated. "If you want to sleep with me tonight…"

Had that been in question? "Yeah," he said. "Trust me, I've been living to make it into your bed." He reached across the table and laid his hand over hers. "The cookie is dead, you know."

She looked down, expression rueful. "I guess it's past saving, huh?"

"I'll toss it outside for the birds, if any of them stick around for the winter." Her stress level noticeably ratcheted up when he said he needed to make a circuit outside before they hit the sack, which meant donning the vest again, and slipping out the door with his gun in hand.

Soaked again by the time he came in, he took a quick shower before joining her beneath the flannel-covered duvet in her bed. This time he made love to her slowly, taking time to learn where she was sensitive, where ticklish, what made her breath hitch or her back arch. She explored with her small, strong hands, discovering his vulnerabilities at the same time until he had to capture her wrists to hold onto enough control to finish this the way he wanted to.

He slept heavily for a couple of hours, then woke with a start thinking he'd heard something. A vehicle passing slowly in front, he realized, probably a Cape Trouble P.D. patrol car. From then on he slept lightly, as he had been nights out on Naomi's sofa, aware on one level of every sound. Twice he got up and walked through the house on bare feet, reassuring himself enough to be able to go back to bed.

Nothing happened on the way into town come morning, but he wasn't about to leave her alone in the kitchen. His reward for the long, slow hours watching Naomi work was a fantastic breakfast and an even better lunch, along with several tastings in between. If he hung around with her for long, he'd have to up the miles he ran to combat the calories, he thought ruefully.

That 'if' wasn't something he was letting himself think about, not yet.

He liked least having to bring Naomi out of the café after it closed. Today, Daniel Colburn showed up, his official car blocking access to the alley from one end.

"Stay down," Adam told her, his gaze sweeping every direction as he emerged from the alley. "Son of a bitch. Where is this guy?"

She didn't say, *Which guy?* She didn't have to. Right now, only one of them wanted to kill her. Unless they'd been wrong all along and there really was one. What if, after the failed attempt to grab her laptop, Cobb had said, "To hell with it. Kill her."

But he didn't believe it. Plus, he'd heard Cobb's voice well enough when she called to think he'd been surprised and alarmed at the news someone was trying to knock her off.

A car Adam didn't recognize sat in front of her cottage as they approached. Mid-size sedan, silver…rental, he diagnosed. Sam stepped out of the driver side as Adam slowed to turn into the driveway. Frowning, Adam wished he'd made his approach more circumspect.

Once he was out of the Tahoe, he summoned Sam with a jerk of his head. "Why didn't you wait until dark?"

"I've only been here a few minutes. Sitting outside the rental would have made me conspicuous, too."

Annoyed at himself, Adam shook his head. They should have made arrangements in advance. He could have left the house unlocked, or the key hidden outside somewhere.

"Let's get inside," he growled.

Sam moved to shield Naomi from the other side as Adam hustled her in the side door. He left the two of them in the laundry room while he checked out the rest of the house. He came back to find Sam studying her openly, but Naomi only sneaking shy – or alarmed – looks.

Despite the standard issue dark suit, white shirt, undistinguished tie and wingtips, Sam Weismann didn't have the ability to make himself as bland as did many FBI agents. Although only in his forties, he was balding on the crown of his head, creating the beginning of a monk-like tonsure, and with his saturnine complexion, brown eyes, bushy eyebrows and the enormous, hooked nose, he was one of a kind.

Having holstered his Glock, Adam tapped his own nose. "See? This is a guy who doesn't do undercover."

Sam narrowed his eyes. "Damn it, will you let up with the nose? It's not that bad."

"It's that bad."

A sound came from Naomi he recognized as a suppressed giggle. Sam's mouth crooked at the sound, too.

"You're definitely not the man I saw," she said.

"Glad we can confirm that." Sam held out a hand. "Pleasure to meet you, Ms. Varner."

"I prefer Kendrick."

"Kendrick it is."

She eyed him, obviously suspicious of the easy tone, and with reason.

"Can we sit down and talk?" he asked.

They chose the table. Perhaps symbolically, Adam sat between the other two, who faced each other.

Yes, Sam agreed, he'd seen the video. What he wanted was to walk her through the entire evening.

He did ask questions Adam hadn't thought to. She explained that guests to a private event entered through a side door that let out into the parking lot on the side. She had discovered early on that if the marquee was lit and people were coming and going through the front, passersby assumed the restaurant was still open and staff had to turn them away. A wrought iron fence and rioting bougainvillea shielded part of the parking lot from the street and sidewalk, allowing relatively discreet arrivals and departures.

"The bougainvillea was already there," Naomi said abruptly. "I didn't intend anything like that."

Sam tapped something into his laptop.

Yes, staff entered and exited through the back door. There was a short hall there behind the kitchen, off which were her office, a pantry and a small room used by staff to hang coats, leave purses and backpacks, and take breaks.

The side entrance was interesting; where staff hung their coats seemed irrelevant to Adam, but this was Sam's show unless he stepped wrong.

By previous agreement, she hadn't seen any of Greg Cobb's guests until her peek through the partially open door. If he was hosting a larger group, she'd set up a coffee urn in advance. For smaller gatherings, as this one had been, he would come into the kitchen himself to say hello and pick up a tray with a carafe and cups.

Had he kissed her? Adam shook off the irritable thought.

"Did he ever send bodyguards to fetch coffee or pass messages?" Sam asked.

"Yes, sometimes, but not that night."

Maybe, Adam reflected, she'd been on edge because Cobb had been even more secretive than usual.

As she did her best to remember everything she'd seen and heard, Naomi closed her eyes, as if to run the reel of the evening back. The stress on her face made him want to stop this. The hand that lay on the table trembled when she talked about taking out her phone and filming, just as it had trembled when she did it. Her eyelids quivered. Adam had never seen her look so painfully vulnerable. It was all he could do not to reach out and grip that hand to offer reassurance, but he'd rather Sam didn't find out how personal this relationship had gotten. Not yet, anyway.

Her whole body jerked when she talked about seeing the men's room door opening just before she whisked back into the kitchen. Adam moved restlessly. He felt Sam's gaze flick to him.

"What did you do after Cobb left? Did you look around to be sure everyone really was gone?"

Naomi shuddered and opened her eyes. "No. I usually did a walk-through before I left, but not that night. I was scared."

Sam nodded in apparent approval for her sensible response to events. "Was your car the last in the parking lot?"

"Yes." She hesitated. "Actually, I left through the alley, so I don't know for sure whether our side lot was empty."

Sam's fingers flew. *Click click click.*

"What difference does that make?" she asked timidly.

"Can't say what matters yet." He lifted his head to look at her. "There is the body found in your kitchen."

She shuddered again. "I haven't forgotten."

"Not someone you'd ever seen before?"

Naomi shook her head.

"But you assumed when you found him that he was one of Cobb's men."

Her fingers curled into a fist. "I didn't assume anything. I got stuck on the dead part. I'd never seen a body before. It…stays with you."

"Especially when the death was violent."

She quaked. "Yes."

Adam's teeth ground together. He knew where Sam was going with this, and wasn't happy. "What's this have to do with Congressman Greer hiring Cobb to kill his opponent?"

"Something," Sam said, leaning back, "or your partner wouldn't have ended up dead in Ms. Varner's – excuse me, *Ms. Kendrick's* – restaurant kitchen. I don't buy the murder being coincidental, do you?"

"No."

He didn't like what he saw in her eyes. Fear. He hoped Sam didn't recognize it, then felt sick. Damn, had he avoided pressing her on Frank's death because he didn't want to know if she'd had anything to do with it?

Yeah. That's exactly why I've been letting it slide. Not entirely; there'd been plenty going on to divert him. Somewhere in there, keeping her alive had risen to the top of his list of priorities.

So I could sleep with her?

He gritted his teeth again.

He tuned back in when Sam removed an envelope from an inner pocket of his suit coat. "I'm going to show you some photos," he said, his normally unrevealing tone giving away a hint of unhappiness. "I know you don't think you'll recognize the man who identified himself as an FBI agent. If you can't, you can't. He may not be here. Some of these photos are of agents who work out of the L.A. office, some are…let's call them control subjects." He took a pile of photographs out of the envelope and slid it across the table to Naomi. "Take your time. Don't force it."

She nodded, not reaching immediately to touch the photos even though she stared at the one on top. Her expression suggested a diamondback had inexplicably appeared on her kitchen table, and it was rattling a warning.

At last, she slowly turned over the top photo, then the next, and the next. From what Adam could see, it was a good lineup. Sam had chosen subjects who weren't all that distinguishable from each other. Brown hair, from short to a little shaggy, some straight, some wavy. Some of the photos could have been mug shots, or taken for a badge.

Naomi hesitated over one, started past it, then went back. After a moment, she set it aside and continued through the pile. She removed one other picture, then started all over again. Finally she looked up.

"I really didn't get a good look. This one—" She gently nudged the first photo she'd set aside across the table. "He makes me uncomfortable. I can't swear it's him, but...well, he's my best guess."

Watching closely, Adam caught Sam's flinch.

"All right," he said, voice sharp. He shoveled the whole pile back in the envelope and restored it to his pocket. "Let's talk about what we're going to do."

He wanted Naomi to return to L.A. with him. Other people would need to talk to her. It was time to bring in the U.S. Attorney's office. Ultimately, her testimony in court would be needed. "You did understand this?" he asked, and she nodded.

He discussed protective custody. She gave Adam a panicky look before turning it on Sam.

"If an agent in your office was involved with Greg, what makes you think he's the only one? As I've told Adam, I saw police officers from three or four different jurisdictions doing guard duty for him. I'm reluctant to put my life in the hands of these unknown agents. I'd prefer to hide on my own and appear when you need me."

"Not an option."

She met Weismann's stare with her own, not backing down at all. "What if I say going back to Los Angeles with you isn't an option?"

"Then we have a problem." His tone was completely inflexible. "I do have the ability to compel you to come with me, Ms. Varner."

Seemingly forgotten by the combatants, Adam said calmly, "No, you don't, Sam. I made promises to *Ms. Kendrick*—" he gave the other man a hard look "— that I intend to keep. She has come forward voluntarily. Agreed to testify despite the inherent risks. You are sure as hell not snapping handcuffs on her."

Sam transferred his glare to Adam. "You overstepped."

"You'd know nothing about any of this if it weren't for Ms. Kendrick's civic-mindedness. *And* her courage."

That momentarily silenced Sam. No way he could deny the courage she'd displayed when she filmed that scene. The tremor of her hand spoke volumes; she'd been scared to death, and by God she'd done it anyway.

After a tense interval, Sam sighed. "Let's put off a decision until tomorrow. You two talk tonight. See if you can come up with an acceptable plan." His tone suggested he harbored grave doubts, but that was Sam for you. In Adam's experience, he never brimmed with optimism. "You got the key to that house?" he asked. "I assume there's a bed?"

"There's a bed. Table and chairs. Not much else." Not anything else, as Adam knew from uncomfortable experience.

Naomi jumped to her feet. "Oh, but you have to stay for dinner! I don't think Adam left any food over there."

Sam's face registered surprise. Asshole that he'd been there at the end, he didn't deserve to be offered one of Naomi's meals, but what better way to soften him up? Something told Adam that wasn't what she was thinking, though; her need to feed people ran deep.

Adam excused himself to do another perimeter walk. Darkness had long since fallen, even though it was barely six o'clock. The rain had let up, but the air felt damp and with every step he felt as if the ground was sucking at his feet. The whole damn Oregon coast must be soggy for months on end. He had the passing thought that an excess of rain might beat an excess of sunshine. Funny, when he'd grown up in southern California, that he didn't love the heat and the brown hills.

He came in to hear Sam talking about his youngest, a girl who played the cello at a level that had her talking about Juilliard.

"You must be proud of her," Naomi said, scraping something from her cutting board into a skillet.

"I am," Sam said. "She got it from my side of the family. I have a grandmother who was a well-known opera singer back in the 1920s and 30s. Musical ability passed me by, but as far as I know it never cropped up in my wife's family."

"Passed you both by," Adam said brutally, remembering the last time he'd heard them sing Happy Birthday.

Sam sneered at him.

Adam inhaled and decided dinner involved curry. His stomach rumbled. Naomi surveyed him and said, "You're not wet."

He lifted one foot in wordless argument. The bottom couple inches of his chinos were soaked.

Her impish smile probably hid a boatload of apprehension, but he appreciated the effort. "Don't be a wimp."

"Wouldn't think of it."

To Adam's surprise, she coaxed Sam into continuing to talk about his family. He went so far as to take out his wallet and show her pictures of his wife and kids, and then of his brother Abe, Adam's sister Ellen and their children. The softening process was going just fine, Adam decided.

Dinner was indeed an Indian curry, and as good as everything else she cooked. In other words, magic. She'd brought home half of a key lime pie that hadn't sold out at the café, giving them each a slice. As usual, she served herself a skinny one and then proceeded to mash it and push bits around more than actually eat it. Sam noticed, too; he watched, then met Adam's eyes.

Adam didn't make any effort to hustle him out. Naomi was probably safer with both of them there than with only him, and he doubted Sam was real eager to head for the bare-bones accommodations he was lucky to have for tonight. The bed beat Naomi's shabby couch.

Her bed was even better, he thought smugly, especially with her in it.

Eight-thirty or so, Sam said, "Walk me out, Adam."

Putting away the last of the clean dishes, Naomi wished him goodnight. She was obviously trying for all she was worth to pretend this was any other evening, and Sam was just a guest.

Walking down the driveway, illuminated only by the weak light beside the door, Sam said, "She's gotten to you."

"She's clean," Adam said flatly.

The FBI agent grunted.

"She picked out the right picture, didn't she?"

Sam didn't say anything for a minute. Then he growled, "Yes. Damn. I didn't want to believe it, but Jim had risen to the top of my list of possibilities. Can't be coincidence she fingered him."

"No." Adam paused. "Jim?"

"Rankin. And you didn't hear me say that."

"I take it he's AWOL?"

"Family emergency. He was a little vague. He's got a twenty year old who has been in and out of trouble. Everyone assumed it had to do with the kid and he just didn't want to talk about it. Wife thought that's what he was up to, too. The boy's in Chicago. As far as I could determine, though, Rankin isn't."

Adam made a sound of acknowledgement. Having faced the reality of his father's sins, he understood why Sam sounded so disturbed.

"Your *Ms. Kendrick*," Sam said, abruptly changing the subject, betraying only a hint of sarcasm with the name, "gets a little closed-mouthed when it comes to the subject of Frank Donahue."

"Finding him had to shake her up."

"Especially with her knife stuck in him."

Adam's jaw tightened. His turn not to say anything.

"Rankin is big on camping," Sam grumbled. "Spent years dragging the family up into the Sierras, even down into the Baja Peninsula. If he's here, my guess is he's hunkered down in the woods somewhere."

"He's not invisible, though. Has to be getting his groceries somewhere, for example."

"You think he's watching?"

The impenetrable darkness around them felt dangerous in that moment. Scattered lights up and down the street were ineffectual against the damp, clouded night. Turning his head to see the dark shapes of neighboring cottages, the bulk of sheds and detached garages, Adam felt the hair on his nape prickle. "Unfortunately, I do."

"You want me to stay? Take turns keeping watch?"

"You get any sleep on the plane?"

"I don't sleep thirty thousand feet up in the air."

"Then you need to grab some while you can. I'll call if I get uneasy."

They left it at that. Adam watched until he saw lights come on inside the house a block down that he'd occupied for so few days. He prowled the yard again, not daring to venture farther from Naomi's cottage and leave her even momentarily unprotected, then let himself in and locked.

She sat at the table waiting, her back very straight and her eyes dark and anxious. "Did he say with the picture…?"

"You confirmed his suspicion."

She swallowed. "Oh."

Adam made his voice gentle. "Bedtime. We can talk in the morning."

She searched his face. "You won't let him take me?"

"No. I keep my promises."

She didn't exactly heave a breath of relief, but he saw a subtle easing of her rigid posture. "Yes. Okay. Do you mind if I take a shower?"

"Of course not."

Much as he'd have liked to make love with her, once they went to bed and turned out the lights, he only adjusted her so her head rested on his shoulder and could knead taut muscles until her breathing became even.

Despite his unease, he did sleep eventually, reassured by the presence of his Glock an arm's reach away.

The first sound he heard was barely a whisper. The scuff of a foot not lifting high enough to clear the edge of the runner in the short hall right outside the bedroom. An indrawn breath.

Before his eyes even opened, reflexes took over. He grabbed Naomi and rolled them both toward the far side of the bed.

CHAPTER THIRTEEN

In her dream, she ran along the cliff above crashing ocean waves, tasting the salty air, muscles flexing. *Wham.* Something smashed into her and she was falling. On a strangled scream, she went over the edge.

She hit a hard surface sooner than she should have, her head connecting with a clunk and bouncing. A hard body came down on top of her, expelling the air in her lungs with a huff. Disoriented, she fought, until she heard a murmured, "Hush."

Adam. In a blink, she was awake. On her bedroom floor. Beneath him. He'd rolled her off the bed, covered her with his own body to shield her. Oh, God. Terror swelled in her. Someone was in the house with them. *Neither of us is wearing a vest.* Feeling him tense, gather himself, she wanted to grab him, prevent him from rising to a crouch, but she didn't. He knew what he was doing. She had to believe that.

Then…there was a strange sound. A cough. No, she'd heard it before. Somebody had fired a gun with a silencer on it. In that weird way a person did in a moment like this, she thought, a suppressor. That's what Adam called it. But…he didn't have one on his Glock. Only, she didn't hear or feel the bullet strike. And she should have, shouldn't she? The bed ought to have shuddered, or splinters have flown from the closet or wall.

Even odder, a heavy thud followed. And then a momentary silence. After which came quick, receding footsteps.

"What the…?" Adam muttered. "Can you reach the lamp without exposing yourself?" he murmured.

She nodded, not knowing if she could or not, but she rose to crawl forward. Sensing more than hearing him move, she groped above her for the lamp switch.

The light blinded her, but Adam, crouched toward the foot of the bed, was farther away. He swore viciously, then rose to his feet.

"No, stay down," he said when she started to sit up. "Jesus," he muttered, then gave her a quick look. "I mean it. Don't move. Don't look."

Her stomach lurched. She smelled raw meat. Blood, she thought in horror. Somebody had been shot and must be dead, or Adam wouldn't be speaking in a normal voice.

"Stay," he said again, and she heard the soft footfalls as he left the bedroom.

Naomi huddled behind the bed, hating the feeling of helplessness and isolation. She couldn't even lie flat to look under the bed. The rolling drawers that held her summer wardrobe and extra bedding would keep her from seeing whoever had just died. She could ignore Adam's order and stand up. But…maybe she didn't want to see.

Adam came back a moment later and said, in a ragged but still somehow gentle voice, "Whoever fired that shot is gone. You can sit up, Naomi, but I suggest you stay put for now."

"Okay." It came out as a squeak. She cleared her throat. "Is…is someone dead?"

"Yeah, a someone who broke in here to kill us." He sounded grim. The next moment she heard him speaking and realized he had his phone. "Get your ass over here." And then, after a pause when he must have dialed another number, "Colburn? I have a body at Naomi's place. Pretty sure it's our renegade fed. And, no, I didn't kill him."

That was apparently all he had to say. The next instant, he rounded the foot of the bed and crouched beside her, still wearing only a pair of navy blue, knit boxers. A day's growth of beard shadowed his jaw. Those clear, pale eyes looked anxious.

"You okay, honey? That was a hell of a drop from the bed."

She blinked at him.

He frowned and slid his fingers into her hair. They found a painful spot that had her jerking. "You've already got a lump. I'm sorry."

"He was going to shoot us?"

"Yeah."

"Then why…? What happened?"

"Damned if I know." With gentle fingers, he smoothed her bangs from her forehead. "No, that's not true. Somebody was right behind him."

She felt like she ought to understand but didn't. Her thoughts swam slowly, each disconnected. She wondered if she was really awake. "I think I'm okay," she managed to say. "You do what you have to."

His intense gaze kept searching hers, but after a moment he nodded, then cocked his head.

"Rostov?" a voice called urgently. Sam Weismann.

"In the bedroom." Adam rose, looked around, and grabbed a pair of jeans from the duffel bag he'd moved to her bedroom yesterday. He was zipping them when Sam said, much closer, "Oh, hell."

"Rankin?"

"A little hard to tell," Sam said dryly.

Her stomach heaved as she guessed what he meant.

A vehicle roared to a stop outside. Naomi heard a distant siren.

"Your back door was open," Sam said.

"I know. Colburn?" he called.

More swearing. Naomi felt peculiar, just sitting there on the floor, her back against the rough wall of the closet, staring at the bed and rumpled covers that hung over the edge. Otherwise, all she could see was Adam, standing with his back to her talking to the other two men.

She shivered, aware suddenly of how chilly the night was. Or shock might be hitting her. Adam's head turned. He snatched the flannel-covered duvet off the bed and was suddenly there, bundling it around her. "I'm going to get some ice for your head. Does anything else hurt?"

"I…don't think so." Well, yes, pain twinged in her hip when she shifted, but she didn't think it was important.

The men stood talking. Someone else joined them with a sharp, startled exclamation. Eventually Adam came back and said, "I'm going to carry you out to the living room. Close your eyes. You don't want to look."

"I can walk," she argued.

"No, I have to step over— We don't want to contaminate the scene anymore than we have to."

Naomi nodded and immediately regretted it. Her head throbbed.

Adam scooped her up and she laid her head on his shoulder. She could see past him to Daniel Colburn, unshaven and rumpled and wearing a faded San Francisco 49ers sweatshirt, and Sam Weismann, in strangely proper flannel pajama top, buttoned all the way up. As Adam circled the bed, Naomi made the mistake of looking down to see if Sam still had on the matching pj bottoms, too.

She'd known there was a body. What she hadn't expected was…his head. What was left of his head.

Her stomach heaved.

Adam swore. "You need the bathroom?"

She nodded frantically, clapping a hand over her mouth.

An instant later, she was on her knees in front of the toilet, losing what little dinner she'd eaten. Adam rubbed her back and kept saying, "Damn, I'm sorry, Naomi." She also heard the word "concussion", but thought he was saying that to someone else. She was pretty sure it was mostly horror driving her nausea.

Eventually, with Adam's help, she staggered to her feet. Trying not to look at herself in the mirror, she rinsed her mouth and then brushed her teeth. Her mouth still tasted horrible.

And I thought a man who'd been stabbed was a ghastly sight, she thought drearily.

Adam used his body to make sure she couldn't see into the bedroom again as he steered her into the living room where she sank onto the sofa. He tucked the duvet around her again, and disappeared, returning a minute later with a bag of frozen corn and a dishtowel. He found the lump on her head unerringly and positioned the impromptu ice pack over it.

"Can you hold this?" The way he looked at her, it was as if they were alone in the house.

"Yes." She lifted one hand from beneath the flannel and put it over the cold pack.

He kept studying her, as if he was afraid she'd keel over, but finally nodded. "I'll be just a few minutes."

A few minutes until…*what*? she wondered. They went back to bed? Um, not likely.

She sat there feeling strangely numb as discussion continued in the hall and other men came and went. One uniformed sheriff's deputy, then others who she suspected were from the medical examiner's office. Or some kind of crime scene technicians? In her peripheral vision, she was aware of flashes from a camera.

Adam checked on her several times. "Just a minute" stretched into what might have been half an hour. When the dishtowel became sodden from melting corn, she set it down. She felt really strange, but decided not to examine why. *Just get through the night.* She envisioned herself in the café kitchen and debated what specials to offer today. Perhaps it was the sagging bag of corn that made her think, corn cakes for breakfast, corn bread for lunch with vegetarian chili. Adam had liked her chili. She hugged herself.

When he sat beside her on the sofa, she started. He cupped her chin and turned her face toward her. "You and I are leaving," he said. "I've got a place for us to spend the rest of the night." He grimaced. "Not that there's much of it."

It hadn't occurred to her yet to wonder what time it was.

He very carefully put her slippers on her feet. "Can you walk?"

"Of course I can walk," she said indignantly.

Adam smiled, his eyes still watchful. "Good girl."

"Don't you have to stay?"

He shook his head. "Not my crime scene."

"It's not Daniel's, either."

"No, a sheriff's department detective is here now. Sean Holbeck." Naomi nodded. She knew the name, at least. He'd been involved in last summer's arrest of the serial killer. Adam continued, "Colburn is heading home now, too."

"Are we going to your rental?"

"No, Sam may. Colburn gave me the key to a place. One of his officers is out of town and won't mind if we sleep there."

"All right," she said docilely. "I want my bag, though. With my computer."

"I'll get it."

He reappeared in a minute with her bag and his own duffel bag, passing through the living room, she presumed, to put them in the SUV before returning.

With Adam's hand beneath her elbow, she did get to her feet. He helped her wrap the duvet several times around herself so it didn't drag on the floor. She paid no attention whatsoever to any of the men whose heads turned to watch as she and Adam walked out through the kitchen. Only on the doorstep did she balk. "You don't have your vest."

"I already tossed it in the Tahoe. Yours, too. With all the activity here, our latest shooter isn't going to be anywhere nearby."

"Oh." She made herself move again.

"I stuck a few of your clothes in my bag, too. For morning."

Another SUV backed out of the driveway to open the way for Adam to do the same, then pulled back in. Her small car sat in the carport, looking forlorn. She wondered if she'd ever drive it again.

It was very dark once they were on their way. Her gaze found the dashboard clock. 3:57. "I'll have to be up in a couple of hours."

"No." He made the turn onto the highway.

"What?"

"No, you won't be opening the café this morning."

"I have to." She sounded, and felt, desperate.

"Naomi…we'll talk about it in the morning."

"We can talk about it while I'm cooking."

"No," he said, his tone inflexible.

She argued; he kept repeating, "No."

Panic swelled in her chest, clearing the dreamy lassitude that had cloaked her. She was barely aware they were in Cape Trouble now, turning through a quiet neighborhood of modest, old homes near the river. "You're going to let him take me to L.A., aren't you?"

"We may have to go to L.A."

"You promised," she said fiercely.

He pulled into a driveway, set the emergency brake with a savage motion, and turned to her. "What do you suggest, Naomi? You just keep placidly on the way you have been?" A streetlight let her see his bared teeth. Shadows cast beneath those strong cheekbones made his face almost demonic. "Tonight, that son of a bitch was five feet from your bed. If he'd pulled the trigger a second sooner, you could be dead. Or do you not get that?"

"You could be dead. You…were closer to the door." *You covered my body with yours.*

"I could be," he said flatly. "Don't you understand? Damn it, Naomi, it's time to finish this."

She wasn't being rational and knew it. *I'm scared.* Because finishing it meant—

No, she didn't have to admit to anything. If she kept her mouth shut, no one would ever know. If she told…he wouldn't believe her. She would lose him.

Only his protection, she told herself, but of course that wasn't what she feared. No, what she dreaded most was his disgust, his fury, his condemnation. The death of whatever he might have felt for her.

After a minute, she nodded.

"Let's go in. Wait until I come around."

She knew the drill. Gun in hand, he hustled her into the house, turned on a lamp, then made her stand just inside while he walked through. When he returned, he held the gun down by his thigh.

"All right. First door on the left down the hall looks like a guest bedroom. Maybe you can get some sleep. I'll go out and get our stuff."

Maybe *you* can get some sleep? Right. Sure.

She hadn't moved a step when he returned.

"Damn it, Naomi!" He scowled at her, tossing the two kevlar vests and her messenger bag onto an easy chair in the small living room and letting the duffel fall to the floor. "What are you still doing here? You're swaying on your feet."

"I won't sleep."

"Try."

He didn't intend to go to bed with her, she realized. In fact, he wanted her tucked away, out of sight. Was probably annoyed because he had to babysit when the real action was taking place elsewhere. Or else tonight's assassination attempt had reminded him afresh that she was really Naomi Varner, the chef who had dated Greg Cobb, whose knife had been found stuck in Frank Donahue's chest.

"I'll sit down." She wound through too much clutter to a sofa that proved to be as uncomfortable as it looked.

Adam stood by the door looking at her, his dark brows bunched.

"The dead man. He was the FBI agent."

His mouth compressed. After a minute he sighed and rubbed the back of his neck. "Yes."

"The one whose photo I picked out."

"Yes," he repeated, then chose a chair about as far from her as he could get and sat. He laid his gun on a side table.

"You think Greg Cobb's guy killed him to save me. Because Greg is still spooked by my threat."

"As he should be."

"But he doesn't think anyone else knows."

"No. And that means we've got to get you into hiding immediately. Cape Trouble isn't remotely safe for you now. Not until Cobb and Greer have been arrested, and maybe not even then."

"Not even—? Oh. Because people in his organization might still be trying to keep me from being able to testify."

"Right."

I don't have to tell him anything. I don't.

"Are we…safe here? I mean, for tonight?"

"I think so. Nobody followed us that I saw. With luck, we've dropped off the radar for the night." For the first time since they had pulled up in front and she'd gotten a good look at his face, it softened. "Go to bed, Naomi. This has been a hell of a night. You need to recharge."

"And you don't?"

"I don't need much sleep. I had enough."

She nodded without meaning anything by it. "There's something I have to tell you." *You don't have to.*

Yes, she did. Only…was this a truth that would taint the testimony Adam and Sam were counting on to put away two evil men? She didn't know, but she couldn't let them be blindsided, either, if Greg were to try to co-opt her by claiming she'd killed a police detective on his order.

Adam had stiffened. "Tomorrow. You've had enough for one night."

"No. This is important."

He stared at her for a long moment, then nodded.

"I stabbed Frank Donahue." Don't be a coward. "I killed him."

He kept staring. Everything inside her clenched, waiting.

But she couldn't stand his silence. "He was going to kill me."

"Bullshit!" Adam exploded to his feet and glared at her. His hands balled into fists.

So now she knew. The hurt was even bigger than she'd expected. She had to finish this, though. She kept talking, her voice dull now. "After Greg left, I told myself I had to wait for a few minutes, in case he had someone waiting outside. I'd told him I had to send some emails. Um, I already told you that. So anyway, everything was quiet and I thought I was alone. He…burst into the kitchen." She sat frozen, not looking at Adam anymore. Instead, she saw it happening again, as she had a thousand times since that night. "He wore a badge on his belt, so I knew he was a cop. I told him he was scaring me, that if he had questions I'd talk to him in the morning. He said…" Her voice shook. She closed her eyes until she was sure she could go on. "No. He said no. There was no good in putting off something that had to be done. And then he pulled his gun and I knew."

"Not Frank."

"He was only a couple of feet from me. Crowding me. You know. I saw it on his face. He looked…sorry. He didn't want to kill me, but he was going to anyway."

"No!"

"I'd had my back to the counter. The minute he came in the kitchen, I sort of…stood sideways, with one arm hidden. My knives were in a block on the countertop. I shifted until I could grab one. And then, as he raised the gun, I…thrust." Nausea rose again, choking her. *Thank God I don't have anything left in my stomach*, she thought. "Under the ribs and up. I saw his eyes…" Her stomach heaved again. She started to stand up and realized she didn't know where the bathroom was and wouldn't reach it in time anyway. She cupped her hands in front of her mouth and retched, long, dry heaves that shook her body.

All the while, Adam stood staring down at her, his eyes blazing, his dark face contorted.

"No," she heard him say again.

Suddenly furious, she lifted her head. "Yes! Yes! He was dirty, dirty, *dirty*, just like your father!"

She hated what she'd done to him the minute she saw the transformation overtake his expression. He backed up a step, then another, bumping into a side table, having to stagger. Naomi had never seen him take a graceless step before. His eyes had dilated until they looked almost black.

"I'm sorry," she whispered, trying to rise to her feet but finding her legs wouldn't hold her. "I shouldn't have said—"

"I'm going out." Adam's voice was hoarse. "Stay here. Go to bed, Naomi."

"But…"

"Not now!" he roared. "Do you hear me?"

Her teeth chattered. She covered her mouth with her hand and nodded.

He turned and blundered out. The front door slammed behind him. She waited for the sound of his SUV engine, but it didn't come. So he hadn't abandoned her entirely. But – oh God – he'd left his gun on the side table, his tactical vest on the chair. He'd walked out without any protection.

Because he's sure we're safe here, she reminded herself. Nobody had followed them; nobody could know where they were. He was just…walking. Absorbing what she'd told him.

Coming to terms with the fact that he'd slept with the woman who murdered his partner, she thought on a surge of bitterness. She'd seen everything in his eyes she'd feared. Oh, not disgust; he hadn't gotten there yet. But rage, oh, yes. And condemnation. Frank couldn't be guilty, so she must be.

How could she have been foolish enough to let herself fall in love with him? Or think for a minute that he might believe her?

Come morning, she thought dully, he *would* hand her over to Agent Sam Weismann to haul back to L.A. Would they cuff her, drawing stares at the airport and on the flight?

Did it matter who stared?

Would they still want her to testify? Or had she just destroyed all possibility of bringing down Greg Cobb and Congressman Greer?

The video. She clung to the thought. It was persuasive. And one of the three men there that night had just tried to kill her. They couldn't argue with that, right?

She stayed where she was for a long, long time. Somewhere a clock ticked. Otherwise, she heard nothing but silence. Finally, feeling unbelievably weary, her stomach hurting and her head aching, she stood and went down the hall until she found a bathroom. After using the toilet, she flushed, then stood there staring at the closed door as if she was a clock that had wound down.

I'll go to bed. Why not? Even if Adam came in, he wouldn't want to talk to her. She might as well…curl into a tiny ball and hide beneath the covers, she thought with sort of black humor.

Her brain issued an order and her feet obligingly moved. She stepped out into the hall, and an arm wrapped around throat, jerking her backward.

"One peep out of you, bitch, and I'll kill *him*."

*****

Adam ground his forehead against the rough trunk of some kind of old fruit tree in the yard, his eyes closed. With one hand he gripped a branch. He should go back in; he knew he should. If nothing else, he felt naked without his Glock. But…he couldn't face her. If she was still sitting there, staring at him with those huge stricken eyes, he might break.

Frank's face replaced Naomi's in his mind's eye. The bags under his eyes turned into plump pouches when he grinned as he gave Adam a hard time about…who knew? And then there was his expression one time when he was talking about his youngest, who'd fallen in love with Scripps College. Spanish Colonial architecture, Frank said. Fountains, wisteria. You ought to see the place. Top-drawer college, expensive as hell. So, what was he going to do? Say, suck it up, kid, you're going to the junior college then transferring to UCLA if you're lucky?

No, Frank had found another way. It was the second time since Adam met Naomi that he'd tasted betrayal, as bitter as gunpowder on the tongue.

He was dirty, dirty, dirty, *just like your father!*

Of course he was. Adam bumped his head against the tree trunk. Did Frank's wife know? How could she not, if her husband was suddenly bringing home a whole lot of extra money?

Adam really believed his own mother hadn't. But Dad had done it all along, while Adam's best guess was that Frank had been a good cop until he made the decision to do whatever it took to give his little girl what she wanted even though putting his boy through college the first three years had been killing him. He'd been mad that the best education cost so much, but what had him ranting was the FAFSA. First time around, with his son, he'd been irked, but Jonah had been content to go to a state school and Frank managed. Sheila, though, she was really smart. Talking about being a doctor. Already stripped of savings to put Jonah through college, Frank had expected

Sheila would qualify for some serious scholarship money. Then he filled out the FAFSA and he went off like a rocket. How dared the federal government tell him and the college how much he could pay? For weeks there, he wouldn't shut up about it.

Had he convinced himself that aiding organized crime was a slap at the government that had been so goddamn unjust to him? How had *that* worked when he pulled a gun with the intention of killing an innocent, terrified young woman?

Imagining the scene Naomi had described, Adam still felt sick. Frank would have murdered her. The chef would have been found dead the next morning in her restaurant kitchen, instead of the police detective. Unless, of course, she'd just disappeared. No – he remembered some puzzlement at the time, because Frank hadn't been carrying his service weapon. He must have just bought a new backup, people said, one not even registered yet.

Uh huh. Sure. Adam shook his head. *I was blind.*

A vehicle engine started less than a block away. Frowning, he pushed away from the tree and turned his head. No motion at all up and down the street. Side street then. The car was moving, the sound receding. Somebody who left for work early. But…it hadn't backed out of a driveway. Had to have been at the curb. People didn't street-park much in this neighborhood; why would they, when they all had driveways, and most had at least detached garages?

Disturbed and suddenly uneasy, he jogged across the yard and took the porch steps two at a time, letting himself into the house as quietly as he could.

The lamp still burned, but Naomi wasn't sitting on the sofa. She'd left the duvet crumpled there, though. She must have taken him at his word and gone to bed.

The furnace kicked on, the sound making him jump. He grabbed the Glock, on edge. He'd swear he felt something like a breeze, but probably it was just the forced air coming from a vent.

Bedroom first. The hall was dark, the bathroom door standing open although he was sure it had been closed before. So Naomi had used it. He flicked on the light, then eased open the door to the guest room. The light fell in a band across a neatly made, empty bed.

Adam breathed a profanity. She'd been upset. She'd gone for one of the other bedrooms. But there turned out to be only one other, empty, too. Ditto the bathroom. Small dining room. He was running by the time he reached the kitchen…and saw the open back door.

And one of Naomi's slippers lying on the concrete patio.

*****

The black ski mask loomed above her. Death mask, she thought again, on a shudder of horror. Only this time she could see the eyes, an ordinary brown although slitted in anger. She knew on a visceral level that this was the same man who'd plowed into her in the alley and grabbed her bag. The one who'd given her that last, hate-filled stare before he fled.

"I saved your life tonight," he growled. "You owe me."

Naomi inched her bare feet up under her on the sagging sofa. She didn't know where she'd lost her first slipper – probably right where he'd snatched her in the hall – but she had managed to let the second one slip off outside, at the foot of the steps leading onto the porch of this old, decrepit lodge across Mist River from town. If Adam got that close, he'd know.

I can't wait for rescue, she thought, clammy with fear. *Why would he think to come here?* No, If she could take Greg's goon by surprise and make it outside, she'd run for the sand dunes, just like Sophie had with a killer after her. This man came from the concrete canyons of Los Angeles. He'd be lost in a maze of sand dunes.

"You work for Greg," she said. *Oh, brilliant.*

He grunted. "All he wants to know is where you've stashed the video. Once he has it, you can't touch him. You can flap your lips all you want, and no one will believe you."

"I've kept my promise. Why hasn't he?"

"I don't know about any promise. I ain't Cobb. I got a job to do, and I'm gonna do it. You hear me?"

Naomi nodded, wriggling a little more. If she could get to a near crouch without him realizing what she was doing...

"Start talking."

"The police are all over my cottage. Even if I have something hidden there, you can't get it."

"Cobb thinks you don't have it on a disk or anything like that. If you do…" The beefy shoulders moved. "Getting it is my problem, not yours. But why don't we skip the bullshit and you just show me?" He jerked his head toward the laptop, which he'd opened on a wobbly table and started up.

"You're going to let me go if I tell you."

He shrugged again. "Why not?"

She could have laughed, but she might not have been able to stop. Hysteria worked that way.

"And if I don't?"

His hand lashed out so fast it blurred, connecting with her cheek in a painful blow that sent her tumbling sideways. Pain bloomed and her vision didn't seem quite right. She lay unmoving even though the upholstery fabric was so filthy a small part of her brain was appalled.

"Then I hurt you," the man in the ski mask said, his tone repellingly unemotional. "And I keep hurting you, until you tell me what I want to know."

CHAPTER FOURTEEN

"I let him have her." Adam had never felt anything like the terror jetting through him. "If I'd stayed with her…" Every time he blinked, he saw the same thing: that fluffy pink slipper lying there on the cold concrete.

He tried not to blink. *Focus on finding her. Beat yourself up later.*

Colburn squeezed his shoulder with a sympathetic grip. "The guy might have gunned you down and gotten to her anyway. You're one man, not an army."

He'd walked out on her. Adam couldn't believe he'd been so stupid, let emotions get to him to the point where he failed Naomi.

"We don't know any more about this guy than we did at the beginning. We don't have a clue where to start looking."

"Not much traffic at this time of morning," Daniel said. "Somebody will have seen them."

Lights had come on at houses up and down the street because of the police activity. He and Adam stood on the sidewalk in front of the house from which Naomi had been grabbed.

"Why didn't he take my weapon?" He'd been further chilled to realize Naomi's bag with her laptop was missing, too.

"Maybe he hoped if everything was undisturbed you wouldn't look in the bedroom. That you'd sack out on the sofa, give him hours before the alarm was raised."

A shout from around the corner had them both spinning toward it. Daniel had called in his entire small force and set them to canvassing neighbors, and Adam knew sheriff's deputies were on their way, too.

It was one of the Cape Trouble officers, a raw-boned kid who looked maybe twenty, who jogged up to them. "Old Mr. Hallquist," he jerked his head that way, "says he doesn't sleep much anymore. He saw an unfamiliar car park there maybe an hour ago and kept an eye on it. Says it showed up right after he saw lights come on in this house." The kid didn't want to meet Adam's eyes. "Had his TV on, real quiet, but he heard somebody slam a door or the trunk of a car and he peeked out again in time to see a man get in and drive away."

So the first slam indicated he'd put something in the trunk or back seat. On a surge of agony, Adam thought, *Naomi*.

"Car?" Daniel said.

"Four door, good sized. Light colored. Maybe silver or tan."

A rental. Sure as hell a rental, Adam thought. "Did he get a license plate?"

"Doesn't see that well. Says it turned left at the next corner, back toward the center of town."

Adrenaline pumping through him, Adam was desperate to give chase, but they still had nothing to go on.

God. He didn't even want to think about what that scum was doing to Naomi while he stood here flat-footed. The minute the asshole terrorized her into admitting she'd already handed over the video to the FBI, she was dead. She had to know that.

Daniel was still talking to his young officer, but no more useful information was forthcoming.

My fault she's gone.

I love her, he thought incredulously.

Please, Naomi. Please hold on.

*****

Three blows later, one eye had swollen shut and her mouth was filled with blood.

"Where is it?"

She spat at him.

Blinded in one eye, she didn't even see his fist coming this time.

She lay on the floor, staring under the sofa, not sure if she could pull herself up again. She decided groggily that she'd rather look at piles of dust bunnies than at *him*, anyway.

"Where is it?"

Maybe, if she didn't move, he'd think he had knocked her out.

That was the moment she noticed the sofa was really more like an ancient futon, the seat supported by wooden slats. Some of which were broken. One not very far from her hand had broken in the middle, leaving two sharp, pointed ends.

If I can stab a man with a knife, I can stab him with a wooden spear.

She made herself move, as if she were trying to struggle up to her hands and knees, except she groped for the slat with one hand. She took hold of it, but it was still anchored to the sofa on the near end. She made her struggle to get up more theatrical as she fought to free the piece of wood.

A kick connected with her belly and sent her sprawling again.

"Where is it?"

He sounded almost bored.

She was just a job to him. Nothing out of the ordinary.

I want to kill him.

*****

Colburn frowned at his phone and lifted it to his ear. "Yeah?" Pause. "Turned which way?" After another moment he said, "Okay," then stowed his phone. "That was Holbeck. Deputies are knocking at every business stirring to life on the highway. A cook came into work about the right time. Says he saw a light-colored sedan leaving town just as he parked. Took a right on the highway. Noticed it because it didn't belong to any of the other people he sees going to work that early, and not many tourists set out while it's still dark, and especially heading south."

Adam closed his eyes. Travelers returning to Portland went north from Cape Trouble. South, there was nothing for miles. Dense, wet coastal forests. The creep could have a campsite fifty feet off the highway, and no one would see it. Or, with Naomi safely stowed in the trunk, he could keep driving, go on for miles.

A campsite during the day wouldn't be seen, he corrected himself. In the dark, though, the guy would need to use a flashlight or start a fire, turn on a lantern. He'd know any small flash of light from the woods would give them something to go on.

And, unless he was deep in the woods…screams tended to carry.

Fear gripped his body. *Block it out, God damn it. Think!*

"The old resort," he heard himself say.

"I sent one of my officers over there last week when we were first trying to figure out where he could be staying. The officer insisted there was no sign of occupancy."

Adam turned that way. The street dead-ended at the river. He saw only impenetrable darkness.

"Did he go inside?"

"Looked through windows."

Instinct tugged at him. "It's a possibility. He might not have been staying there, but he'd hear talk, know it was empty and that there are no neighbors to hear anything."

Daniel barely hesitated. "Worth a look," he agreed. "But put on your vest first." Of all men, he must understand Adam's desperate need to take positive action. And doing something was more useful than nothing. He could keep taking phone calls, and they wouldn't be far away if there was a contrary lead.

By the time Adam returned, Colburn was done snapping out orders to his men and was instead talking on his phone. "I'm blocked in," he growled. "You drive." As he jumped in the passenger side of Adam's Tahoe, he went back to his phone conversation. "Yeah, the state patrol," he was saying. "In case this guy keeps going. If he has Ms. Kendrick unconscious, he could plan to drive for an hour or more."

Unconscious. Adam's hands tightened on the steering wheel until he heard the plastic creak. It took every bit of his considerable self-control not to speed.

Daniel ended the call. "We have every jurisdiction up and down the coast watching for him."

Adam didn't say anything.

"The cabins are falling down. The few intact roofs leak. It'd have to be the lodge." His tone was strange. "You heard about last summer?"

"Yeah."

"Place is haunted, as far as I'm concerned."

Adam almost asked if they were sure they'd found all the bodies buried over twenty years ago by a serial killer, but thought better of it. He didn't want to think about dead women right now.

They reached the highway and at last he could accelerate, his headlights piercing the darkness. There was no other traffic.

"Look for the turn as soon as you're over the bridge," Daniel said. "Entry should be blocked. Let me out and I'll pull it aside."

The river was nothing but deeper darkness beyond a low railing. Adam slowed, watching tensely for the driveway. He found it, and his headlights picked out first a No Trespassing sign, then a second that declared No Hunting Allowed. He strained to see something else in the undergrowth, then realized it was the remnants of a rotting wooden sign. He also saw that a saw horse had been pushed aside, allowing room for the Tahoe to squeeze through.

More adrenaline peaked. "He's here."

Daniel grunted. "Everyone ignores the No Trespassing sign. Could have been somebody walking their dog on the beach today."

The lights of town were to the right, across the river, woods to the left. Ahead, Adam spotted the first cabin, rotting back into the soil like everything made of wood did in this climate.

"Turn your headlights off," Daniel said suddenly. "Better yet, park. If he's here, let's surprise him."

Adam braked where he was, shoved the gear into park, and turned off the engine. He paused only long enough to switch off the dome light, then rummage in the glove compartment for a flashlight. The two men jumped out, neither closing his door, and without exchanging another word, jogged down the track.

*****

"Where is it?"

The board came loose with a noise Naomi tried to mask by lurching half to her knees and falling against the sofa. She drew the slat beneath her. Would he let her slowly push herself to her feet, for the pleasure of knocking her down again?

Maybe. Maybe not.

She turned her head so she could see him through the one slit of vision remaining to her. He was bending over, she saw, pulling up his pants leg. A sheath… Oh, God. It was a knife. She hadn't thought she could be any more scared, but she'd been wrong. The blade was wickedly long. If he started slicing her…

I have one chance, she thought with sudden clarity. *I have to thrust the jagged end into him with everything I have, and then run like hell.*

That was assuming she could stagger to her feet at all.

Into the belly. Up beneath the rib cage. Done it once. Can do it again.

"Where is it?" He sounded like a broken record. Same intonation. Over and over.

She kept scrabbling, trying to look more disabled even than she was. *Feet under me. Get balanced on them. Then spring. Have to get him dead on.*

Dead. Funny.

She gathered herself.

*****

The unending roar of the Pacific Ocean filled Adam's ears. This close, he saw shimmers of white ahead, where surf crested then foamed. Clouds were breaking up. It wasn't just his eyes adjusting; he was catching fleeting glimpses of a half moon between scudding clouds.

The rutted lane curved to the left to follow the beach. Some cabins were still recognizable as such, while others were little more than skeletons with odd angles jutting out. Adam lost sight of the ocean and realized sand dunes blocked his view. The lane climbed toward a slightly higher elevation.

Now he could see the black bulk of the lodge. No lights, no vehicle. Could be around the side or back.

Another shaft of moonlight let him realize that he was actually looking at the side of the massive old lodge. The broad porch with peeled log supports faced the ocean. The soil beneath their feet was hard and gritty now.

Daniel suddenly gripped his arm. Adam slowed, then obeyed a hand signal and slid into the greater darkness close to the porch. Both had their guns in their hands now as one moved forward, followed by the other.

Adam reached the foot of the stairs first. For an instant he thought he was delusional. *Blink and you'll see that slipper.* He moved forward, crouched, and felt baby-soft fluff under his hand.

She'd dropped her second slipper out here, trusting him to find it.

Pride and rage filled him to overflowing. "She's here," he murmured.

"I'll take the back door," came the near-soundless whisper. "I know my way. Give me the count of thirty."

Adam nodded and silently mounted the steps.

*****

He grabbed a handful of hair and yanked her head up. "Where is it? Last chance, or I start cutting."

Now.

Naomi leaped to her feet, driving the crude stake at his belly with all the force she could muster. She couldn't even tell if it penetrated his shirt, but he yelled and fell back. She kept shoving, shoving, shoving, and heard herself screaming like a banshee at the same time. He slammed against a wall and she kept shoving, even as he grabbed the slat with both hands, pushing back toward her.

Cutting through her scream came a sharp, "Police! Hands up!" *He* looked past her, forgetting her for a foolish moment, and she gave another thrust that had him doubling over with a ghastly, gurgling sound.

"Naomi." Adam's voice this time. His hand closed on her arm. "Let go. We have him now."

"I want to kill him." The words were so slurred through her swollen mouth, she didn't know if he would even understand them.

But he did, because he said gently, "I know. But let us take care of him now."

She sagged. Began to tremble as, finger by finger, she let go of the wooden slat. Amazing that she could feel her hands sting. *Splinters*. She didn't know who was with Adam. She could hardly see the monster, only enough to know he was still bent over, clutching the piece of wood.

The knife. Where was the knife?

The shakes intensified. She tried to back away, but her knees seemed to be folding. A hard arm caught her before she went down, and then Adam swung her off her feet and carried her to the sofa.

He was swearing now, a non-stop litany. Another man passed him, a gun held in rock-steady hands.

"Turn around. Face the wall."

She knew the voice – Daniel Colburn's.

"Bitch tried to kill me," *he* snarled.

A smile was beyond her, but, oh, she tried.

Her mouth formed a word. "Buffy."

"What?" Adam set her down and crouched in front of her.

"Vampire slayer," she whispered, and this time she could tell he made out the words, because he grinned, edgy and dark. Then he cupped her chin with one hand, turning her head so he could survey the damage. Through the slit allowed her, she saw the terrible look in his eyes.

"I want to kill him, too," he said.

"You found me." Even her tongue was swollen.

"Followed the bread crumb."

"Slipper?"

"Yes. *God.* My fault."

She tried to shake her head, but it hurt too much so she gave up. She seemed to be listing sideways, even though the last thing she wanted was to find her cheek pressing into that disgusting fabric again.

"Get in here!" Adam called, and moments later he stood back and she knew vaguely that she was being transferred to a gurney.

Suddenly Daniel was there, bending over and peering at her face. "Naomi. Did he say who he works for?"

"Greg."

"I'm sorry. I don't understand. Can you say it again?"

Behind him came Adam's voice. "Greg. She said Greg."

"Is that right?" Daniel asked, and she nodded, the tiniest possible bit.

Daniel gave a fierce grin. "It's time to arrest that son of a bitch, before he finds out what happened here tonight."

He stepped back. Naomi turned her head, trying to locate Adam, succeeding when he gripped her hand.

"I'll be right behind the aide car. See you in a few. Okay?"

"'kay," she whispered, and let her swollen eyelid sink closed.

*****

Adam spent most of the next few hours prowling the halls of the small community hospital. Naomi was examined, subjected to Xrays, wheeled off for a CAT scan which took time because technicians had to be roused from bed and given time to come in. Eventually she was sedated for an endoscopy to look via her sinuses for damage.

Her kidnapper was brought in, too. Turned out she'd done some damage with her make-shift stake. Not much, unfortunately, but the point had penetrated the skin and left splinters as well as significant bruising.

Daniel told Adam quietly that the stop here at the hospital was part of a plan to drag their feet, giving Weismann time to arrange to have Greg Cobb arrested before his boy here got his one phone call.

"Naomi sounded okay," he said, gaze on Adam's grimly set face. "The swelling makes her injuries look worse than they are. He says he barely 'tapped her'."

Adam imagined the creep estimating how hard he could hit her without knocking her out or – God forbid – killing her before he got the information he'd been sent for.

"Gutsy woman," Daniel commented with satisfaction.

Oh, yeah. Adam was still stunned by the sight of her trying to drive that broken slat through the big, muscular man's belly. She would have failed, but…damn. She'd held on. Kept fighting. He remembered setting eyes on her for the first time and thinking there was no way she could have taken down Frank Donahue. What did he know?

By the time they tucked her into bed, she was done for. He wasn't about to leave her, however curious he was about what was happening at the police station or in Los Angeles. He sat in a chair at Naomi's bedside, close enough to hold her hand, laid his head back and allowed himself to court sleep.

*****

Naomi woke up and discovered she couldn't see. She cried out and struggled to sit.

"Hey." Hands on her shoulders restrained her. "Naomi. You're okay, but the doctor wants you to relax. What's wrong? Can you tell me?"

Adam. She quit fighting. Slumped back against the pillow, she tried to dampen lips that felt huge and strange with her tongue. "Blind."

"Not blind," he said. "Your eyes have just swelled shut, honey. Swelling always gets worse before it gets better. The nurse is putting ice on your face off and on. It'll go down."

"Sure?"

"I'm sure." His voice was kind.

"Happening?" she asked.

"Ah. You're in the hospital. Guess you figured that out. Because you lost consciousness, the doctor wants to keep you under observation for at least twenty-four hours. He'd have really liked to get an MRI, but the closest that can happen is Seaside or Lincoln City, and he wasn't crazy about the idea of having you transported. Since you weren't displaying any confusion, he decided to wait and see."

She wished *she* could see.

"You have hairline fractures in your cheekbones. Broken nose, too, thus the tape across your nose."

She reached up and touched it, noticing for the first time her hands were wrapped in gauze.

"A couple of teeth are loose. The E.R. doc thinks they'll, uh, settle back in on their own, but you may need to see an orthodontist."

Maybe it was just as well she *couldn't* see. She must be hideous.

"They've got you on pain meds, of course, plus a decongestant to keep your sinuses from swelling. A steroid, too, to bring down the inflammation."

She had a vague memory of the doctor telling her some of this, but it hadn't really sunk in. "Surgery?"

"He doesn't think it will be necessary. It appears Cobb's guy was trying to scare the shit out of you while not doing so much damage, you wouldn't be able to think and talk."

She bit her lip, then winced. "Knife. Said…cut…"

A foul word escaped Adam. After a moment, he said, "Greg Cobb is under arrest." He sounded hard now, all cop. Except he held her hand in a gentle, reassuring grip, and he was here, at her bedside, instead of being part of the action. "Turns out Greer was flying home to California today from D.C. Agents plan to meet him at the airport."

"Stay here?" she managed to ask. No, beg.

"You know that's not possible," he said regretfully. "Once you're able, you'll have to decant everything you know, probably over and over again. And keeping you safe is still going to be the priority."

Only because they wanted her testimony in court, she knew. She wondered if he'd told Sam yet about her killing Frank. She couldn't bring herself to ask. *So, am I going back to L.A. in cuffs, or not?*

Instead, she turned her face away from him.

"Naomi," he murmured, his fingers momentarily tightening, but she ignored him.

It had hurt, walking away from her restaurant in southern California, but she thought she'd miss the cafe even more. It had been…not so much an achievement as a refuge. *Comfort cooking*, she thought.

She wondered when she'd have a chance to do it again.

*****

Maybe it was the ability to see again that gave her the courage to ask hard questions. The swelling was receding, allowing her to open both eyes a slit.

Adam had finally left for a few hours, time she'd spent sleeping, and she could tell he'd showered, shaved and changed clothes while he was gone. His midnight dark hair, brushed back from his face, was still wet. He stood at her bedside, his eyes clear and intensely focused on her.

"How do you feel?" he asked her.

"Better." Her mouth was working, more or less. "When will I be released?"

"Probably tomorrow."

"And…and when will I go back to L.A.?"

"Not until the doctor clears you to fly."

A reprieve. She almost would have liked to get it over with sooner. "Are you leaving right away?"

Shock showed on his face. "Am I leaving—? For God's sake, Naomi. I'm not going anywhere until you can go with me."

She blinked. "But…what about Sam?"

"He's taking off in the morning, prisoner in custody."

"Oh."

Adam's expression softened. "You're going to L.A. with *me*, Naomi. You'll be staying with me." His mouth compressed. "If you trust me to keep you safe, after I let you down last night."

"What?"

"Dealing with what a fool I'd been took me a few minutes. I left you unprotected while I stewed. There's no excuse for that."

"Wait."

Lines in his forehead creased. "Wait for what?"

She clutched the white cotton blanket. "What were you a fool about?" *Me?*

Never looking away from her, he dragged the chair close to the bedside and sat, then covered one of her knotted hands with his. "Frank. What else? You were right. Of course he was dirty. I'd seen the signs. I just didn't want to admit it."

"Signs?"

He talked about his partner's rage at his inability to give his daughter what he thought she deserved. "And then, damned if she didn't start at her expensive private college anyway. I asked him how he was managing, and he claimed she'd gotten some good scholarships. About the same time, he started not answering his phone sometimes when I called. I handled a few scenes on my own when I couldn't reach him. Covered for him so the lieutenant didn't find out. He claimed he was picking up some traffic gigs, that kind of thing." He grimaced. "Like my father did."

Suddenly she was holding his hand, not the other way around. "I'm sorry."

His mouth curved into a sad smile. "Nothing for you to be sorry about, Naomi. I've never been a big fan of self-delusion. Nothing like finding out I've been doing a whole hell of a lot of it. I feel free, in a way. I'd turned my head into an obstacle course. I had to dodge this way and that to avoid seeing straight ahead. Now I don't have to do that."

Stunned, she examined his face. "You mean that."

His smile widened. "I do."

"You believe me."

"I do," he said again.

She tried to withdraw her hand, but he wouldn't let her.

"Did you tell Sam?"

Adam shook his head. "I decided to leave that up to you. I can't see that it makes any difference at this point."

"Except to his family."

"Yeah, and I have to wonder whether his wife knew."

"What happened after he died? Did his daughter have to leave her college?"

"No." His expression was cynical now. "She's still there. I think we both know who is paying her tuition."

"He'd have had life insurance, wouldn't he?"

"Sure, but Cobb would want everyone to know he did the right thing for people who worked for him."

Naomi nodded, thinking about it. Of course he would.

"He's in jail."

"Going for bail, but the U.S. Attorney is doing his damndest to see that he doesn't get it. Even so…"

"He'll still think getting rid of me might help his troubles go away."

"I'm afraid so." He lifted his free hand to smooth her hair from her forehead. "We still have some trouble ahead, Naomi. But we'll get through it."

We. She closed her eyes, the better to savor his touch and that one, small word. "Maybe I can sell the café instead of just closing it."

"Could you hire someone to keep it open until you can get back?"

Her eyes flew open. "Get back?"

"Assuming that's what you think you might want to do."

"You think I might be able to come back to Cape Trouble?" Was he giving her advance notice that his sole intention was to keep her safe until she could resume her life – and him his?

"Maybe." He had an odd expression. "Lot of rain, but it's a nice town. We found you because a couple of people you probably don't even know paid attention when they saw something a little out of the ordinary. And I sure can't fault the support we've had from law enforcement, city and county."

No. She thought of all the times Daniel had come in the middle of the night. And Sheriff Mackay personally delivering the vests.

"Place has grown on me," Adam said, voice casual but his gaze sharp. "Just so you know, I've had a job offer here."

"What?" She gaped at him.

"Yep. I'm getting way ahead of myself here, but in case I ever decide I'd like to live in Cape Trouble, Mackay has let me know he'll have a detective job open for me. Colburn made a point of letting me know he won't be extending his contract when it's up in another year, too. So, hey, Cape Trouble may be looking for a new police chief, too."

Tears gushed so fast she didn't have a hope of stopping them. Crying *hurt*, but she couldn't help herself. On a sudden exclamation, Adam shifted to sit on the side of the bed and take her gently into his arms. She sobbed against his shoulder, holding onto him for all she was worth. It was a long time before she could pull back and let him gently dab tissues on her damaged face to clean her up.

The minute he tossed the tissues in a waste basket and sat back, she whispered, "You mean…?" But she couldn't make herself say it. Her courage, it seemed, didn't extend to believing he could possibly be implying what she wanted to believe: that he loved her.

His mouth crooked. "Yeah. We haven't known each other that long, but we've packed a lot into a few weeks. I figure if I start throwing out hints, you'll come around to my way of thinking." His expression became entirely serious. "You're dreading going back, Naomi. I need you to know I'll be there for you, as long as you need me."

Her lips formed a word she still wasn't brave enough to say aloud: *Forever.*

And Adam Rostov smiled. "That's what I'm saying," he murmured huskily, and leaned forward to press a tender kiss to her forehead.

About The Author

Janice Kay Johnson is the author of more than ninety books for children and adults, including the Cape Trouble novels of romantic suspense. Her first four published romance novels were coauthored with her mother Norma Tadlock Johnson, also a writer who has since published mysteries and children's books on her own. These were "sweet" romance novels, the author hastens to add; she isn't sure they'd have felt comfortable coauthoring passionate love scenes!

Janice graduated from Whitman College with a B.A. in history and then received a master's degree in library science from the University of Washington. She was a branch librarian for a public library system until she began selling her own writing.

She has written six novels for young adults and one picture book for the read-aloud crowd. ROSAMUND was the outgrowth of all those hours spent reading to her own daughters, and of her passion for growing old roses. Two more of her favorite books were the historical novels: WINTER OF THE RAVEN and THE ISLAND SNATCHERS, written for Tor/Forge and now available in e-book format for the first time. The research was pure indulgence for someone who set out intending to be a historian.

Janice raised her two daughters in a small, rural town north of Seattle, Washington. She spent many years as an active volunteer and board member for Purrfect Pals, a no-kill cat shelter, and foster kittens often enlivened a household that typically includes a few more cats than she wants to admit to.

Janice loves writing books about both love and family — about the way generations connect and the power our earliest experiences have on us throughout life. Her Superromance novels are frequent finalists for Romance Writers of America RITA awards, and she won the 2008 RITA for Best Contemporary Series Romance for SNOWBOUND.

Visit her website at www.JaniceKayJohnson.com.

A Note from the Author:

Thank you so much for purchasing my book. This is my second independently published effort, so if you enjoyed the book, I hope you will take a moment to help me get the word out to others by posting a review on Amazon or Goodreads - or "like" my Author Page on Facebook to see future updates.

I also love to hear from readers, so please feel free to contact me on Facebook or via my website at www.JaniceKayJohnson.com.

Also Available from Janice Kay Johnson

Cape Trouble, a tiny Oregon Coast town, was named for the dangerous off-shore reefs. But some of its citizens seek refuge from their own troubles…which have a way of following them.

SHROUD OF FOG (Cape Trouble, Book 1)

The secrets of the past haunt the present…

Sophie Thomsen's life had a Before and an After – marked by the terrifying morning when she found her mother dead in the foggy sand dunes, an apparent suicide. Now, twenty years later, Sophie returns to Cape Trouble, only to find her aunt brutally murdered. Although she swore never to set foot again on Misty Beach, Sophie takes over her aunt's crusade to save the falling-down Misty Beach Resort and its wild sand dunes and beach from development. But Sophie's memories threaten a killer…who doesn't dare let her remember too much.

Having come to Cape Trouble to heal his own wounds, Police Chief Daniel Colburn investigates the present day murder, but begins to suspect Sophie's mother was another murder victim, not a suicide. Everything he learns increases his fear for the woman he is coming to love.

Sophie's fate may be to die in a shroud of fog, just like her mother before her, unless she can trust Daniel to help her uncover her past in time.

TWISTED THREADS (Cape Trouble, Book 3)

The faintest creak of the floorboards her only warning...

Emily Drake has clung to her solitude for four long years after the tragic death of her husband and child, filling empty days stitching quilts that will be heirlooms for other families, never her own. It takes a terror-filled escape from a midnight intruder to open her eyes. She desperately wants to embrace life again…if death's next approach isn't utterly silent.

Detective Sean Holbeck is powerfully drawn to his new neighbor, a woman threatened by an unknown enemy. He's already investigating a murder that he fears is just the beginning. Until he knows why the victim was chosen, he can't stop a killer…or protect Emily, who may hold the key to understanding an enraged man set on vengeance.

Dark threads of past and present, guilt and grief and pain, have twisted together until only love and trust might untangle them before a killer strikes again…

What people are saying about the romantic suspense novels of Janice Kay Johnson:

- "If you are in the mood for a wonderful romantic suspense story that will have you so engrossed in it that you lose track of the time, than look no further."
  - Night Owl Reviews (on Shroud of Fog)

- "SHROUD OF FOG will immerse the reader in a world of suspense and intrigue. Elements of romance throughout this captivating read will capture your heart. I kept guessing as to whom the killer was up until the very end. Janice Kay Johnson has penned a deeply satisfying story that is appealing to mystery lovers as well as romance aficionados. If you are looking for a tale that has plenty of plot twists and amazing characters that will remain with you, then you should rush out and get a copy of SHROUD OF FOG!"
  - Romance Junkies

- "[G]uaranteed to have you looking over your shoulder more than once in this explosive, fast-paced thriller."

  \- Linda Silverstein, ROMANTIC TIMES (on Dangerous Waters)

- "Studded with tension and skillfully riveting, [it] will capture you from the first page and won't let go until the end."

  \- Kay Gragg, AFFAIRE DE COEUR (on Dangerous Waters)

- "I've never read Ms. Johnson's work before and all I can say is I will be finding everything else she's ever written. This story is so masterful it takes you inside this small town and really makes you think you are there."

  \- Sara HJ, HARLEQUIN JUNKIES (on Everywhere She Goes)

Turn the page for a sneak peek at the first chapter of SHROUD OF FOG - and find both books available online now.

SHROUD OF FOG - Excerpt

CHAPTER ONE

Why on earth wasn't Aunt Doreen answering her phone?

Disgruntled, Sophie Thomsen sipped her coffee from the travel mug as she waited at the red light. The tinge of worry, she could probably blame on the eerie effects of coastal fog. For most of her life, Sophie had hated fog. This morning it was thick enough that she felt peculiarly alone even though she was driving down the main street of Cape Trouble. The tourists passing on the crosswalk in front of her appeared and disappeared, ghost-like and colorless in their anoraks and heavy sweaters.

The morning fog might or might not burn off. You never knew on the Oregon Coast, and especially at Cape Trouble, infamous for hidden, dangerous rocks offshore and the peculiar mist that rose from the river that flowed into the Pacific Ocean and formed the southern edge of town. Sophie had spent enough time here on the coast to guess that yes, the sun would be out in another hour or two, the sweaters would be shed, the kites and beach towels would emerge, and some brave souls who didn't mind standing in waders by the hour in icy water would be spotted casting their lines in Mist River – named, of course, for its mysterious propensity for cloaking itself in drifting tendrils of gray.

She and her aunt had made vague plans to meet this morning at the storage facility, but hadn't set a time. There wasn't any real reason to feel anxiety. One thing you could say for the friendly town of Cape Trouble – sarcasm fully intended – was that if there'd been a car accident or an aide car had been summoned anywhere within a ten mile radius, everyone including Sophie would already have heard every gory detail.

Probably Doreen had simply gone ahead and was happily working inside the storage unit, sure Sophie would show up eventually. Aunt Doreen was very capable of being scatterbrained.

Lucky she'd already given Sophie the code to get in and even a key to the lock.

The light changed, the green less visible than the red through the fog. Sophie looked carefully to be sure the last pedestrian had stepped onto the sidewalk. She drove more slowly than usual along Schooner Street, lined with small seafood restaurants, coffee houses, boutiques and gift shops, their lighted windows made indistinct through the gray shroud of fog.

Although it had been twenty years since she'd spent more than a few days at a time here, she knew the town well. Like other picturesque Oregon coast towns, Cape Trouble had been commercialized, but the changes were mostly cosmetic. The Victorian era homes were nowhere near as grand as those in Astoria far to the north, but charming enough to be a draw along with the lighthouse, the broad sandy beach, the never-ending waves, the much-photographed sea stacks and the whale watching tours that departed from a pier that thrust out into the river.

Sophie's family had spent summers here when she was a child. Before. That's how she thought of it. Before and After. Before the great divide that had riven her life and left her a different person on the other side of it. Sophie would gladly never have visited Cape Trouble again, or even the Oregon Coast, but unfortunately the one person in the world she truly loved lived here, so she'd resigned herself to those occasional visits.

What she didn't understand, Sophie thought with the unsettled sensation she'd had ever since arriving last night, was why she'd let herself be talked into spending the entire month of June here to help with the auction intended to raise money for a cause she didn't personally support.

Not that she could tell Doreen so. It would mean talking about things she didn't talk about. Not with anyone.

Two stoplights and one turn later, she broke out of town, heading away from the ocean, the fog thinning as she drove. She passed first the Safeway and hardware stores, the laundromat and a pharmacy as well as neighborhoods of more ordinary houses where the locals actually lived before reaching the least attractive part of town, never seen by most visitors. Two garages, an auto body shop, some kind of metal fabricating business, plumbing supply, lumberyard, two seedy bars, a wooded stretch and – finally, two turns later – the sprawling storage facility made up of long buildings encased in metal siding, covered with metal roofs, and enclosed in a high chain-link fence.

The metal siding and roof presumably explained Aunt Doreen's failure to answer her cell phone.

With a sigh, Sophie rolled down her window, punched in the eight digit code preceded by a * and ending with the # key, then waited while the huge gate rolled jerkily to one side.

Sophie glanced again at the notebook page on which she'd jotted the information. The auction committee had unit…4079. The buildings weren't clearly labeled, so she turned down the first aisle and discovered herself passing 1001 on one side and 2045 on the other. Which didn't altogether make sense. Well, the first row on her right – the 1000s - proceeded in numeric order, but the ones on her right were given to odd fits and starts.

She wasn't the first here this morning. A moving truck was being loaded at one space, a plump woman, a boy of perhaps twelve or thirteen and a man with a pot belly currently wrestling a sofa up the ramp. The man was shouting at the woman and boy, who weren't lifting their end up as high as he'd like. The woman began screaming back just as Sophie carefully maneuvered through the narrow lane between truck and the storage spaces on the other side. She flinched at the language.

Around the corner, another woman seemed to be poking rather desultorily inside a space that was packed, literally, concrete floor to ceiling and bare-stud wall to wall with…well, household possessions, Sophie guessed, glimpsing the white side of some appliance as well the plush back of a chair, the top of an end table plus lots of cardboard boxes and some bright plastic tubs. If the poor woman was hoping to put her hands on one thing, Sophie didn't envy her.

That was unit 3006. On the other side of the next aisle was…3093. The 4000s had to be here somewhere, didn't they? And surely she'd spot Aunt Doreen's aging white Corolla.

Sophie passed other tenants either putting more possessions into their rented spaces or taking them out. The place really was huge. There were occasional doors that likely opened to short hallways where tenants could access small spaces – maybe five by ten feet or ten by ten – but most units seemed be at least fifteen by twenty or more. And there were parking spaces for RVs, boats on trailers, cars covered by canvas, a horse trailer and… She stared. Good Lord, was that a carnival carousel? She'd swear it was.

A last jog, and she found herself facing a shorter row of buildings that formed an L to the rest of the facility. And yes, she was finally among the 4000s.

It wasn't until she reached the end and turned again that she discovered a couple of units were caps to the rows, and 4079 was one of those. Aunt Doreen's car was not parked in front. And she couldn't miss the lock clipped over the hasp of the closed metal door designed to roll up.

Well, damn.

Sophie parked and tried her aunt's number again. Four rings and she was back at voice mail. She had already left several messages. Wonderful. Well, she had the key and she was here, so why not open up and see for herself the stuff the auction committee had procured? Not to mention how well organized the amateur enthusiasts were.

But when she got out and tried fitting the key her aunt had given her last night into the lock, it didn't fit. Not even close. Sophie frowned. The brand name on the key didn't match the one on the lock, but she hadn't expected it would. She knew her aunt had had copies made of the original keys so practically every member of the auction committee had one – something Sophie thought hadn't been smart. So she supposed it was possible the keysmith hadn't done a good job. But…so bad the key wouldn't even go in the hole?

Had someone replaced the lock in the past few days? Without telling Doreen, who was the auction chair? That didn't make sense unless the committee had decided to expel Doreen but hadn't gotten around to telling her. And that seemed unlikely, given that Sophie's aunt was the moving force behind the whole enormous effort.

Sophie drove back to the office she'd passed at the entrance and went in. A middle-aged woman behind the counter said, "You looking to rent a storage space?"

"No, I was expecting to meet my aunt – Doreen Stedmann – here at the space she rented…"

"Oh, you're Doreen's niece Sophie." The woman beamed. "I'm Marge Hedgecoth. Why, Doreen talks about you all the time! Says you're some kind of fancy event planner."

"Well…"

"She was so excited that you were coming." She frowned. "I haven't seen her yet this morning, although I don't open until ten, you know."

Yes, Sophie had noticed the sign on the door. Tenants had access to their units from six a.m. until midnight with special arrangements required for other times, but office hours were more limited.

"She's probably just late," Sophie said, then explained that the key she'd been given didn't fit into the lock. "I'm wondering if I might have written down the wrong number for the space."

Marge verified that, indeed, the auction committee for the Save the Misty Beach campaign had rented number 4079, beginning in March when the first of the donations had begun pouring in.

"Well, Doreen gave me a key, which is unusual, but she wanted to be sure anyone who needed to drop something off could get in. So let me get my cart and I'll follow you out there."

She flipped the sign on the door to a picture of a clock that indicated she would be back in ten minutes and and climbed into a golf cart parked by the back door. Sophie was able this time to drive directly – more or less – to her aunt's unit, which faced the chain link fence at the back of the property and the woods beyond. As Sophie parked again and got out, it occurred to her that it was really rather lonely back here, blocked by the bulk of the building from being seen by any other units except the one other that faced the same direction.

The golf cart arrived. A small, wiry woman with short, graying hair and skin that was beginning to look leathery, Marge got out and confidently poked her key at the lock.

"What in tarnation…?" she muttered.

Sophie saw immediately that she wasn't having any better luck.

After a minute her hand dropped. The two women looked at each other in something approaching consternation. "Hmph," she said. "I suppose they're entitled to change the lock."

"But Aunt Doreen gave me this key only last night. Could she have forgotten…?"

"Did you call her?"

"She's not answering." Sophie couldn't put her finger on why she was so uneasy, but she was. "I went by her house first, and she wasn't home. Her car wasn't there, either."

"I've a mind to cut that lock right off," Marge declared.

Sophie stared at the metal door. "I'll happily pay for a replacement lock."

"Well, then, you just hold on and I'll be back in two shakes."

The morning was chilly enough Sophie began to pace. Wisps of fog lingered. If she went one way, she could see down the aisle at the far side of the property, which was currently empty. The other way, she could see the same people working in their units that she'd earlier passed. A few covered vehicles were parked back here, too. She ended up at the chain-link fence, staring into a forest that looked surprisingly primeval, considering how long this area had been settled and that it had likely been clear-cut at one time.

There wasn't much forestry on this side of the coastal range anymore, though; winter storms and ocean winds kept trees small compared to farther inland and therefore unprofitable. These were hemlock, spruce and cedar, she thought, although she couldn't have told a hemlock from a spruce from a fir, if the truth be told. The evergreens were underlaid with shrubbery, some native, some not. Oregon grape, she thought, the ubiquitous salmonberry, huckleberries, the ferns that loved the damp climate, and other bits of foliage and even a few late spring flowers she didn't recognize.

Movement, caught by the corner of her eye, made her jump until she saw that a squirrel was scampering up the trunk of a tree. It paused on a branch to gaze at her with suspicion before darting out of sight.

She was smiling when Marge returned with a pair of lethal-looking bolt cutters.

Sophie hit re-dial on her phone and, at the sound of her aunt's voice saying, "I'm too busy to take this call," shook her head at Marge, who marched over to the door and applied the bolt cutters.

Marge appeared entirely too scrawny to cut through a quarter-inch or more of steel, but with a snap, the lock fell open. "There you go," she said with satisfaction.

Sophie took the lock off, set it on the concrete to one side, turned the hasp and heaved the door up. With a squeal and clatter, it rolled on its tracks.

Beside her, Marge gasped.

The interior was shadowy and astonishingly full, but Sophie was instantly riveted by the mess. Boxes were open, items spilling out. Smashed ceramic and shattered glass sprinkled the concrete floor. A framed picture lay face down, glittering glass around it and a hole stomped through the back. Somebody had broken in, was all she could think. Rifled the contents without caring what was destroyed. What a disaster.

Dear God, Sophie thought in shock, had Aunt Doreen seen this? Might she have gone to the police?

The committee or her aunt had obviously bought multiple shelving units, the kind that could be easily assembled and then taken apart to be moved, because a number of them lined the walls. Most were still packed with boxes of assorted shapes. Peering in, Sophie saw framed pictures carelessly stacked to one side. Tall or awkward things filled the middle. Was that a cat climber? A huge basket that had been covered with cellophane spilled gourmet foodstuffs across the floor.

Along with her dismay at the implications of the mess, it was the clutter and the dim lighting that explained why her eyes didn't immediately focus on the figure crumpled at the back. Even when she saw...what she saw...she rather stupidly gaped at the drying pool of a dark substance that had crept far enough from the – body? – to soak the corner of a cardboard box and possibly damage the contents.

It was only then, reluctantly, that her eyes focused on that ruined head, and she saw the face.

"Oh, dear God," she whispered, at the same moment as Marge whirled, raced to the fence and lost her breakfast through it.

*****

The gate to the storage facility stood open when Daniel Colburn drove up in his squad car. Marge Hedgecoth stood just inside, waiting beside her golf cart. She didn't look so good.

Rolling down his window, he asked, "You okay, Marge?"

She summoned a smile that didn't help much. "I've been better."

Daniel nodded. "Around back, you said?"

"Far corner." She waved. "4079."

"Once I see what's what, I'll need to talk to you."

"Yes, Chief. I'll be in the office."

"Good," he said. "In the meantime, I want you to shut down the gate. No calls, either," he told her sternly. "Don't let anyone in, or anyone out. Ask folks to wait until I can talk to them."

She agreed. He figured he could trust her. He'd gotten to know Marge since he took on the job as police chief of Cape Trouble ten months ago. During his tenure, the fence around the facility had been cut a couple of times, a car stolen once, a lock cut off a unit and the contents ransacked another time. There'd been some vandalism. Marge was a tough lady.

He eyed the people he could see industriously doing whatever you did in a storage space, but drove directly to the far corner where Marge had told him the victim's niece waited.

He noted the isolation of this particular unit and automatically scanned eaves and fence line for a camera. He knew there were several sprinkled throughout the facility and that Marge kept an eye on monitors during the day in her office. He'd arrested the idiot who drove away in the very collectible, shiny red, 1962 MG roadster by watching video footage that showed the guy clear as day. But – didn't it figure? – Daniel didn't see one back here.

The car parked to one side of the gaping door was a sleek, four-door blue Prius. A woman sat behind the wheel. She got out when he parked and walked to meet him.

His immediate reaction shook him a little. Crap. He liked to look at a sexy woman as well as the next guy, but this was piss poor timing. He couldn't let himself forget that this woman was involved in some way with a death and therefore a potential investigation. And the feeling of a fist in the gut meant he was doing more than looking.

She wasn't even beautiful, not exactly. Medium height but leggy, maybe a little short-waisted which might be making her breasts look bigger than they actually were. Wavy dark-blonde hair – yeah, he did like blondes – bundled carelessly up on the back of her head with tendrils already escaping. A pretty oval face without noticeable cheekbones but somehow…delicate. As they got closer, he saw how fine-textured her skin was.

Uh huh, and how waxy pale. His nose had already caught the scent of puke. Not surprising. Rookie cops invariably puked at their first murder scenes or after seeing the gruesome result of a major vehicular accident.

"Chief Daniel Colburn," he said, holding out his hand. "I'm afraid Marge didn't mention your name."

Her eyes were green. Hazel probably, but mostly green.

"Sophie Thomsen," she told him. "That's, um, my aunt in there." She nodded sideways without looking into the storage unit. "Well, sort of my aunt."

"Sort of?"

"She's my stepmother's sister. Doreen Stedmann."

Oh, hell. "I know Doreen."

Ms. Thomsen nodded unhappily. "Everyone in town does."

"Please stay here while I take a look."

She didn't appear to be sorry to stay behind.

Daniel knew all about the auction, which was being held as part of the effort to raise the funds to buy a sizeable piece of land the other side of Mist River from town. Forty or fifty acres, he understood, of prime river- and ocean-front land that included forest, dunes, an old lodge and a string of cabins, now all but falling down. The long-time owner had passed away and his heir wanted to unload the property, which had resort chains salivating. Locals were determined to keep their pretty town pristine and save it from the evil giant condo developments that were sure to take over if that land was chopped into pieces and made available. The heir was apparently giving them a little time to raise the money. Daniel didn't see much hope, but you never know.

Doreen Stedmann was a local character, an eccentric woman known as an activist but lacking real solid follow-through, gossips said. She started a lot of projects but finished few. From the bulging contents of the storage space, she'd been doing surprisingly well on this one.

Until somebody had gone berserk in here, that is. And until she'd died or decided to kill herself amongst the auction items, if that was what had happened. He hadn't had the impression from Marge's frantic call that there'd been an accident. She hadn't asked for an aide car. She hadn't even asked for police in a generic sense. She'd wanted him, Chief Colburn.

He stepped carefully around the clutter and the broken bits, trying not to touch anything, ready to begin revival efforts if there was any chance at all. But he could tell from twenty feet away that it was too late, and had been for a couple hours, at least. What's more, Doreen hadn't killed herself. Somebody had taken care of that for her. She was definitely dead, and the sight wasn't pretty. No wonder the sort-of niece appeared about ready to keel over.

He stood for a long time, doing nothing but studying the scene. Taking in her position, the sizable dent in her head, the cord tied around her neck as a finishing touch. The hefty, cut crystal vase that had been tossed to one side and the blood and tissue that marred its sharp cut edges.

No obvious sign of a struggle. The auction stuff closest to her was still neatly piled. The cat climber might have been rocked; it sat unevenly now, one corner of the base on top of something he couldn't see.

Why that cord around the neck? Symbolic, or had the killer been unsure the blow to the head did the job?

"Damn it," he muttered, and carefully retraced his steps. Once in the open air, he made some calls, then turned to the niece who stood with her back to him, staring into the trees on the other side of the fence. He followed her gaze, scanning for an opening cut in the chain link, but didn't see one. The ferns and salal and salmonberries appeared untrampled. Moisture from the mist glistened on leaves. From here, he couldn't see the back gate required as an emergency entrance. He'd be wanting to verify that it was still locked as soon as he had a minute.

"Why don't we sit in my vehicle," he suggested. "I've got the medical examiner coming and some crime scene folks I'm borrowing from the county."

She shivered and turned. "Yes. All right."

"Marge didn't mention cutting the lock off," he said thoughtfully. "When she called, she said only that you and she had found a dead woman. I was half-expecting a heart attack victim or suicide."

Ms. Thomsen explained about the keys not fitting this lock, and how she'd felt uneasy when she couldn't reach her aunt by phone after they'd made arrangements to get together this morning.

"I intended to change the lock anyway," she admitted. "I gather that any number of people have keys right now, and that's asking for trouble."

That was one way of putting it, Daniel would concede. Murder probably wasn't quite what she'd had in mind, though. Unless, of course, after murdering her aunt she'd just happened to have a new lock in hand because she'd intended to replace the old one anyway.

A patient interview later, he thought he knew everything she'd done from the time she drove into town last night, but her reserve was so deep, he had to wonder what she wasn't telling him. Either Sophie Thomsen was holding back on him, or she was one complicated woman. He was leaning toward the second explanation, because the one thing that rang clear was her affection for her shirt-tail aunt.

When he temporarily ran out of questions, she asked, "Was…was she strangled?"

"The cause of death will likely have to wait for the autopsy," he said gently. "That head wound looks to me like it would have been fatal."

A shudder wracked her, the most profound sign of distress she'd yet displayed. "I wonder if she saw it coming."

"Likely not. It was on the back of her head."

"I hope not," Ms. Thomsen burst out. "I hope she had no idea."

He hoped for the same. That way, Doreen's death, while brutal, was also a good one. One minute, she was involved in life, productive, maybe happy, the next, wham, one blinding moment of pain and she was gone. No lingering, knowing her fate, no misery. There were certainly worse ways to go.

Which did not mean he felt any more merciful toward the man or woman who'd killed this decent woman for no justifiable reason.

"It had to be quick," he said. "You don't have to worry about her suffering."

Some of the tension left Ms. Thomsen's shoulders. "Thank you for telling me that."

He nodded.

She breathed audibly for a minute. He was about to make his excuses when she said, "Does the gate record when people come and go? Or does everyone have the same code?"

Interesting that she was thinking so analytically. Almost like a cop.

"No, each tenant has a unique code." He already knew that much, from previous investigations. "So the answer is yes, we'll be able to pinpoint arrivals and departures based on what code they used." Maybe. The gate moved with ponderous slowness. He'd observed before that two or even three cars could pass through once it opened. If the guy was patient, he could have ridden someone else's tail coming and going and left no record of his presence at all. "You're wondering where your aunt's car is."

"Well…yes."

He'd been mulling that over himself, and now said, "I had a thought about that." He jumped out of his squad car and walked over to the row of vehicles that were being parked here presumably because of the security. He ignored the RV on the end and the camper next to it, as well as the aging but well-cared-for Cadillac that inexplicably lacked a cover. Nope, it was the vehicle on the end that was hidden under a canvas tarpaulin. He lifted one side only enough to confirm his suspicion, then let it drop.

Ms. Thomsen had gotten out, too, he saw, and stood watching him.

"White Corolla, rusting bumper?"

Looking numb, she nodded.

"The question is, how did *he* get out of here?"

"Or her."

He looked at the niece.

"From what I can gather, most of the people working on the auction are women. Doreen has mentioned only a couple of men."

She blanched at speaking her aunt's name, but hadn't let herself cry yet. He'd begun to suspect she wasn't the one who'd puked. Marge had looked considerably more rattled than this woman when he arrived.

Ignoring the approaching sirens, he asked, "Why do you assume the killer is an auction volunteer?"

She frowned. "Are you suggesting it was someone who just happened to wander by?"

"I didn't say that."

Her eyes widened in alarm. "There were a whole bunch of people already inside the gates when I got here. What if they leave?"

"Marge won't let 'em." He turned when a white van rolled around the corner and stopped behind his city car. "The troops are here, Ms. Thomsen. You said you're staying at the Harrison cottage? Why don't you go back there, and I'll be by to update you later. Say, mid-afternoon."

She gave a half nod, then changed her mind. "Will you ask everyone to be really careful when they're working in there? I'd hate to see anything else get broken."

He stared at her, struck by her coldness. "Why would you care at this point?"

She transferred her stare to him, startling him with the pure ferocity in her eyes. "Because Aunt Doreen cared. She cared a whole lot. And I'm thinking the only thing I can do for her now is finish something that mattered to her. Make it my memorial to her. That, Chief Colburn, is why I care."

After a minute, he said, "Got it."

She nodded and walked to her Prius. For maybe thirty seconds his brainwaves altered, letting him see only *her*. The confidence of her stride, the delicacy of her bone structure, the sway of her hips in snug jeans, the way she carried herself with shoulders squared and head high. Then he blinked and called, "Wait!"

He lifted a hand at the two men and one woman who'd gotten out of the van, but jogged to Ms. Thomsen.

"Is there any chance you – or someone – have a list of what should be in there?"

"Yes, in theory."

He raised his eyebrows at that.

She grimaced. "That's one of the reasons I'm here. It became apparent to me, talking to Doreen, that while the group was doing a heck of a job begging donations, they weren't doing nearly so well organizing the stuff once they had it. Apparently somebody had volunteered to enter donations as they came in and work on a catalog, but she's been full of excuses and not really doing it."

"And who would that be?"

"Rhonda…Rhoda…something." She lifted her hands. "I have a list of volunteers with contact info back at the cottage. I haven't met any of them yet, except for a few I already knew from visits to Doreen."

"All right," he said. "See what kind of inventory you do have, too." He stared at the daunting contents of the storage locker. "Do me a favor, though. Please don't call any of the other volunteers or accept any calls. In fact, don't talk to anyone, okay? I'll want to give each of them the news myself."

Still remarkably composed, she nodded. "I wonder what happened to the lock."

"I think the fact that the lock was replaced suggests the killing of your aunt was thoroughly premeditated. He – or she – came prepared. The replaced lock was likely intended to slow down the discovery of the body. Any volunteers who came out here would be puzzled and possibly annoyed because their keys didn't work, but most of them wouldn't have demanded Marge cut the lock off." Which, the more he thought about it, made Ms. Thomsen an unlikely killer. Why would she put the damn lock on, then immediately insist Marge cut it off?

"No. No, I suppose not." She hugged herself. "No." She stole a look toward the cluster of people now waiting for him outside the space and the grim sight past them, then hurried the rest of the way to her Prius.

A moment later, she drove around the corner of the building without looking back.

www.ingramcontent.com/pod-product-compliance
Lightning Source LLC
Chambersburg PA
CBHW070930180626
46817CB00003B/1227
9780989041874